Fault Zone: Detachment

San Francisco Peninsula Branch of the California Writers Club

Fault Zone: Detachment

Published by Paper Angel Press
San Jose, California
paperangelpress.com

Cover design: copyright © 2023 by Laurel Anne Hill
Cover Production by Doug Baird Productions
Cover Art Direction by Laurel Anne Hill
Cover art includes a photograph by Inga-Av, licensed for use through iStock.

Library of Congress Control Number: 2023950557

ISBN 978-1-962538-16-9 (Trade Paperback)

FIRST EDITION

10 9 8 7 6 5 4 3 2 1

Fault Zone: Detachment is an anthology of fiction, creative nonfiction, and poetry. In fiction, characters, locales, and events are the product of authors' imaginations or are used fictitiously. Any similarity of fictional characters to actual people living or dead, or to real locales or actual events is purely coincidental. Creative nonfiction may incorporate real events, describe real locales, or mention actual people; however, in each case, events are recreated solely from the perspective of the individual author, recognizing the natural flaws of memory. Events, locales, and characters may be adjusted, compressed, or otherwise changed in the furtherance of effective storytelling or to protect the privacy of individuals. Poetry may incorporate elements of both fiction and creative nonfiction, and the above disclaimers apply as appropriate.

CONTENTS

CREATIVE NONFICTION

Contents

INTRODUCTION

SHINING FORTH

O VER THE COURSE of this past year, I have had the privilege of watching this anthology take shape, butterfly emerging from larva and cocoon. I helped the poetry emerge; Laurel Anne Hill midwifed the prose; Lisa Meltzer-Penn, Audrey Kalman, and Vanessa MacLaren-Wray graciously put in the hours under their individual editorial eyes to strengthen, nurture, clarify—in short, to make this collection what it now is, a focused presentation of the best work of the members of the San Francisco Peninsula branch of the California Writers Club.

This, the tenth issue of *Fault Zone*, also represents our first foray into the world of formal contracts and copyright—a valuable experience, I trust, for those whose work appears here. We have Vanessa MacLaren-Wray and Steven Radecki, our publisher, to thank for leading us through the thickets of potentially daunting legalese into the light of professional publication.

Doug Baird put in hours on our cover, based on a photo selected by our prose editor, and generously shared his skills in graphic design. I chose the poems presented here from a slew of vivid submissions: club members responded generously to our call for their work, making the choices challenging.

It's been said that writing's not so much something we do as it is a place we go. In that spirit, and as a poet myself, I've added a few lines as "bookends," marking our entry into, and return from, that alternate world—poetry as passport.

Finally, let me sing the praises, in particular, of Laurel Anne, in whose footsteps I follow, whose efforts culminate here in one more well-edited, well-mentored *Fault Zone*—the product of both painstaking attention to detail, and also an overarching vision of what each prose piece she fostered could, in fact, become. Her hours of dedication to her fellow club members shine forth in the collection you hold in your hands: she organized a series of revisions for each author, keeping track of each stage of development for every story, so that they would all shine brightly, showcasing the work of our membership. Whatever we've achieved, much of the credit goes to her.

Here's to our next *Fault Zone*, which will be—*Faultless?*

Kate Adams
Editor-in-Chief
Redwood City, California

You turn the page, you take a sip of tea,
drifting out across an open sea
of vivid fantasies.

You shut the book and start to see
how words can catch elusive feelings,
rendering realities.

Cold Trap

VANESSA MACLAREN-WRAY

Who put this golden bridle in my hand?
The linen dress I wear was never mine.
A stranger braided flowers in my hair.
I shiver in the dew—my feet are bare.
The morning air blows cold and smells of time,
Its touch so dire it shakes me where I stand.

They brought me here as bait to draw the eyes
Of lambent prey that walks the wood at dawn
To sip the water from this forest pool.
Men lie in wait to ply their trade so cruel—
To snare the beast whose hooves will pace the lawn,
That mythic soul whose horn is all they prize.

How did I let them dress me for this part?
They ready their ropes, knowing I long to run,
To flee until my blood flows warm again.
My punishment for listening to men—
I let them trick me to this treason.
It freezes my veins. It shatters my heart.

I Named Her Lola

Lawrence Cohn

CITIZENS OF THE JURY, I know you won't judge me too harshly when I tell you how I slowly sank into this longing for Lola. How I quietly turned the radio off and smoothly rolled up the windows of my old Chrysler, anticipating Lola might today decide to slide into my car next to me. Most days she shunned my advances as I hugged the curb and opened the window and yelled hello or whistled and barked like a yapping dog. The more she turned the other cheek as I moved around the corner, the closer I came to an absolute yearning. If I wasn't so lonely, I would have forgotten about her, but every night in my dreams she was in my bed.

It started on a Friday around 5:30 p.m. As usual, cars raced along Middlefield Road from Palo Alto through Menlo Park, Atherton, and finally into Redwood City. Hungry drivers and their carsful would stop at the taquerias, burrito joints, and bars along the way. Their left turns kept me from speeding. All that hunger stayed inside the cars that kept motoring. I was one of them. They never slowed except when Lola was out on the sidewalk with her crazy red hair and mini skirt and beige legs.

I was feeling down and thinking about how empty my rented room would be. Who can't understand the depth of loneliness when a home is four walls and a hot plate and a bathroom that has seen 100 renters doing their business? I found myself whispering her name. I was imagining "Lola" with her worn pocketbook and poker face staring down at passersby. Though she was straight-up gorgeous I knew the truth. The flimsy dress and porcelain cheeks gave her away. To this day, I believe Lola was more than an enchanted mannequin.

Yes, I knew she was inanimate in real life, but to me, she was magical. The sign she carried outside the buffet diner read "Eat All You Can $12.69." With a wave of her slender arm, she smiled and invited me in. She and I both knew her smile wasn't for everyone and that soon it would be just for me.

It had been a rough week. I wasn't sleeping and my stomach was sour. The hunger left me delirious.

Maybe it was the job. I'm a line engineer. My doctor swears it's the electrical transmissions that gave me unrelenting insomnia. Maybe he's right: my brain waves were altered by the artificial electromagnetic fields (EMFs). Why else would I have fallen in love with an inanimate soulmate? Have you ever loved an object so much that you would kill to keep it? Maybe a tiara or a red wagon or a child's loved doll?

That Friday, I needed to settle it for certain. I shook my head to wake myself and parked right in front of Lola. I leaned over and looked through the open car window to scan her silky beige legs. I slowly moved my gaze upwards, over the rough texture of Lola's milky-white skirt, the brilliance of her white shirt, to reach up to her perfect visage. For a moment, I was spellbound.

I paused, then gracefully slid out of the car. Sweat trickled down my neck. Suddenly, a bicycler whipped out of nowhere, almost smashing into my open car door. Without a break in his motion, the rider flipped me off. The moment took me out of love's oblivion. I waved at his receding form, his arm still raised high.

As I headed for the restaurant door, Lola's powerful presence flowed over me. My stomach growled. Something in my loins stirred. Or was it the electrical magnetic fields?

Inside the buffet, a small sign read "Dolores Is *Not* for Sale."

So, Dolores is her real name, my inner voice chimed. *Mary of Sorrows— another name for the Virgin Mary.*

"I like 'Lola' better," I grumbled, as I grabbed a tray, plate, and silverware and lined up for the hot dishes.

It wasn't an abduction. The *Post* said I had "mannequin madness," but that's not it. Citizens of the jury, have you forgotten what it is to fall deeply in love? Nothing else you can think of will occupy the mind. There is no room for anyone else. It's not in your heart. It's invaded your whole system. You just *crave.*

Even so, I logically and stealthily planned our tryst with precision. There was no madness in my methods.

By the time I finished dinner, I had a plan: a detailed sketch on my napkin.

I moved my Chrysler to the other side of Middlefield Road and sat outside all evening, waiting until the restaurant workers turned off their front lights and locked the door.

11 p.m. Noted. I waited.

At 12 a.m., staff opened the door, hurried to their cars on the street, and left for their cozy homes. Also noted. Some carried bags—leftovers for their families.

1 a.m. The manager and the cook came out to do a final close. I studied Lola's body and the slim shadow she cast under the streetlight. How could she stand so sensually when she was so thin, so cold?

She knew I was watching. She winked.

The manager grabbed Lola's feet. The cook caught her by the head. They carried Lola inside. The cook brought in the support pole. Then they locked up.

They were gone at 1:08 a.m. Noted.

At 1:15 a.m., I crossed the avenue and peered at Lola through the dark and locked door, just to make sure she was truly safe. I explained my scheme for our getaway.

She smiled and whispered, "I love you, darling." I could read her sensual lips plainly. How could I leave her? I was not a burglar.

I slept in my car until 3:30 a.m. and woke from the night chill. I realized I needed to come back that night and leave a copy of the plan in Lola's pocketbook. I needed her to remember our scheme. I rubbed my blurry eyes and drove home with determination.

When I trudged to the 5th floor of my 5th Street tenement-quality apartment house, I remembered that the elevator was out. No worries. Lola couldn't weigh more than 30 pounds and I didn't need the pole. She was perfect, you see. I could have named her Emerald because Lola had eyes of sweet gemstones. She was *Rockin'*!

I had to work on Saturday, but as soon as I got off, I rushed home to shower and dress. I spent some time cleaning my ears. Tinnitus is a constant battle. Not just the ringing but those phantom roars and buzzing like flies. Sometimes, it makes me cry. It makes me deranged. Did I tell you my doctor says it could be the EMFs?

I patted some Old Spice on my neck and shaved face.

I found my notes and letter and headed for the Chrysler. I ran down the flights and leaped into the car. I was out of breath. I would get to the diner by nine o'clock. I was ready and brazen.

At 8:30 p.m., I parked across the street from the diner, in front of an auto wrecker. Lola was dressed to the nines. It seemed so appropriate that tonight she looked so lovely. She smiled and jutted her chin towards the diner. I locked up the Chrysler and headed across the avenue.

Nonchalantly slipping the plan into Lola's white clutch, I looked the other way, with my body turned toward the diner door. No one could have suspected that I was flirting with Lola as I passed. I felt lightheaded and giddy like a schoolboy crush.

I opened the glass door and headed for the booth. Then an outrageous conversation took place. Another customer remarked, "Whoa, Dolores is gorgeous tonight—one look at her, and I just had to come in."

I'm not a jealous person but a bolt of electricity hit me in the gut and my heart started fibrillating.

He went on about her sexy outfit and jewelry and overall enhanced features. He wished he could take her home—all the time laughing and spitting food like a perverse pig.

I swung around, ready to do battle with my butter knife when the owner strolled up to him. "Good evening, I'm August, the owner. Would you like to hear her story? It's a tale of true love.

"We were in love, Dolores and me. After she died in childbirth, I saw her everywhere. I couldn't sleep. Every woman who crossed the road or came into the business was Dolores. I didn't know what to do. I was losing my mind and my life. One day, this "Got Junk" truck parked in the lot. While the driver was eating, I walked outside to empty the trash.

"For just a moment, I thought I saw my wife ... but then I realized it was a mannequin. I decided to buy her—it only cost me two free lunches! I brought her in and dressed her in my wife's clothes. I placed her on the sidewalk to welcome eaters. Not only did we get busy, but all the men remarked on how friendly we all are.

"Tonight is our anniversary, so I dressed her to kill. She's wearing my wife's party dress and real gold jewelry. When I started posing her, I stopped seeing my wife everywhere. Now, the only Dolores I have is a mannequin. But, yes, she is a beauty."

The pig-man laughed. And the owner laughed with him. I was sickened.

I abhorred Lola being used as a marketing come-on. The owner saw her as no more than a dressed-up mannequin—how insulting! He couldn't see the vital and sensual being who smiled at me every day—even on weekends.

Tonight, particularly, she was a knockout.

After finishing my dinner, I popped a Certs and rewrote my plan on a diner napkin, so it was fresh in my psyche. My love was trapped, so I was confident in doing the right thing ... Wouldn't you want to save someone if you could? It was logic—not madness or EMFs.

I paid cash, so I wouldn't leave behind any credit card info and said goodnight to August. He was happy and perhaps I might someday sympathize with his loss ... or not.

Now, I simply had to wait. I put on the radio and listened to the blues channel. The love-lost songs filled my ears, one after the other until I fell asleep. When I awoke, it was after midnight. All the employees were gone except for the manager, cook, and August. I turned off the radio and sat by. Finally, the cook and manager left. August finished his cigarette and came out to carry Lola. He may have been drinking too, as he seemed to whisper to her as he stroked her arms. He lifted her gently, bringing her inside the door, together with the support pole. She was elegant in the doorway while the neon diner sign flashed her shadow. Then the light went dark, and August drove off in his old Fleetwood.

From eavesdropping on the staff, I knew there was only a local sound alarm and that the batteries were going. I crossed the empty street and used my work tools to pry open the door. The weak alarm sounded like a low nasal off-key singer. There was nothing to alert the police, and all the businesses in the area were closed. I slid one very large green opaque lawn bag over Lola's head down to her waist. I held the second lawn bag while she stepped in, to cover her legs and hips. Then I wrapped the wonderful duct tape to keep everything neat. The pole was left inside the door.

I carried her to my car. *She is such a light lover,* I thought. I laid her in the back seat. Even hidden beneath the bags, her form consumed me. I hurriedly climbed beneath the wheel and nervously dropped the keys. In the dark, I felt for the right key and slipped it into the ignition.

Nothing. The battery was dead. The radio killed it.

I had several wild thoughts about what to do. I could bring Lola back, wrapped or unwrapped, and try again another time, though I may not have such a chance again. August could install a better alarm or make it impossible to find her. He might chain her inextricably.

That's when I realized that we had forgotten to leave the gold jewelry. Lola was wearing gold chains around her neck, a thick gold bangle bracelet around her wrist, and a gold chain lightly caressing her lovely, thin ankle. I was determined to make sure no one thought this was a heist.

It wasn't an abduction, either. It was an extended romantic tryst. I started to hear buzzing.

Getting out of the Chrysler into the deserted avenue, I stopped to breathe and counted my breaths until I calmed myself down. I needed to unfold my Lola from the lawn bags. I carefully unfastened the gold jewelry and carried it across the street to the front door of the diner. I slipped the jewelry into the mail slot.

Done. Then, I quietly walked across the street to my car.

My ears began drumming. Damn EMFs. I lifted Lola into my arms and locked the car. Then, I walked through the neighborhoods, heading for my apartment house almost two miles away. At 2 a.m., no one would be outside, so it was likely I would evade the police.

It worked.

I carried my love into my apartment building and up the stairs. The ringing in my ears stopped and I could think. We were safe.

I pulled the bags off her and discarded them down the garbage chute in the hallway. No one had seen us. We were stealthy.

I won't reveal any details of how Lola and I showered together, standing in the stained bathtub. But when we were done, I dressed her in a white robe I had purchased at Nordstrom. It was quite expensive, and I knew Lola would appreciate it. She wrapped a towel around her wet hair. We were both exhausted and so we lay still robed under the covers of my king-sized bed.

It was so sweet to have Lola share my bed—no longer just a thought or a dream. We were out cold in minutes.

Per Sherlock Holmes, criminals often go back to the scene of the crime; however, I was not a criminal. I was a customer, a regular, so I went back to the restaurant the next evening. Besides, I needed to get my car jumped.

By chance, August was talking to customers about his stolen mannequin. He retold the story of his wife and the expensive gold jewelry "Dolores" had been wearing. He planned to include it in his insurance claim. So, it was the gold that August was most concerned about. As for the missing mannequin, he would use the jewelry to make her loss a felony crime. He would claim the stolen jewelry had a value over the California threshold. A "felonious felony," he said. "A phony felony," I thought.

The auto wreckers helped me jump my car.

•   •   •

I confess, Lola was a bit hard to sleep with. She was bony and would only change her position if you maneuvered her. After all, she wasn't a blow-up. I was gentle of course. Her thin lips were always ready for mine. Whenever I awoke next to Lola, she was smiling and bright-eyed. She watched me sleep, listened to me snore, and never criticized me.

I was loved.

For nearly a month, I left work on time and floated home, knowing that Lola would be waiting. The EMFs seemed to dissipate.

Then something unexpected occurred.

One evening, I arrived to find my apartment door ajar. I discovered the landlord and two policemen questioning Lola. She looked nonplussed and refused to answer their questions.

Frustrated, the police left her standing in the corner and handcuffed me when I walked in.

Apparently, my bathroom toilet had leaked, seeping down to the apartment below. When the landlord entered to make the repair, he found Lola. He recalled the local article in the *Post* about Lola and the reward August had posted. He called the police, who arrived quickly, recognizing her as a missing person.

The police read me my rights. But I ask you, did they ever read me my human rights? The right that I could remain in love with Lola?

Thank you, citizens of the jury, for listening to my tale. Now, I ask each one of you, is true love dead? How can I be guilty if our love was consensual? Finally, what would you have done in my place?

Monsieur Ventilateur

AUDREY KALMAN

T HE BOX HE CAME IN said his name was Mr. Fan. When he was new, he whirred in the corner of the scientist's office, swiveling on his base to view the room.

Eventually the scientist got a promotion, moved to a building with air conditioning, and brought Mr. Fan home, where he served the family for many years. He cooled Uncle Fred's neck during Fourth of July barbecues and blew through the nursery, making white noise that helped the baby sleep. All summer long, as soon as he finished one job, the scientist's wife moved him somewhere else and cranked him up again.

During the winter, Mr. Fan rested his five arms and contemplated how he might convey, without face or voice, the expressions of emotion he observed among the family members. Uncle Fred's grin as his neck cooled, the baby's smiles as he drifted off, the tender kiss of the scientist's wife on her son's brow before she tiptoed from the nursery.

Perhaps his too-plain name, assigned by a marketer at the Chinese manufacturing company that had assembled him, was holding him back. He began referring to himself as *Monsieur Ventilateur*, having learned a bit of French from the scientist's wife. He took a cue from the music she blasted while vacuuming the carpets.

"I'm just a girl, I'm just a girl in the world," he repeated to himself.

However, neither straining against his nature nor renaming himself in the image of a gentleman altered his stiff plastic countenance.

One year, Mr. Fan remained buried at the back of the closet as spring turned to summer. The squalling baby had morphed to a sullen teen. Mr. Fan listened through the closet door to a female voice that did not belong to the scientist's wife. The room grew hot with breath and lively with yips and sighs. The overripe air seeped into the closet. Mr. Fan practiced outrage, compassion, indignation. If only they would take him out to clear the stink! But he stayed in the closet.

"Maybe this is it," he thought. "Maybe I will never spin my arms again." He sank into the dusty muff of a folded baby blanket.

Amongst the sleeping bags and stuffed animals, Mr. Fan cycled through hope and despair. The only time anyone opened the closet was to stash another unwanted household item. The accumulating objects buried him deeper with each passing year. The baby blanket shifted beneath him so now he rested on the hard lid of a plastic bin. The end of a metal curtain rod poked through his frame. He could no longer see the lip of light around the closet door on the rare occasions when someone entered the room. Still, he practiced, imagining how he would make his plastic arms curve into a shape that would resemble a smile.

•   •   •

The Apocalypse arrived slowly. A thousand-year flood here, a million-acre fire there. The once-pristine suburbs, adjacent to the gleaming edifices of human ingenuity constructed atop lost apricot orchards, heated up like a pie in God's oven. Fire swept down from the canyons. Like other houses in his neighborhood, the scientist's home had been built at a time when air conditioning in this part of the country was unnecessary.

The scientist's children were gone and his wife had long since stopped taking much notice of him wandering nude around the house. He tossed the thin sheet aside and stomped naked through the stifling rooms to peer into the closet of cast-away things. The fan's plastic handle showed from behind a pair of hockey skates that had once belonged to the scientist's son.

"There you are," the scientist said.

He set the fan on the dresser in the bedroom.

"Oh, thank goodness," the scientist's wife said.

The first turn of the blades spewed dust. The scientist coughed and twisted the dial up to three. He stood for a moment, letting the flow of air dry the sweat on his chest. Then he joined his wife on the bed.

•   •   •

Mr. Fan observed the scientist and his wife. He felt a familiar ache beginning in his motor and visualized his arms spinning happiness. His blades beat at the heavy air. A warm glow spread outward from his core.

The scientist placed a hand on his wife's naked hip. She turned her face toward Mr. Fan. His manufactured breeze ruffled her hair.

Minutes later, he began to suspect the warm glow was something other than the manifestation of a newfound ability. One of his blades began to wobble as a fissure, thin as a hair on the head of the scientist's wife, extended across the plastic. If only she would turn the dial back to one! His frame shuddered and hopped him to the edge of the dresser-top. He had only a moment to contemplate the descent before he found himself lying on the floor, still spinning.

The blade did not sever completely until after the fall.

The scientist's wife lifted him from the floor and stared inside the plastic frame where the broken blade clattered against the intact ones.

"*Merde, merde*," she said. She clicked off the fan.

Mr. Fan squeezed his remaining arms together, two on each side, and stared up at the scientist's wife.

"Look." She held Monsieur Ventilateur up for the scientist's inspection. "Doesn't that seem like a smile?"

THE STONE

TIM FLOOD

B Y THE TIME BERYL RETURNED to the house in the early afternoon, the skies had left the ground with another layer of snow. When she opened the door, she found Michael lying on the kitchen floor, his body still and cold. Her world stopped. She could not move.

"Angina," the doctor had called it. She had pried that piece of news out of her husband one morning three months earlier seeing him double over in pain out by the barn. It wasn't his first episode. Turned out he had been seeing the doc for the problem without telling her. "Oh, it's nothing, Beryl. I didn't want to worry you none."

Winter had come early that year. With harvest concluded, he plowed his fields and laid down next year's seed, now dormant in the frozen ground until its time in the spring. A prairie farmer's life is never dormant. This year the harvester needed cleaning, the fence out on the north forty had to be mended, and the barn roof required patching. And of course, there was the livestock with the usual calving. "What's a farmer to do?" he had said. "The work has to be done." Michael had persevered. He was stubborn like that. *All these farmers are like that!* Now he was gone.

Then Beryl sat at the kitchen table for nearly an hour, staring at her fallen husband's body.

When she was able to move at last, a flood of events took up her life: the coroner, the pastor, their children in the city, the obituary, arrangements for the memorial service, prairie women offering help and sympathy, and at the culmination of it all, the service and cemetery.

Now everyone was gathered at the house she and Michael had shared.

Beryl quietly opened the bedroom door, holding the picture of Michael she had neglected to set on the dining room table, where prairie folk congregated for the wake. Michael had been much beloved. There wasn't enough room for everyone. Some even stood in the snow outside.

But whispers down the hallway stopped Beryl before she'd opened the door all the way.

"She's always been a harsh one, hasn't she?"

"Cold-hearted, I'd say."

She stepped into the hallway and smiled to let them know she had heard. She felt a little pleasure at their reddened faces.

"Oh, you must be so grief-stricken, Beryl," came the quick recovery.

At my husband's very own wake, Beryl remarked to herself, calmly showing them Michael's picture.

"Such a fine-looking man."

"We'll all miss him. The dearest soul."

Yes, everyone loves Michael. She nodded and walked to the dining room.

•   •   •

It began suddenly, as a sensation in the back of her neck and a feeling she could not dismiss. By the time she had placed his photograph on the dining room table next to the food set out for the guests, she knew for certain. Something within her, tightened by years of habit, strength of will, and boredom loosened just a little. She felt no longer in her body, detached. She saw herself as if from a space a little above in this room of strangers. *Yes, that's who these people are to me—strangers in my own house.* She had known most of them all her life, these familiar strangers, dressed in black and wearing long faces. *Who are they, really?*

Just as suddenly, her usual presence returned. *There's no time for these shenanigans*, she admonished herself. She stiffened her back and inhaled deeply. *None of this must touch you. Keep it usual, Beryl. Be strong.*

But nothing was usual. Genuine grief for Michael affected everyone. Even some of the men seemed teary-eyed.

"Beryl, you are so strong. How're you able to hold up?" the one with the plain face asked.

"Oh, I'm just putting one foot in front of the other, Myrtle."

Give them what they need. Keep yourself to yourself.

Myrtle looked at her a bit oddly, she thought, and Beryl felt unusually self-conscious. *I won't allow myself the emotion of it. Michael would have felt the emotion.* But that was Michael.

For a moment Beryl felt a bit envious of him. Of all of them. She shook it off.

People won't mourn me in the same way when I go, I know that. All this emotion just leaves a person weak-kneed.

She straightened her back again to hold her head high. *Always stand a bit aloof*, she reminded herself. Not enough to be unliked, just enough to let them know you're stronger. *You have a certain stature, after all.*

Command respect, her father taught her. Beryl had grown up watching him with admiration.

Hat in hand, one of the farmers approached her, his face flushed with worry about the right words to say. "Yer as tough as a rock, Beryl. Tough as they come. That'll see you through this difficult time, sure. Anythin' you need . . ."

She nodded, smiled, thanked him, and moved away. *Never settle in one place among them. Always do the right thing. Don't let them see too much.*

She returned to her bedroom to fetch a sweater for a guest, then to the kitchen to put on another pot of coffee. She paused a moment to look out the kitchen window where her grandchildren and some of the prairie kids were working up a sweat from throwing snowballs. She heated water on the stove, then called them in for cocoa. As they noisily sipped at the kitchen table, Beryl stood alone at the window again, looking out over the acreage that spread white to the horizon. There stood the snow-covered granite stone Michael loved. In the living room, her son and daughter caught up with old friends they hadn't seen for years. She gazed at the snow covering the seed Michael had sowed.

Maybe some of these people here loved him more than I did myself. I was loyal, though. Never strayed. I was grateful for what he did for me. And I showed it. Never asked anything of him. Didn't have to, did I? He just always loved me. That was his nature. Can't say I loved Mike the same way he loved me, though, not as a girl might love her man. But I did all the things a wife should. After all, he was just an ordinary farmer—the best on the prairie, but all these farmers are plain folk.

Her father had always said, "Beryl, there's something special awaiting you."

It was the city awaiting me. Knew it from the start.

•   •   •

A few days later, the quiet of solitude lay over the house, disrupted only by the creaks as Beryl crossed the worn oak floor. That morning, she had met the attorney to settle affairs. "Michael prepared for the worst and left you in good shape," he assured her. "It won't be hard to find someone to do the farming. You'll have enough to get by."

After lunch, she stood again at the kitchen window, staring at the large granite stone in the distance. Michael's rock, the one he took her and the children to on every harvest moon. An emptiness lay between her and everything. An expectation of something to be done. But what?

Michael's rock will be my permanent reminder of him. That old rock has seen a lot of things.

The memories came. *Thought I'd be whisked off to the city—to adventure, romance, and passion. Quite the dreamer I was back then, I was.*

She had thought Michael was nice and a good-looking fellow. He was bent on farming like the others. But Dagmar had promised he'd take her away.

I knew Dag wouldn't make a suitable husband, but he'd get me out of here. 'Course, he skipped town once I told him I was pregnant. It's a sin to kill an unborn child, the preacher said. Then Michael showed up at my doorstep. She wasn't going to let him in at first. She was too embarrassed to see anyone on account of the way she'd started to look. That was mostly in her head. *Mother said I wasn't showing much at all yet.* But there he stood in the doorway with that worshipful look in his eye. So she invited him in, bid him sit, and fetched him a cup. Something—Beryl never knew what—made him know she was carrying.

"I'll marry you if you'll have me," Michael offered simply. "I love you, Beryl. I'll give you a good life. I promise."

At first, Beryl thought he was making a joke. It made her angry. Then she came to her senses. *He was throwing me a lifeline. I wasn't going to get off the prairie that easily, was I? I'd have to figure out that part later.* She dealt with the situation and married him. What else could she do?

Only afterward did she come to appreciate Mike. When the harvest was good, he bought her things she wanted. She was comfortable. She'd wanted a life of passion and excitement. When it didn't happen, she'd had to muscle her way through. Life on the farm filled her with a kind of drowsiness. It was busy, and the kids came, and she lived there with them in a kind of sleep world. Acceptance set in. *A girl's expectations can get her into trouble.* She held everything inside the way her father taught. *People won't understand. Make sure you don't show how anything affects you. Never let people get too close.*

The stone lay mute in the distance and beyond it the eastern horizon and the city—the unreachable, somewhere beyond the plain and the distant mountains separating her from a dream. Behind her, the sun was setting, the clouds above the stone and the distant hills billowing in orange, red, and pink with reflected light.

She'd meet tomorrow with George, who had offered to work the farm.

I'm free to go to the city now. I could find Dagmar. It wasn't too late, now that his wife had died.

Beryl had seen Dag again at the summer picnic a few years back. How good he looked, handsome and tall, a grown man with his pretty wife and young kids. She saw how he looked at her, though. *No mistaking what his eyes told me or that suggestion in something he'd said. What was it again?* It made her think *there's a chance.*

She eyed Michael's rock again, and the sky's azured deep.

Aw, they're just old dreams. She looked down at the clean, empty sink. *I settled for this. And this here is what I got.*

She looked up again at the granite stone.

When Mike took her and the children there, when the harvest moon hung fat over the granite stone, he'd say, "We're connected to this earth." His carrying on like that was a little embarrassing, actually. "We give to the earth and it gives back. Just like we give to each other and receive what others have given to us. It's our ancient connection." That's what he called it. Beryl never understood what he was going on about, really. *He was an idealist, Mike was.*

As she watched the changing colors, Beryl remembered her kids at the wake—all grown now with little ones of their own. Becca and Paul grieved, each in their own way. They had asked what they could do for her and offered to stay a while or to stay with them until she adjusted.

"No, I'm fine. I'll be fine."

They were all gone now. Back to the city, to their houses and careers. *They got away like I should've. None of us is connected at all, Mike.*

•   •   •

Beryl made it through winter and spring. Harvest arrived in early September. George had done a good job with the crop. Prices were low, but Beryl had pored over Michael's books and learned how to track income and expenses.

Lying awake one warm night, she thought she heard something from across the field, from the west, the direction of her longing. She turned over. *It's just my imagination.*

Sleep followed. In the morning she looked in the almanac. Tonight was the harvest moon. *Well, I'll be.*

She busied herself that day with cleaning, humming to herself as she put the house in order. In the afternoon, she gathered a few pumpkins from her garden and hauled them to the fairgrounds.

The moon's red face will stare at me tonight. She couldn't get Michael's ritual out of her head. The memory had a mind of its own, she conceded, and fought it no longer.

When she rose from the supper table to carry her dishes to the sink, she paused to look out the window. The sun behind her was nearly down.

The urge came on like something she had to do against her better sense.

It would take her several minutes to get out there. She sighed, grabbed a flashlight and jacket, and trudged toward Michael's stone. There was a chill in the air.

Guess I'm doing this for him.

She felt the give of the soft, loosened earth under her feet.

Maybe there's something more . . . No, no.

She sighed. *No, Beryl, when you break it down, it's just crop yields and margins, yields and margins, year in, year out.*

The last pink of the sky faded into dark maroon. She turned on the flashlight.

As she reached the large granite stone, she noticed the usual few sprigs of wheat near the stone left uncut where the tractor couldn't get near enough. She reached down, and, out of habit, pulled one up from the earth and brought it to the rock—the way Michael always had. Against all reason, Beryl climbed onto the rock's flat surface and lay down, as he always had them do, to face the sky with a wheat sprig on their chests. She felt the stone, still warm from sunlight, on her back.

"This is the surrender," he used to say. "We're not in charge of this—any of it. Even this stone knows that."

I never understood a word of what he was going on about.

Beryl fell asleep for a while.

When she woke, the stone was still warm. It filled her with a kind of reassurance. Above her spread the vast black loft of moon and stars, beneath which she and Michael and all the prairie, and even the city far away, were small. She felt a bigger kind of yearning enter her.

Maybe I'll just lie here for a while. This could be as beautiful a sight as I ever might see.

A tear willed its way into one of her eyes, forcing her to squint to take in the grandeur that spread across an endless above. And for the first time, everything seemed different to Beryl, in a Michael kind of way.

A LIFE IN FIVE BATHS

NIRMY KANG

I N THE PUBLIC BATHS on the Ladypool Road, an additional sixpence will buy you a private room, two towels instead of one, and all the hot water a body could need. He pays the extra every week. Not out of extravagance, or because of his hair, which when released from the confines of his turban streams in black jets halfway down his back and needs a whole towel unto itself. Nor out of vanity, for he is no longer the lean man-boy of a few years ago who arrived in this damp gray country that needed him but did not want him with three pounds in his pocket and no words but "please" and "thank you" in his mouth. Now he is a patchwork of drudgery-darkened hands, pale feet that see no light, arms made steel by labor, and a belly made soft by the English ale he drinks to dislodge fine soot from his throat. No, he pays the extra because he is reluctant to bare his brown body to distrusting eyes. Eyes that see not citizen, friend, hard worker, or neighbor but foreigner, invader, usurper, outsider.

With the first rinse, he washes away the grime of foundry filth. *Ablution*. With the second, the ache of longing for his mother's touch, his father's smile. *Absolution.* With the third, he submerges his body until no space remains between the bathwater and his tears.

•   •   •

At a chipped enamel sink stands a nineteen-year-old girl whose glass bangles—an exact match for her magenta *salwar kameez*—tinkle as she mixes scalding water from a pan on the stove with frigid water from a kitchen tap that drips. While her forehead beads sweat, the rest of her is pitted gooseflesh and she is as cracked open as the cracked linoleum upon which she stands. She dips her elbow, that maternal gauge, and though the water feels right she looks over her shoulder for the comfort of her grandmother's always encouraging smiles, the reassurance of her mother's always scolding love. They are not to be found, for she has left all that behind, across seas, in the Land of the Five Rivers.

Outside, all is quiet under the weight of months-old *angrezi* snow. Inside, she is as drained of color as the beginning of the movie that the kind stranger—who is also her husband—had taken her to see. She has no ruby slippers to take her home, just a pair of embroidered *moje* that hold no magic but memories. Holding her solemn-eyed babe in the crook of one arm, she uses a cupped palm to wet the soft black curls as she whispers her grief—*my little bird, may you never fly too far from the arms of the ones you love*—and baptizes her with the salty tears of a homesick heart.

•   •   •

Shadows lengthen across fields laden with golden corn and the air shimmers with the scent of champac and chameli, nargis and gulab. From the swing under the peepal tree, a mother and father—she of the tinkling bracelets and he of the patchworked body—blow on cups of fennel tea and watch their children as they giggle and jostle with cousins and second cousins to line up at the hand pump for the evening ritual. Bittoo, the jack-of-all-trades who came to this farm as a boy and will leave someday in a shroud and lives in the space between family member and servant, works the pump with one hand and with the other soaps behind reluctant ears and scrubs the backs of dirty knees. Then, with a final inspection, he sends them one by one into the waiting arms of aunties and grandmothers who massage sun-warmed almond oil into smooth limbs and, like birds feeding their chicks, murmur sweet words and ardent prayers into still-damp ears to ward off evil eyes. Yet as they watch their children being held in the very arms for which they themselves had so long yearned, their joy is tinged with an unexpected melancholy that floats its own scents into the air. A truth they would never have believed: that once you have drunk the waters of distant lands the sweet waters of home may no longer quench your thirst.

●　　●　　●

They return to that other green and pleasant land. Home is now a faded Victorian beauty in Birmingham with servants' bells that clang with no answer at the end of a rope. The days of chamber pots and claw-foot tubs are long over. Instead, there is an outhouse with temperamental pipes and, bizarrely, a bathtub in the kitchen. Bath nights are on a Friday— kitchen becomes bathhouse—and as with all things the children go first. Their hair is washed with Vosene until it squeaks and a careful capful of Matey is added for some bubble bath fun. Then it is fish and chips for dinner and soon the only sounds are the rustling of newspaper and soft sighs, as fat chips and flaky hot fish are popped into mouths and lips become as crinkled with salt as fingertips are with water. A last treat—a chocolate biscuit and a cup of milky tea—and the children are sent to bed. Finally, in tepid water, they take their own baths. They are worn as thin as the threadbare towels they use to dry first themselves and then the condensation from the walls. Weighed down by this constant struggle to make ends meet, weighed down by the sounds of the booted feet that march through their streets chanting slogans of hate, weighed down by speeches that talk of rivers of blood. How much will it take before this country sees that we all bleed red?

●　　●　　●

Endeavor has borne fruit. A home with four bathrooms, in the grandest part of town. Toil-drenched bricks hidden behind porcelain tile. Shelves of perfumed oils and unguents and thick cream-colored towels and hot water that flows and flows. *There are more bathrooms than people now,* she thinks, as she wanders from room to room to the echoes of long-ago laughter and the awful shouts that arose when East clashed with West. *Never in my life did I think I would have to bear such disrespect. If I had spoken to my mother in that way she would have given me two tight slaps. All my friends are allowed to. But we're not in Punjab anymore. I'm British. We should have gone back when we still had the chance.*

How hard it has been to be a daughter of more than one land. Brown bodies in white countries. White countries in brown bodies. Homesick hearts and clipped wings. Ancestral reckonings and second-hand dreams. *My children,* she thinks, *my children, who now have children of their own, will carry more lightly the burden of the immigrants' lot. Their mother tongue will not leave them silent for their birth tongue has all the right words.*

She runs her bath and submerges her body until no space remains between the bathwater and her smiles.

The Man Who Loved Bridges

Luanne Oleas

PETER SPENT EVERY DAY painting the Golden Gate Bridge. It was the most secure job he had ever had. As soon as he reached one end, he would go back to the other and start painting again. It wasn't much different from his previous job operating a drawbridge on the St. Joseph River for the state of Michigan. However, that job had ended every year on December 15th, whether the river froze December first or not until the 31st. Work had started again in March, whether the river had thawed or not.

Back then, he would stand for hours at the control board in his office housed above the river. He opened the drawbridge at fifteen-minute intervals and watched the ships pass through. One day, a car attempted to cross the bridge just as it was opening. Peter pulled the emergency lever, leaving the car balanced atop the angles of the partially-open bridge.

Everyone in his small town heard about the accident. For weeks, folks would stop him on Main Street with comments like, "How many cars you catch today?" Or "Kind of like operating the jaws of life over water, eh?" or worse, "You give a whole new meaning to the Peter Principle." It embarrassed his girlfriend so much that she dumped him. Finally, he left town to escape the torment and headed for the West Coast where they didn't report Michigan drawbridge accidents.

He wasn't sure what he missed more, the girlfriend or the bridge.

The best part of painting the Golden Gate Bridge was no one told him how to do it. He figured no one wanted to climb up to where he worked and give instructions. The second-best part was being at the very top of the bridge towers and calling his new girlfriend.

Peter had met Kathleen one rainy day when he couldn't paint. She waitressed at Lori's Diner, a '50s era café doing well in 2022. It was complete with a jukebox, pinball machines, and the front half of a '57 Chevy embedded in one wall and remodeled into a booth.

On the day they met, he had ordered a chocolate-banana malt. "It's my favorite drink," she said when she brought his order, "since they don't serve Singapore Slings." Somewhere behind her dark eyeliner and fake eyelashes hid mysterious brown eyes. Eyes in famous paintings seem to follow you everywhere, but Kathleen's never seemed to follow him anywhere. Certainly not to the top of the Golden Gate Bridge.

He would call her every day while he sat perched on the scaffolding, eating his lunch. Sometimes a seagull would brush past his cheek. Sometimes he would describe his view. Maybe the fog was so thick he couldn't see the water. She might tell him about the last customer she waited on, who had insisted on having more water, then never drank it.

While Kathleen was talking, he would imagine straddling the suspension cable and riding it all the way down like a giant slide. For Peter, looking down was easier than looking up. Looking up, he had no frame of reference and would start to lose his balance. He felt safest looking across the bay toward the financial district. On clear days, the distinctive pyramid building punctured the sky. On foggy ones, its pointed top appeared to float on an endless cloud.

Peter always called Kathleen from up there on his break, but she never called him. She claimed to be too afraid his ringing phone would frighten him and cause him to lose his balance. He tried to explain the safety precautions he took, but she wouldn't listen.

One rare clear afternoon, Peter tapped the icon on his phone next to her number. Above him hung the plaque with the names of the eleven men who died while building the bridge. He watched a barge glide below him.

"Hello, Paul," she answered.

"What?"

"Oh, I mean, h-h-hi," she said.

"You called me Paul," Peter said, turning his back to the bay and looking out to sea. He pushed back his hard hat and wiped the warm day from his brow with a rag.

"No, I didn't." He could hear a loud banging sound from her phone.

"What was that?" he asked.

"Flies," she said, which made no sense. "We're having a terrible time with them. Hang on a sec—"

The line went completely silent, almost as if they'd been disconnected. He was ready to hang up after thirty seconds, but she came back on the line.

"What did you say?" she asked. He thought he heard a faint "bye" and a door shutting in the background.

"What was that?" Peter asked again.

"Nothing. Are you coming to see me?"

"Not tonight."

He jammed his paint brush into the bucket and shoved the rag into his back pocket. He always called her. He always went to her diner. She never called or came by the bridge. She claimed it would give her the creeps to watch him.

"I'll call later," he said and disconnected without a good-bye.

He picked up his paint brush and began coating a section of the massive metal tower nearest him. He knew each tower contained 600,012 rivets. He had painted every one. Some nights, he saw international orange—the color of the bridge—in his sleep.

He had a job going nowhere, a relationship going nowhere. And right now, he felt as if he was going nowhere too.

"And who is Paul?" He often talked to himself while working. No one heard him. He started to climb, then paused on the suspension cable nearest the memorial plaque. Ten of the workers had died in one day when a section of scaffolding that supported them fell through the safety net. It took $35 million to build the bridge and experts expected to lose one man for every million spent. Apparently, losing only eleven was a minor triumph.

At times, Peter felt their ghosts still walking the bridge. Today, they followed him as he climbed. The wind carried their voices in the whistling wires, saying the same word over and over. *Paul. Paul. Paul.* He painted a four-foot section, balancing on the highest cross beam of the center tower, before he called Kathleen again.

"Hi there," she answered. Her hollow tone meant she had their call on speaker. "I thought you were mad."

"I was," he said, one hand on his phone, the other on his safety line. "I am. You called me Paul."

"Sorry, hon," she said. "I was talking to Paul when you called."

"Paul who?"

"Just a customer." She sounded out of breath.

"Are you at work?" he asked. He didn't hear '50s music in the background.

"Of course," she said. "Are you?"

Her strained reply conveyed an attempt at honesty shaded with misplaced indignation.

"Yeah. Listen." He held the phone high over his head, knowing she would hear the whistling. He brought the phone back to his ear. "Can you hear that?"

"It sounds like traffic," she said.

"It's the wind," he said, watching the fog start to roll in. The sun was setting and lights blinked on around Alcatraz Island. The boats in the Sausalito harbor were lit up with Christmas lights. Picture windows from tall apartment buildings near Ghirardelli Square reflected the last of the sunlight, glaring back at the bridge like blank, rectangular eyes. Far below, car headlights created streams of white lines in one direction and red lines in the other. This was his world, the one she never knew.

"Come and see me." He looked down the tower to the roadway. "I want to show you the bridge."

"You know I'm working," she said.

"I thought your shift ended at 5:00."

"Yes, well, by the time I got to the bridge, you would be ready for dinner. Maybe tomorrow."

"What time?" He braced himself against the steel girder and felt the cold metal through his jacket. He kept his feet spread wide on the crossbeam as it grew moist from the fog.

"I don't know," she said. "I mean, I have to work."

"I want you to come to the bridge now. It's beautiful here." He knew he should climb down before the sun set. "Think about it. I'll call you back in ten minutes."

He put the phone back in his pocket and began methodically making his way down the beam. He knew each step. On a good day, he could rappel down the tower in five minutes. But it didn't feel like a good day. Distractions were deadly, whether descending a tower or building a relationship. Still, he pondered why Kathleen didn't want to share his world.

As he came closer to the ground, the sounds of the cars clacking over the sections of the roadway grew louder. The lights from the old toll booths flickered in the distance. Beyond it, outside the bridge office, stood the statue of Joseph Strauss, the chief engineer who had built the bridge. A plaque below Strauss' statue described Peter's world, calling the bridge an "eternal rainbow that he conceived and set to form."

Not everyone worked on an eternal rainbow. If the day was clear and the weather kind, Peter found it hard to come down off the bridge. He wanted someone who would share this part of his life, who would understand why he did what he did, and see the view that lived in his soul.

He looked across the bridge, feeling connected to the 80,000 miles of wire it had taken to construct the 4,200-foot span. The majesty of the bridge echoed from its two fog horns. The one sitting mid-span bleated out the first tone. The other replied from the south end of the bridge.

Only men who loved bridges could understand why Joseph Strauss had viewed the bridge from Crissy Field and been inspired to write *The Mighty Task is Done*, the poem he had read at the opening ceremony. Who else could love steel arms that linked two shores?

Nothing compared to the swift parade that crossed the vast span or, below it, the promise carried by ships arriving from far-flung ports. The bridge embodied all the hopes and fears of those forgotten men who had lived and died, braving wind and weather, to build it. There was nothing selfish about a bridge.

Peter called Kathleen again when he reached the road level.

"Kathleen, I need you to come to the bridge." He crossed the bridge on the walkway and moved toward one end. Above and below him were warning lights meant for travelers both by sea and by air. "Come and be with me."

"Tomorrow," she insisted. "I'll come tomorrow."

But he knew that tomorrow would never come. It never had and it never would.

He stood silently by the south tower beneath the plaque placed there the day the bridge opened to foot traffic on May 27, 1937.

"Tomorrow will be too late," he said. "I need you to come today."

"No, Paul."

He heard her voice, but she wasn't talking to him. Beyond her reply, Peter heard odd, two-toned laughter, one tone a man's and one Kathleen's.

"What the—" Peter started. Should he bother to tell her it was over between them?

"Did you say something?" she asked.

He yanked his arm back and hurled his phone into the bay.

It flipped over and over, disappearing into the dusk. He never heard it hit the water. He stared down the length of the span and a song echoed in his ears. *Like a bridge over troubled waters.* Maybe he should just give up on people and stick to bridges. Bridges that Strauss said feared neither war nor time nor storm.

Peter picked up his paint bucket and headed home.

TO MY CANADIAN FRIEND

ELLEN MCBARNETTE

Losing a parent is like having the roof ripped off of your world
You never realized it was there
This layer of protection
But now that it's gone
Gravity doesn't seem strong enough
One could trip and fall off into the infinite.

Now, you can feel the cold winds that blow between the stars
In the chill across the crown of your head
And down your spine

But, then,
There is your mother's voice,
Beside you
Inside you
Reminding you
Always

To put on a hat

THE VISIT

D.L. LAROCHE

A COLD RAIN DRIZZLED onto black umbrellas and a tape somewhere played "Annie's Song." We stood under a green tarpaulin that kept the main entourage dry as we lowered our heads to somber words that slid out from a preacher's mouth. I stopped listening.

•   •   •

Alma called.

"Alvin!" Like Mom, she called me Alvin when wanting to set an imposing tone.

"Alvin, call your mother. You haven't been home to see her in five—*five*, Alvin, think of it—*five years*. And you haven't called her since Easter. Yesterday was Thanksgiving, Al, and you didn't call her then . . . *Jesus*, Alvin."

"Uh-mm . . ."

"You know, she talks about you all the time. She asks me—*me*, Alvin—how you are getting along. How the hell would I know? You don't call me either. Remember me, Al? I'm your sister."

"Yeah . . ." It was the same old message dozens of times, and I tried not to listen.

"Yeah? Now, what's that supposed to mean?"

"It means *yeah*. Look, if it'll calm you down, I'll drive over in maybe a week—a couple weeks or so. Tell her that—I suppose it's my duty."

"It's not a duty, for God's sake. She's your mother! I go every day or so. We talk—mostly about you. She cooks, and we have dinner, a bottle of wine. She's lost weight, you know, but is still attractive. Of course, you wouldn't know. She never leaves the house, Al . . . not since Dad died . . . since that panicky thing . . . never. She'd really enjoy a visit."

"Okay." She was pushing harder than usual.

"That's not enough, Al, say it. Say you'll visit before Christmas."

"Yes, Alma, I'll drive over. I have some time coming, and I'll take a few days. Okay?"

"Listen, Al . . . I understand. You're the oldest. Got all the pressure. Well, in my estimation, it wasn't that much, but anyway, it's gone now. She just wants to see you, and you'll have a good time."

"Bye, Alma."

"Bye, Al."

•   •   •

Mom . . . back in the day, she was hell-bent and racing most of the time—insisted I come along. But she set the bar a little higher than I was interested in jumping, and mostly, I suppose, I just crawled under. She pushed, and if that didn't work, she got out in front and pulled. Get Alvin out of the mire, over the line. Get that boy moving.

She had her tools: the old hands-on-the-hip exasperation, the stern look from eyes about to leak, the tongue-lashing ambush, and the kicker— that family-expectations thing. There were others. She was inventive.

Even the old man—considerably more experienced with avoiding her ambitions—died early. I think, in the main, to escape.

I suppose she was well-intentioned; I'll give her that. "It's for your own good," she would say. It didn't occur to me until later that it wasn't me or Dad she was pushing along. She was simply being "Martha"— pushing her nature. She would push as long as we were there. Not being as dramatic as Dad, I packed a bag.

36

She had a humor, though, that woman, and we had some wonderful times when she left her prod in the toolshed. And Alma had it right; Mom was appealing—on the tall side with coal-black hair, athletic and tanned, the brightest brown eyes I've ever seen, exciting and piercing. When she looked at you, you knew you were looked at, and if she caught you eye-to-eye, there was no getting away.

She loved having friends around or being at the Club with her golf pals. Parties? Yes, parties: bridge games, the Women's Club, and any excuse for a celebration at Quimby's. A real butterfly, and my guess— she'd have been a lot better off without kids.

Did I say parties? Dad would sit in his old recliner with a double-barreled scotch, and Marty—they called her Marty then—would flit around newly winged, spreading goodwill pollen wherever she'd light. "Marty, over here! What's new, dear? And did you know?"

And she knew how to laugh. On a warm night with the windows open, you could hear her clear down the block.

Yeah, there were the good times and, I suppose as I look back, see these scenes flipping by, there were things about her—many things that were admirable.

•   •   •

"Mom, it's Al. I'm driving over next Tuesday—that okay?"

"Oh Al . . ."

"Yeah, I know it's been a while; it's the job. I'll leave early and ought to be at the house about three."

"That will be wonderful, Al. It seems forever."

"Okay then, about three."

"We'll have a marvelous time, Alvin. We'll talk all night. You can tell me all about your life . . . I know you're doing well. It's been so long. I'll invite some of your friends, those you haven't seen for a while. We'll have a reunion. You *will* stay a while, won't you, Al?"

"Couple days, Mom . . . no friends."

"All right dear, it'll be just you and me if that's what you want. It's been such a long time. Did I say that? Anyway, I suppose I can wait 'til Tuesday. Your sister will come over one night, maybe two. I'll call her."

"Don't make any plans, Mom, no parties. See ya on Tuesday. Bye, Mom."

"Bye, Son."

At least she wasn't telling me to bundle up.

• • •

I pulled into the driveway precisely at three. Before I could knock, she opened the door, and I swear, if not for the house, I might not have recognized her. She was pale, almost white. If you asked me to describe her in a word, "gaunt" would come to mind. I tried not to look startled, and while I was dumbstruck, it lingered only a moment.

She still dressed to a "T"— a green brocade dress with long tapered sleeves and a flash of silver embroidery. Emeralds dangled from her ears and another around her neck.

"Hi, Mom. You look great."

"Oh, Al, I'm so glad to see you."

Her broad smile and those beautiful white teeth were the same. We embraced, and she covered me with kisses and then a long hug—both arms around my neck. But she left me feeling like she was only partially there—so light her impression.

She took my hand and led me into the kitchen where she mixed us a drink, and I was beginning to feel better about coming, about being there—a thaw on a long winter's day. I was at home.

"Now, let's sit here for a minute with our drinks," she said. "I want to look at you. Then you get your bags. I've made up your old room and when you are settled, come down, and we'll start our talk. I want to hear everything. Alvin dear, it is so nice of you to visit, to have you home again."

• • •

"Al, you're up early. Did you sleep well, dear? I did. We're having your favorite—poached eggs, muffins, and that caramel honey you like so well. I loved our talk last night; I'm so proud of you. And your job . . . it sounds so important. Isn't that a new car you drove up?"

She went on, making mountains of my molehills. She had been doing it my whole life—bragging about the things she was pushing me toward as if I'd already arrived.

"Don't make so much, Mom. I'm a little spoke in a big wheel, nothing more."

"You've always been modest."

"Yeah."

God, she was thin, and her eyes, though still demanding, seemed set back and darker than I remembered.

"Is there salsa for the eggs?"

"In the fridge, dear—top shelf where it's always been."

Her voice trailed off as if she were back on the tee box, teasing and laughing while waiting her turn. As I said, she could be a lot of fun and often was, but what I remembered most clearly was different.

The scenes came back, flipping through my head like those twenty-five-cent movies at the amusement arcade, though mine had sound.

•   •   •

"Alvin, you are capable of better—much better. Now, you get back to your desk, young man, and apply yourself. I want a researched paper—facts, not blather. Mrs. Atherton says you can write. We are both disappointed with your work ... if you can call this work? Don't come down until you've done an 'A' paper. You write like your father."

I tried not to listen, but ...

•   •   •

"Alvin! Take off those old jeans and put on a decent shirt. You're not going on a hayride! Ellen will want you to look nice—and so do I."

"Mom, we're just going up to the Green-Lea for a sundae."

"I don't care where you're going. No son of mine is parading about looking like a street urchin. You represent our family when you go out. Fred, talk to him ... though I don't know what good that would do. You're two peas in the same damn pod."

I tried to tune out.

•   •   •

"Now, isn't he the most handsome young man you have seen? That's our Alvin. He's going to Dartmouth this fall, and I'm so proud. He'll do big things; you can bet every dime on it."

"Marty, I've known a lot of mothers, and you take the cake—seven layers. No one I know pumps like you do about their kids, especially Al.

Now make me another gin and tonic, and Jim wants one too. When do we eat, darling? We've been listening now for more than an hour."

•   •   •

We had shared some good times. The frames in my movie changed, and our shopping sprees came up. She loved to shop at Christmas—the music, the joy, the displays, and later a drink at Quimby's.

"Mom, after breakfast, what say we toddle off downtown—see the sights. Decorations will be up, there's music. We can stroll down Main and do window shopping like we used to when I was a kid. Sound like fun?"

"No, dear, not for me. You go if you like, though I thought you came to visit with me."

"Ya know, Mom, whenever I've thought of us, I'm led first to those excursions downtown—the two of us traipsing through stores, you talking with everyone, and lunch at the Forum. They'll be playing carols today, and it'll be like old times."

"Yes, I remember. And it was fun, but no, Al, you go. I'll stay here and fix a nice dinner."

"Mom, we'll dazzle them—me back from who-knows-where and this lovely woman on my arm."

"Alvin, I simply don't feel like it, and that will have to be that."

I got up, went over to her, and put my hand on her shoulder. I wanted to give her something to remember. Who knew when I'd be back?

"Look, I'm not givin' in. We're going downtown and stroll the avenue, window-shop, have lunch, and a hot toddy at Quimby's. We'll have fun, Mom."

"Oh, Jesus, *okay!*"

•   •   •

She seemed a little tense and didn't talk as we drove. Snow began to fall, and I turned on the wipers. The Mannheim Christmas played softly on the radio.

"Lighten up, Mom. We're going to do like we used to. You'll take my arm, and we'll do Main."

"Al, I d-don't feel well. Can't we go back?" I recall a tremor in her voice but passed it off as excitement.

"Remember when I was little," I said. "I'd have to dress up—that bow tie you liked and I didn't. We'd come on the bus and do a whole day, one shop after another. I loved those pot pies at the Forum, and remember . . . I had to eat everything or suffer the consequences." I put my hand over hers, tightly clutched in her lap and cold.

"What were those consequences, Mom?"

"I don't remember." Her words were flat.

We swung into Sturtevant's parking lot. They had the best displays. I was thirteen again as I killed the engine.

"What do you say to a stroll down Main to Quimby's? After that, back here to Sturtevant's and then over for pot pie?"

"Alvin, I'd really like to go home. Will you *please* take me home now?"

"Not a chance . . . We're here, and you'll enjoy this."

I opened my door and heard music. I took a deep breath and looked around. Garlands, silver bells, red bows, and the smell of evergreens in the air. People tucked into warm winter coats, collars up to their ears, all bustling about and wearing big smiles. The spirit enveloped me.

I got out of the car and looked up. The flakes falling seemed like so many stars. I spun around, arms outstretched, opened my mouth, and felt the snow on my tongue. I was the kid I used to be. Alma was right. I was having a good time.

Over to Mom's side, I opened the door. She seemed frozen in place—and as I remember it now, her eyes were vacant and staring ahead. I reached for her hand and pulled.

"C'mon, Mom."

We walked past the Sturtevant windows where Santa and his elves were staged. Out front, a guy with a red bucket rang his bell and sang out.

"Merry Christmas, young man—and to the lovely woman on your arm. You have a wonderful holiday, Ma'am."

The old soldier laughed, and I dropped a tenner in his bucket. Mom hung tightly to my upper arm and said nothing as we made our way down Main, people laughing, carols playing.

"Alvin, won't you listen? *Please*, let's turn around." She pulled on my arm.

"You'll be fine, Mom. We'll have a Tom and Jerry or an Irish, and it's only a block to Quimby's."

The heavier snow was sticking, frosting shoulders and hats. Cars left black tracks on the snow-covered street. I hummed with the music. She tightened her grip on my arm. A glance in her direction brought me a drawn face and startled eyes, and it began to leak into my mind that something actually might be wrong. Quimby's would fix it.

We stood at the Main and First intersection, waiting for the crossing light to indicate our turn, when suddenly she let go of my arm and screamed out.

"Taxi! Taxi, wait for me. TAXI!"

With one arm waving high in the air, she dashed diagonally into the intersection and the oncoming traffic. The very next thing, she was on the hood, then over the roof of a Yellow Cab—a Barbie doll tossed up in the air by a playful terrier . . . except for the screaming.

Scenes played out in my arcade frames—a black purse, unattached through the air. A taxi sliding sideways. A crumpled body in the street. Cops in yellow slickers. A cab driver mumbling, shoulders drooping, alone in the falling snow, his hands in his pockets, his eyes to the ground. Silent scenes, as if sound had stopped right after a blast from the taxi horn, a paramedic wagon, men with kits bending over. Mouths gaped, and eyes widened behind yellow tape. Christmas shoppers pointing.

Frame followed frame. Silent shuffling frames, and then I felt shaking.

"Sir, do you know that woman?" It was a policeman with his hand on my shoulder.

"She's my mother."

"I'm sorry, son. You wanna ride with her? They'll need you to confirm her ID."

"Yeah, I guess." What else would I do?

"Come with me—over here now and watch your step. The streets are slippery."

•   •   •

"Alma, it's me, your brother."

"Hi, Al. Are you having a good time? I'll be over for dinner tonight."

"Uh, Alma—It's . . ."

•   •   •

I waited on a bench in a pale green hall where the windows were embedded with wire. At the far end, I saw the elevator light blink.

Alma came marching. She plopped down beside me and was quiet in her earsplitting way, and I noticed again, for a small woman, she took up a lot of space. I opened my mouth to explain, and she shushed me.

In her time, she turned to me, her face smeared with tears and mascara.

"Do you ever listen? I know I told you! It's been coming on since Dad died. I've told you and told you. Jesus Christ, Alvin."

She turned away, and again it was quiet—Alma rocking and mumbling, "Dear God. Poor Mom. Dear God."

I stared at the pale green wall.

•   •   •

My eyes wandered through the mist and drizzle, my shoulders heavy as a ton. I could make out a few faces. Of course, it weighed heavily, the whole damn business. I just went to cheer her up—urged by Alma.

So out here in the freezing rain, on the side of a hill—cold and scattered flowers. Heads bowed, water dripping off the edge of the tarpaulin, and John Denver singing about Annie.

Why John Denver? She liked Sinatra and Martin, a little of Bach now and then, and she enjoyed dancing. You can't dance to Denver.

Alma's eyes are stone, staring at the coffin—ebony with silver handles and trim—must've cost someone, I suppose Alma and me, a few pretty big ones.

I'm on this side, and she's on the other. Alvin comes home to visit his mom after five years, and the next day she is dead.

I could hear the murmur.

Yes, Alma had called. She called frequently with the same message: "Visit Mom, Alvin." If she had said "agoraphobic" during any of those calls, it wouldn't have registered. It was always this pleading with me to visit, and in keeping with my well-engrained if damnable inclination, I'd simply tuned it out because the calls were always the same.

Ricky the Robot

TOM ADAMS

M Y DAD PARKED his red Ford Lightning at the harbor on our way to see my mom. The air smelled of salt and dead fish. Ricky the Robot and I got out and chased a bunch of crabs back under the dock.

"So what's it going to be there, Matey?" My dad squinted one eye and talked out of the side of his mouth. "Is you going to play with yer robot or is you going to guides us to the jetty where we can see some surfers?"

His pirate accent wasn't as good as my mom's when she'd roll up one pant leg and limp down the beach like a peg-legged captain. She'd pull a scarf down over one eye and we'd search for doubloons at low tide. When her pockets were full, she'd get down on one knee and point into the fog, searching for her ship, "Will ya look at her mast, there Matey?" And I could almost see it.

When my dad joined me and Ricky at the jetty, I asked, "When do we get to see Mom?"

My dad licked his finger and held it to the wind. "Blimey, Matey. We sees the mother this very day, we does."

I leaned into his side and looked up. "When? Can we go now?"

He took a deep breath, "Your mother is getting a special treatment today. We can't go until the doctor calls. But once he does, we'll be full sails to see the mother."

A surfer rode a big wave so close to the jetty I thought he might hit a rock. The phone in my dad's pocket buzzed. "Terry, it's the Domestic Alliance Hospital. Why don't you wait for me at the truck?"

My dad walked along the jetty while I ran back to the truck with Ricky.

Me and my mom had made Ricky before she got so sick that she had to live in a hospital. We'd stretched out on the floor with a kit she'd ordered from Domestic Alliance, the place where my dad works. My mom had scattered wires and circuit boards and little robot body parts all over the rug.

"Don't get attached to the robot." She wore thick glasses that made her eyes look like a fish's. "He won't last forever." She scratched around the rug, "Terry, can you find the feet? We need big ones so he can walk on the sand."

I found two big feet and helped her attach them with a ratchet.

She brought the foot-tall robot real close to her glasses and pressed the start button on its back. The robot shivered to life.

"Would you look at that, he's alive." Her eyes sparkled as she placed the robot in my hands.

The robot looked me up and down, "Hello, what is your name?"

When I hesitated, my mom gave my wrist a tiny squeeze. "Go ahead. It's okay. The robot will be your friend."

"My name is Terry, what's yours?"

"That's up to you, Terry. What would you like to call me?"

He sounded like a smart, human boy. I picked him up and said, "Ricky. Ricky the Robot. Is that okay?"

"Hello, Terry. I am Ricky the Robot. I am your friend."

•   •   •

I took Ricky to school for show and tell. He jumped from my shoulder to the podium and said, "Hello, I am Ricky the Robot, I am Terry's friend. Did you know that the name Terry means, ruler of the people?" My face felt hot when the kids all laughed.

46

At recess a big kid with red hair and a pimply face pulled Ricky from my grip and said, "My name's Greg, what does that mean?"

"Hello, Greg, my name is Ricky. Greg is a word that means vigilant, watchful."

"That's stupid, now watch this." Greg threw Ricky on the concrete walkway. Ricky bounced twice and came to rest looking at me with still eyes.

How could Greg have done that? I picked Ricky up, "Are you okay?"

Ricky blinked, "Hello, Terry, I'm sorry. I did not see that coming."

•　　•　　•

My dad returned from the jetty smelling of mint and cigarettes. We got in the truck, and I tucked Ricky between me and him. The motor purred on, and the headlights searched out toward the jetty. My dad said, "Your mother got a special procedure today. Supposed to let out bad memories."

"Like when she cancelled Christmas last year?" I asked.

"Oh, no, much farther back than that."

"Like when she saw me with Vicky?"

"Now don't you go saying that again. You were just kids. Your mom over-reacted, that's all."

I didn't say it again, but I remembered Vicky. When we were four years old, she'd taught me how to play doctor, in my garage. Vicky had said, "Pull down your pants so I can examine you." She held one end of a strand of rope to her ear and the other on my privates, just like a doctor checking a chest for a cough or a wheeze. We were laughing when my mom, holding a basket of dirty clothes, opened the garage door.

She dropped the basket and shrieked, "Oh my God, Vicky Barkley, you get out of here right this minute." My mom held my shoulder with one hand and spanked me with her other, all the way to my room. She made me get down on my knees and ask Jesus to forgive me. Her vision had gotten worse after that.

•　　•　　•

The tires crackled and popped as we drove over gravel to the exit. "Dad, does it hurt when they remove a memory?"

He turned onto the road. "Oh, I don't think so, Terry, it's like brushing your teeth." He smiled with lots of teeth. "They hook her up to a little electricity, flip a switch, and poof, the memories be walking the plank."

I remembered grabbing a live wire that hung over my dad's workbench in the garage. My hand and arm got so stiff I almost couldn't let go of the wire. It had felt like a thousand ants crawling around inside my arm.

My dad jammed on the brakes as a white truck with a big Christmas tree in the bed stopped to let a family cross the road.

"Fucking idiot," my dad yelled. Then he got quiet, like last Christmas when he and my mom had yelled at each other for so long they forgot to tuck me in. My dad had stomped to his room and slammed the door. I thought my mom would pull out her vape and listen to choir music. At nine she'd tuck me in and say prayers. But she'd just flipped off the lights and went to bed without a word. I'd never felt so alone.

I hoped that in the morning I'd hear the heater ticking and the toilet flushing. I'd walk into the den and find piles of presents. Mom would get up and we'd start with the stockings. Then we'd open the rest of the gifts. We'd devour piles of waffles and bacon.

In the morning it was quiet. I crept down the hall to the den where my mom slept on a sleeper sofa. "Mom?" I stayed a few feet away and watched her outline under the quilt, like when we played hide and seek. "Mom, are you awake?" I waited for her to throw back the covers, pull a scarf over one eye, and shiver me timbers back to life. But she didn't move. She didn't get out of bed all day. There had been only a couple of presents. I had gone outside and shot my toy ray-gun at a mockingbird perched in the lemon tree.

•   •   •

We pulled into the hospital parking lot and found a spot by the fountain. "Dad, can we bring Mom home today?"

He slid his vape from his shirt's pocket and took a long puff. "I'm sorry, Terry." He breathed out smoke on every word. "She can't come home yet."

I pulled Ricky to my chest. "But why? Why can't she come? She needs Christmas, too."

My dad reached over and dusted sand from my sneakers. "The doctors here take special care of her all day long."

"I can take care of her," I said. "We could make robots. We could get a Home Health droid. Some of my school friends have them."

He kissed me on the forehead, then took another puff off his vape. "We can't afford a droid, Terry." He got up and walked me to the thick metal door and pressed a button next to the Domestic Alliance Memory Unit sign.

"But why? You work at Domestic Alliance."

A medical droid, dressed in white with black shoes, opened the metal door and said, "Welcome to Domestic Alliance." He led us to a desk where my dad wrote something in a tablet. The droid unlocked another door and motioned us to follow.

The place smelled like our bathroom after Mom used that stuff in the green bottle that seemed to clean everything. The smell burned my nose. My dad took my hand and guided me into Mom's room. She wore bracelets on her wrists and ankles that were strapped to the bed with thick leather. Her body looked so thin. Her eyes opened a slit and stared at the ceiling.

A tall man in a stiff white jacket hurried into the room. The man pointed at me and told my dad that Mom had a tough day, and I shouldn't be here. Her bracelets rattled.

"Ahh, ate, you," her mouth was stiff like she'd been chewing bubble gum for too long. "Why'd you bring him?"

My dad cupped his hands over my ears and steered me toward the door. Was she yelling at me?

"I hate you," she yelled.

My dad sat me in a big blue chair, right outside her room. "I need to speak with your mother alone. Can you stay here and wait?"

I nodded yes. When he went back into the room I looked Ricky in the eye. "She knows it's my fault."

Ricky said, "Macular degeneration and depression often go together."

"You don't understand." I shook Ricky, so he'd know I was serious. "She saw me do something that made her lose her sight."

"Terry, according to Domestic Alliance medical records, your mother started losing her sight before you were born. It wasn't your fault, she was always going to be blind."

My dad pushed the button that closed my mom's door. I leaned forward for a last look when Ricky slipped to the floor. The closing door swept him against the frame and kept the door from shutting all the way. I saw a tiny slice of my dad holding my mom's hand.

He whispered, "I love you. There, there, I'm right here." Her hand stiffened like when I held that electric wire. Her fingers tightened into a fist.

"How could you do this to me?" she yelled. "If I had a gun, I'd shoot you."

Two big medical droids rushed into my mom's room. Ricky jumped onto my lap. My mom screamed, "Terry," and thrashed against the bracelets like a wild horse and then it was quiet. It was like the day when the men in white suits came and took her from the house all tied up in a jacket with all those buckles. I wanted to help but didn't know how.

• • •

When my dad left her room, his face looked like it was going to cry. But then he said, "So, what shall it be, Matey?" His voice sounded hollow. "Should we gets us a smoothie or maybe a barrel of ice cream?"

We got ice cream on special occasions, but this was not special. This was an emergency.

"Let's go home and make Mom a Christmas tree. We could paint it and bring it to the hospital."

We got a gallon of Rocky Road ice cream on the drive home. We ate our bowl-fulls sitting on my dad's workshop bench. Ricky the Robot sat by my side; his torso cracked from the door to Mom's room. She'd been right, Ricky wouldn't last forever. My dad tried to smile. I could still smell the hospital on him.

I said, "Maybe they'll remove some more memories and she'll be happy again?"

"She just needs a good night's rest. We'll wait a few days and go see her again." He laid out a wide piece of wood and sketched a tree with a flat red pencil. "So Matey, we should cuts this tree together, we should."

"Aye aye, captain. Full speed ahead." But I wondered if maybe my mom wouldn't last forever either.

My dad put safety glasses over my eyes, ear protectors over my ears and then covered his own. He flipped the switch and the band saw buzzed to life.

THE HOMECOMING

CAROL READE

I T WAS A TYPICAL MORNING, at least it started out that way. I plunked down at my desk with a cup of coffee, switched on my laptop, and began scrolling through emails. Unexpectedly, there was one from Dad. He didn't write often and when he did it was generally a forwarded joke or petition for political action to protect the environment. This one, though, had the subject line "Fwd: Question from France." Curious, I opened it.

"Hi Hon," began the email thread, "I was just contacted by a woman in France who says she has information about my father. See her email below."

> Hello, my name is Danielle. I am French and live near Paris. I found your email address on the internet searching for the name Marcel Turckmann. I have several boxes with letters and papers that belonged to a man called Albert Turckmann. They were in the attic of my grandparents' farm in Normandy. He died on the farm during WWII. He lived with my grandparents there from 1937 to 1943. Our farm was a safehouse for political resisters and Jews. I read some of the letters. It

51

seems he had a son Marcel in the States. I guess that because of the war
he couldn't come back to the States. Maybe you are related?

My heart skipped a beat. Could this really be our Albert, my long-lost grandfather? His son, Marcel, my Dad, was eight when his father was deported back to France. The way he tells it, he and his mother, Emma, went to the train station in San Francisco that day to say farewell. It was mid-April, 1937. They stood on the platform outside Albert's train car. Albert smiled and blew kisses. Marcel beamed with delight though he sensed something was not quite right. When the whistle blew, the train lurched forward, and Marcel walked alongside. His father handed him a paper cup through the barred window. Marcel grabbed it, quickening his pace to keep up, his gaze fixed on his father's face, not fully realizing it would be the last time he'd ever see him. The train gained speed, pulling away from the station and leaving young Marcel alone by the tracks. He looked into the paper cup in his hands, all that remained of his father, and frowned. The cup was empty. Every time Dad relived this story, there was a palpable hurt, a betrayal even. He and his mother endured hard times with no support from an absent father. An empty cup, Dad would say, that's all I got.

In her email, Danielle went on to apologize for reading Albert's papers and personal correspondence. She'd initially assumed they were written by someone in her own family. She gathered that Albert was an engineer and had worked many years in Russia. Engineer? Russia? My excitement mounted. This matched the broad contours of what we knew about Albert. Reading through her email, I kept pinching myself in disbelief. I never thought I would find out what happened to my grandfather. We'd always speculated that he had perished in the war, perhaps in a concentration camp. Now we knew that he lived his last years in hiding on a farm in Normandy. Danielle offered to ship the boxes to Dad.

•　　•　　•

"Come on, Dad," I implored over the phone, "open the boxes, tell me what's inside." For as long as I can remember I longed to know more about my grandfather. I had learned a few details about him over the years. He was from the Alsace region of France, had studied engineering in Paris, and had migrated to the US but never became a citizen. He'd been deported for political reasons, I was told. He was supposedly a communist. He was also supposedly something of a lady's man, having gone to Russia in the early 1930s on an engineering consulting assignment and returned to San Francisco with a mistress. Such story nuggets were channeled to me through Dad, coming mainly from his mother Emma. I wanted to know more. I didn't even know what my grandfather looked like; we had no photographs of him.

"No, I'll wait till you get here," Dad replied with some hesitation. "Let's open the boxes together." If the boxes had come to me, I would have ripped them open immediately and devoured the contents. But Dad was holding back, slipping into a familiar pattern when talking about his father. Growing up, Albert had been like a phantom in the house, a faceless presence that furtively shaped family identity, choices and dynamics. While he was never physically present, the few stories we had about Albert were powerful conduits to an Alsatian heritage that bound the family together. Yet, two different Alberts were always at play. There was the well-educated and worldly Albert whose mere persona inspired our attempts to hold conversations in rudimentary French at the dinner table, our search for French films, and Dad's choice of Alsatian wines over all others. Then there was the Albert with the empty cup, the father who had abandoned his son, who sometimes triggered Dad into silent withdrawal. This dark undercurrent appeared to be behind Dad's apprehension to open the boxes.

"Okay, Dad, we'll wait." It wasn't like I could easily stop by to join him in opening the boxes. He and Mom had retired to the Oregon coast. It was an eight-hour drive from the Bay Area, and my next visit would be at Thanksgiving. That meant another three months of suspense.

What would the boxes contain? Would the contents reveal details about Albert's relationships, feelings, dreams, and disappointments? Would they uncover uncomfortable truths for Dad, for all of us? Would they heal family wounds, or wrench them further apart?

•　　•　　•

Thanksgiving Day arrived on the cool, misty Oregon coast. While the turkey roasted in the oven, and a fire roared in the wood-burning stove, Mom chopped vegetables in the kitchen while catching us up on the latest happenings in their small coastal community. Not much news, really. This was a town where front-page headlines often featured someone who had caught a prize-winning fish or won a pie-baking contest. I sat with my husband at the family dining table, a sturdy wooden table that had seen many holiday gatherings. Dad carried in three boxes, each the size of a half case of wine, wrapped in brown paper and tied securely with stiff twine. Without a word, he set them on the gold-carpeted floor between our two chairs, took out a pocket knife, and slit them open.

There they were at last, three cardboard boxes crammed with letters and papers belonging to my grandfather Albert. Where to begin to make sense of his life? I pulled several handfuls of papers and envelopes out of one of the boxes and spread them on the dining table. Dad plucked up a letter and began reading it silently. My husband examined a finely drawn blueprint of a machine. I was attracted to a clipped stack of loose-leaf binder pages filled with handwritten entries in pencil. Scrawled across the top was "San Francisco to France – 1937." A journal from the year he left! I felt a rush like a miner spotting a glint of gold in the pan. My eyes fastened onto the first entry.

> *April 19, 1937. What a surprise at the Station! The first sight of the prison car with barred windows in which I was to travel. Then almost in the same moment, Emma and Marcel. My first sight of Marcel since he bounced in his crib in the car on the way West eight years ago. I did not know how to act at this first meeting with my boy. So many things had happened in those eight years. So many emotional carnivals.*

A chill shot up my spine and formed goosebumps on my neck. He's writing about that day at the train station!

> *Emma looked such a fine woman, stouter and still youthful. I think I kissed her first, and she did not expect it. Then Marcel, who seemed to hesitate an instant to come to me, looked first to his mother for approval before giving himself to me. The poor little fellow. I can understand how strange this father who he had never seen and who never paid any attention to him throughout his childhood must have seemed.*

I hadn't realized Dad didn't know his father at all. Before that day at the train station, Albert had been working as an engineer in Russia, and he was deported shortly after his return. That day was both the first and last time Dad remembered seeing Albert. Maybe that's why Dad never talked about doing things with his father. The only direct experience he had with his father was the day at the train station. Albert continued.

A gentle boy, tall for his age, and a little quiet and timid even as I was at his age. I can only wonder what his reaction towards his heartless father will be in later years.

"Is this my father?" Dad barked, his voice full of disgust. He held up something that looked like a passport. "He looks like a Nazi!"

I abruptly set down the journal and got up from my chair. In his hand was a German travel pass, issued in 1935, allowing Albert to travel through Germany from Russia to a seaport in the Netherlands. The photo, in sepia, showed a somber man with round horn-rimmed glasses, suit and tie, and receding hairline. It looked not unlike other sepia photos from that period. The travel pass listed him as having light brown eyes, gray hair, no distinguishing birthmarks, and being of medium height. So, this was Albert, my grandfather. He was ordinary-looking. There was nothing in the photograph to suggest he was a Nazi. Why would Dad go to such extremes? Albert lived in a safehouse, hiding from Nazis, and Dad knew this. Yet Dad's gut-level reaction to his father's photo spoke volumes. The young boy in him saw a heartless father, just as Albert had feared. It was like Albert had become the empty cup, devoid of human emotion. This animosity from my gentle father spewed forth like an angry geyser from a deep, wounded place.

Mom joined us for a moment at the dining table. "Hmph, so that's the infamous Albert! You're much more handsome, dear," she said to my father, and returned to the kitchen.

I gazed hard at the photo, searching for a family resemblance. In Albert's face I could see Dad's broad forehead, his large, pensive eyes that sloped slightly downward toward high cheekbones, the strong Gallic nose. Didn't Albert, too, mention a resemblance with his son in his journal? Upon seeing Marcel at the train station, he wrote that his son seemed quiet and timid, just like he was at that age. To bring up these resemblances to Dad, though, would be painful; the old wounds were still too fresh. I sat back down and picked up where I left off in the journal.

I kept calling Emma, Alice. For no reason except that my subconscious may have connected her with my first wife Alice. The two being so much alike in form and appearance.

"Who the heck is Alice?" I blurted out.

"Alice?" Dad looked up from a letter he was pulling out of an envelope. I read the journal passage aloud. A few seconds of silence passed.

"I don't think my mother knew about a first wife," said Dad, a shadow passing across his brow.

A first wife. Well, this was quite a revelation. Were there any children from that marriage, aunts and uncles I didn't know I had? What other surprises were in store? We'd barely scratched the surface of what was contained in the boxes. While some mysteries were being cleared up, like what Albert looked like, new questions about Albert's life were rapidly emerging.

"Dinner's ready!" announced Mom from the kitchen. "Clear the table, please." Dad and I quickly gathered up the papers to make room for a table setting. I laid out dinner plates and silverware while Dad brought out our green-stemmed Alsatian wine glasses reserved for special occasions. Albert was put back into the boxes for the time being.

A sumptuous feast appeared on the table, plate by plate, where the kaleidoscopic fragments of Albert's life had been strewn moments earlier. The comforting aromas of turkey, gravy, and mashed potatoes wafted across the table, placating the raw emotions that had erupted before dinner and still seemed to linger. The sun was setting over the Pacific, throwing a rosy glow into the room. The fire crackled, exuding a warm contentedness. Dad opened a bottle of Alsatian wine. We raised our glasses to "Family."

Dinner conversation began with Albert but Dad quickly changed the subject. I felt Albert's presence at the table, and Dad's tension with his father. The phantom, now with a face, continued to shape family dynamics. After dinner, Dad immediately withdrew to his half-read science fiction novel. The rest of us quietly became absorbed in our own amusement. Mom picked up her knitting, my husband, a copy of the Wall Street Journal. I went to the kitchen to brew a pot of coffee, then grabbed Albert's journal out of the box. Curling up on the couch across from the wood-burning stove, I re-entered Albert's world.

Escorted to my seat on the train by the immigration official who accompanied me to the Station. He surprises me with a gift of coffee in one of those Dixie cups with handle, and wishes me a good journey. A gruff but decent man. About 12 passengers in the car of whom two are released convicts from prison.

There is a railroad detective guarding each end of the car. Two more immigration officials board the train. Emma and Marcel wait on the platform. We blow kisses to each other. The train leaves at 6 p.m. with Marcel running alongside the car, one hand outstretched toward me. I reach for something to give him but only have a cigarette and half cup of coffee. On impulse I thrust the cup through the barred window, spilling most of the contents on myself. We are then out of sight. Memories of sunny California, the Bay and the Bridge, Emma and Marcel, seen for the last time?

I set the journal down and stared at the low, bluish-orange flames that licked at the last piece of firewood. Albert's impressions mirrored Dad's childhood memory of that day at the train station in many ways, yet how different these perspectives were of a father and an eight-year-old child, especially around the significance of the paper cup.

The coffee maker beeped.

"Coffee's ready. I'll pour some," Dad offered. He handed me a heavy earthen cup with cinnamon-colored glaze that he had made in a pottery class. The cup was brim-full of coffee. I savored the aroma and took a long sip. In that instant, a subtle shift occurred in my consciousness, like pins in a combination lock falling into place at the right number. The cup in my hand was full and solid like the relationship my father and I had built over the years. And yet, wasn't the paper cup at the train station that day full of good intentions? Didn't Albert in that moment attempt to connect, to bond with his son, however fleetingly?

Reading the first journal entries earlier in the evening, I couldn't help but think that Albert deserved Dad's negative characterization, and saw it coming. He knew he'd spent little time with his son, and would likely be viewed as heartless someday. Would Albert really have been surprised to be likened, however inappropriately, to a Nazi? The more I read, though, I saw in Albert a genuine compassion and care for his son, and a sense of regret for how things had turned out. Was I making Albert out to have parental instincts that he didn't really have? One thing was certain, the train left the station impervious to individual feelings, memories, and interpretations.

I finished my cup of coffee and watched the embers spit a flurry of orange sparks. My grandfather had been forcibly taken away that day and lost to the family ever since. Now his life was being revealed one journal entry at a time, one emotional layer at a time, in his own words. He was eloquent, he was interesting. He was sincere, and painfully aware of his shortcomings. For the first time, I was developing my own relationship with Albert, distinct from my father's experience. Dad's wounds would take time to heal, if ever.

I felt Albert's presence next to me on the couch, more corporeal this time, fleshed out with his face, his build, and glimpses of his personality. I wondered what more I might discover about his life in these boxes, seventy-five years after that fateful farewell at the train station.

"Albert," I whispered, "welcome home."

THE CAR WASH

AMY KELM

I SAW MY DAD TODAY, sitting on the curb outside Delancy's Carwash—the one next to LiquorLand over on Washington Avenue. My stomach dropped the second I saw him and I can still feel the panic bouncing around in my chest. I used to spend a lot of time fantasizing about what I would do if I ran into him. How would I act? What would I say? But these days, I don't think about him at all.

He was slouched over, elbows on knees, facing the street and drinking from a rumpled brown bag. I'm guessing it was Smirnoff, but then again, times have changed. His hair was matted and longer than I remember. Thinner too. His jeans were soiled and he looked very much the cliché my mother always threatened he would become.

Shirley was with me. I was performing another test of my devotion by spending the day running her errands rather than studying for my own finals. I don't know why I continue to try so hard with her. As per usual, she was unimpressed and, I was pretty sure, looking for an excuse to break up with me for good this time. She was in the middle of telling me a story about some girl named Josie when we passed him. I think she

59

guessed something was up, but she just kept right on talking and pulled me towards a bench a few feet away where we waited for her Tesla to be waxed. I feigned interest in her story, and even managed to mutter a few "uh-huhs" and "ohs," but I simply couldn't take my eyes off my dad. Finally, she punched my arm and said, "See, Thomas, this is what I'm talking about. You never pay attention to me."

I was trying to remember how many years had passed since I had seen him last. I've never been great at math, but I concluded twelve. And still, even after all that time, I would have known him anywhere. There was something about the shape of his shoulders, the curve of his back.

"Thomas!" Shirley said, evidently for the second time. "I asked if you wanted a soda?"

"No. Uh, thank you," I managed to say before she stood up. She just shook her head and walked away from me.

I wanted to tell her that I knew this man on the curb we had just stepped past. But how could I? And where would I even begin? I'd tried once ... earlier in our relationship but chickened out and never tried again. Now I imagined her furious and saying something like, "how could you not have mentioned this before?" But mine isn't an easy confession to make. Especially to someone like Shirley who reveres their own childhood. When I was only seven years old, my father was arrested for murder. And if that sounds bad, wait until you hear it happened on Christmas Eve. Now, before I go on, I should tell you not to worry. He didn't actually do it, but we hadn't known that at the time. And when all was said and done, and he had finally cleared his name, we had all lost a hell of a lot more than Christmas. Although I was small, I still remember most of it. At least the important parts, anyway.

Somewhere around dinnertime on Christmas Eve, my mom was in the kitchen and the smell of the ham roasting wafted deliciously throughout the entire house. I was never much for food—only dessert—but ham was my favorite main dish. My mother always made it with canned pineapple slices and those little red cherries that I helped her stick to the outside. On this particular night, it was already dark outside. The Christmas tree, covered in tinsel and lit with these big red, green, and white bulbs, made our living room sparkle with color. My older brother and I had been battling one another over the Lionel train controls when a knock on the front door distracted John just long enough for me to wrestle the joystick from his pudgy hands and lord it victoriously over him. However, when my mother opened the front door and we saw those two men in blue standing on the other side, the train was all but forgotten. The men were asking, hats in hand, if they might have a word with my father. My mother let them in and shooed us out of the room, but John and I hovered in the hallway and strained to hear from behind the partially closed door.

It turned out a neighbor lady down the street, Doris Langley, had been found lying dead in her living room and my father, a local building inspector, was thought to have been the last person to see her alive. She had just finished having her kitchen remodeled, and my father was the lucky bastard assigned by the great city of Madison, Wisconsin to inspect the wiring, check the lighting, and test the plumbing. The whole thing might have ended right there in our doorway that night, had the police not been so thorough in their investigation. You see, they'd found a pair of crystal whiskey glasses in Doris' sink and asked if my father knew anything about them.

For a tense few minutes they asked, my dad answered, and we all learned more than we wanted. It turned out that when my old man, who was already an alcoholic, arrived for the site inspection and saw the nice lady drowning her sorrows in the middle of the day and was asked if he might like to join her in the partaking of a little holiday cheer, his desire for the sauce got the better of him. He happily sat down and helped her drain the bottle, justifying his drinking-on-the-job as an occupational act of seasonal charity he was simply bestowing on the less fortunate.

Understandably, this admission from my father was enough to pique the interest of the officers, who were now becoming annoyed they wouldn't be making it home in time for their own holiday hams. They offered a respectful apology to my bewildered mother for their unfortunate timing, then asked my father if he might accompany them down to the station for "a few more questions."

As the car sped away, my mother wiped her hands on her apron and told us to wash up for supper. John and I didn't move until she swatted at us and scolded, "now!"

You see, when my mother, who knew her husband to be an alcoholic but not a philanderer, heard my father admit that he had in fact spent the day with this neighbor lady inspecting more than just pipes, she was overcome with vindication, and as she watched my father slide into the back of the squad car she would later admit the emotion she felt greater than all the others was that of relief. She welcomed the moment of solitude to collect her thoughts and determine just what in the hell she would do now as a single parent, with two kids, and no other source of income to rely on than that from her alcoholic, confirmed-philandering, and now suspected-murdering, spouse.

My father eventually cleared up the whole, unfortunate misunderstanding of his involvement in Doris' death. But not before spending a couple of weeks behind bars during which time he lost his job, our life-savings to lawyer fees, and many of his closely-held secrets. And my mother, who during this same time concluded that she had given enough of her youth and patience to this miserable man, determined she wanted a better role model for her two sons. She'd packed our bags and retreated home where she was met by her own father who was standing, arms open wide, welcoming us, and reminding her that my old man was a bum and that he had told her so long ago.

Shirley returned with our drinks. "I got you one anyway," she said, handing me a Coke. "But you look like you could use whatever that guy is having." She gestured towards my dad, who was still slumped on the curb. "What a loser," she snickered and flopped next to me on the bench.

My stomach tightened. I had not been that close to my dad since that terrible night; or at least I don't think I have. He was filthy. He needed help. A shower. A change of clothes. A rehab facility? Watching him sit there, all I wanted to do was kick that bottle out of his hands, shake him and ask how it had been worth more than our family. But I wasn't sure if he would even recognize me.

Over the years his silence had spoken loudly. He had made it clear he preferred the past to stay where it was. As my mother explained it, when my old man returned home from jail to find the house emptied of his dependents, he embraced his newfound freedom as an unexpected opportunity to wipe the slate clean and head west. He simply packed up, she said, and left. We never heard from him again. If you ask my brother, he will say it's for the best. John still thinks we're better off without "a jerk who would leave us like that." But I've never been sure.

I'd asked my mother about him on a few occasions. I guess I just wanted to know why he had never come looking for us. She explained she was in touch with his mother at the time, my grandmother, who took our forwarding address. My mother confessed to her that while she couldn't live with the man, she wouldn't stop him from seeing his kids, under supervision, of course. My grandmother said that while she was very sorry to hear it, she understood my mother's position, and wished her well. She couldn't account for her son's behavior but felt it best for everyone that she not get involved in his "affairs." To this day my mom says she wasn't sure if my grandmother was referring to us or Mrs. Langley. My grandmother promised to pass along our new address and swore she would encourage her son to be in touch with his children. We never heard from her again either.

"Thomas, for God's sake, are you coming?" Shirley asked, and once again she walked right past my old man. I don't think she even saw him this time. They had finished polishing her car and she was going to retrieve her key from the attendant.

I looked back at my dad and wiped my palms on my jeans. As I said, with the exception of Christmas Eve, I don't really think about him these days. If I do, it's usually in a very far off and distant way. But when I saw him, hunched on the curb in front of me, he was so close that I could no longer wonder how I might behave.

"Not just yet," I told Shirley. "There's something I have to do."

She wasn't interested in what that something might be. Instead, she found her fight and stared at me with her hands on her hips. "Great, Thomas," she said. "Just great." I started to explain, but she spun around and stormed off. I think she expected me to chase after her like I normally do and when I didn't, she simply slammed her car door and peeled loudly out of the parking lot.

For the next few minutes, I stood there with my hands in my pockets and tried to stop them from shaking. John will tell you that between the two of us, he is the stronger one. And maybe on the outside, that is true. But on the inside, where it counts, I hold my own. So, I just did it. I walked slowly over to the man on the curb.

"I'm Thomas," I said. "May I sit with you awhile?"

He stared up at me for a good long while, and then, very tentatively, accepted my outstretched hand.

ALONE IN THE GARDEN

CHERYL RAY

1951

I LAY ON THE SOFT BED of grass with my arms stretched out to form the letter "T." My cousin, Michael, next to me, touched my leg with his bare toes. With our fingers curved into round tubes held over our eyes like binoculars, we stared into the sky.

"What's up there?" I asked. "Do you see God?"

"The sunlight's up there. Don't look at it." Michael's eyes must have squinted. He said, "I don't see God. What do you see?"

"Clouds piled high as whipped cream. Yum." I licked my lips.

My cousin and I were nine years old and lonesome for our fathers. Michael's father had returned home from the war and discovered there was a new baby. He wasn't the father. My daddy had returned home from the war, bought a new car, and got a girlfriend. She wasn't my mother.

Michael's father had moved away from San Diego to San Francisco. Mine still lived in San Diego, and he'd married his girlfriend, Shirley. I needed to call to ask if he would come and take me to their house. On a weekend, he might say "yes." If I didn't call, would I ever see him?

When I stared into the sky, I believed God was there. Sometimes at night before going to sleep, I pretended I was sitting on God's lap. He wrapped his arms around me, holding me close. Then I was safe.

1973

The sun scowled through the kitchen window while I fixed cold breakfast cereal for my two boys, five and eight, and then sent them off to school. My husband traveled for work and had been gone for the past two days. I needed coffee despite its bitter, nauseating aftertaste. Next to the chair where I'd sat last night, an ashtray brimmed over with cigarette butts from the pack of Marlboros I had smoked while I drank to an alcoholic stupor.

My drinking had started during yesterday's late afternoon with the customary lie, "I'll just have one more gin and tonic to relax before I fix dinner." Yet after that drink, the alcoholic demon said, "One more won't hurt." And the count stopped. With all the liquor I downed, I should have slept last night and all today. But I woke early, and my head pounded. I needed to close my eyes.

I staggered up the stairs to my bedroom. The dark-out drapes were closed, but a hideous hint of daylight escaped a side edge of the curtain. The burgundy patchwork bedspread lay crumpled on the floor. I stretched out diagonally across the unmade king-size bed.

Face-down into my pillow, I pleaded, "If there is a God, please help me."

Three months after my appeal, I drunk-dialed myself into a recovery program during another drinking bout. The woman who answered the call told me she would pick me up the following morning and take me to a meeting. She arrived. I barely remembered the telephone call. What had I done? Too late to get out of it. Hungover and with the stink of alcohol, I went with her to my first meeting. How could it be that I never drank again? Did my imploring prayer to God save me from ruin?

For most of this life, I'd searched outside myself for acceptance from people I believed were better than me. I resented my womanizing father and blamed my insecurities on him. I wore a mask of confidence to cover my inside loneliness and my notion of being an outsider. I felt either in or out with most people. With my father, I mainly figured out. With God, I wasn't sure. I'd been adrift in a deep sea of neediness.

During my early days of sobriety, my husband, for a hobby, purchased a sailboat. He learned to sail, which enthralled him. That gave me plenty of time to attend recovery meetings. There I learned how to live without alcohol—to collapse the lifebuoy of justification that held my thoughts of "if only such-and-such had happened, things would be different." The program instructed me to get off my "pity pot" and come to rely on a Higher Power. I could not believe in God, the man clothed in flowing robes I had viewed in pictures. Yet I needed and wanted help. For that, I was willing to replace the unfaithful spirit of alcohol. I accepted a power that held the universe together. My sobriety saved my marriage, my children, and my life.

1986

After thirteen years of sobriety, I moved with my husband from Southern California to the San Francisco Bay Area. I still hadn't settled on a satisfactory concept of God. I remembered happily going to the Unity Church in San Diego as a child with my grandmother. So, I asked my friend Grace to go with me to their local church. Soon after, we attended. We approached the entrance, and I delighted in the vibrant purple wisteria that cascaded over the roof edges to greet us. Inside, we walked up the center aisle in search of seats. Friendly-looking people filled the long wooden pews that stretched across the large sanctuary. Above the stage and podium, high on the silver-gray concrete wall in large white letters, were the comforting words, "With God, all things are possible." Beautiful music flowed through the fingers of the man at the piano. When the Love-Love-Love choir sang "Wind Beneath My Wings," chills covered my body, tears ran down my face, and childhood memories of my grandmother filled my mind.

The church my grandmother and I attended didn't have its own building. Instead, the service gathered in the main meeting room of a funeral home. The children's Sunday school class met in a small space hidden behind thin black curtains—a room for the mourning families. I loved the singing, the Bible stories, and the other children. Before I went to class, my grandma and I sat with the whole congregation and listened to a short talk by the minister. We sang from the hymnal—my favorite song: "I Come to the Garden Alone." Some days I sat at my grandmother's piano and pretended to play. I had sung the words: "He walks with me, and he talks with me, and He tells me I am His own."

Rediscovering Unity Church as an adult, I worshiped and volunteered there for five years. I enjoyed the music, learned life lessons from the sermons, and met kind people. But then I stopped going, and I don't recall why. Maybe I got busy doing other things, like going back to school. Or perhaps the God of this church wasn't working for me or what I needed. I knew my search would continue.

1999

"Sailing is magic," my husband told me. It took twenty years, thousands of ocean miles, and three sailboats before I began to understand his enchantment. My conversion was enough that I volunteered as his co-captain on a Pacific Ocean adventure from San Francisco to South America. At a unique point in this voyage, I awoke to a shift in my consciousness—an insightful spiritual experience. I held gratitude for the wind's driving force as it filled the sails and moved the boat toward our destination. I listened to the music of the surf stroking its waves on the boat's hull as it cut through the water. Indeed, the sea offered me continual blessings: otters that floated on their backs, a whale that came to the surface to breathe, dolphins that jumped alongside the boat, and turtles that ducked below when they sighted us. The essence of this mystical journey awoke my inner aliveness with the wind, ocean, and sea life.

Upon reaching Panama, we anchored in the crystal-clear cyan water of a protected island. One afternoon, we set out to snorkel. We rowed our dinghy to a close-by reef. I lowered myself into the tropical sea, and my skin tingled. I placed my mask over my eyes and nose and then put my face into the water. As my breath slowed and my body relaxed, I realized the beauty surrounding the ocean floor. This spiritual awareness became a floating meditation. Below me, schools of tropical fish—yellow sergeant majors, blue and yellow parrotfish, gray-yellow foureye butterflyfish—swam and dashed in a splash of color around the coral fans.

In the early mornings, I sat outside in our boat's cockpit while I enjoyed my coffee. Overhead, lime green parrots flew in pairs. Their boisterous chatter boomed so that I wanted earplugs. Hundreds of these birds glided out of their tree beds where they had spent the night. The birds were nature's perfect morning wake-up call. Later in the day, I watched another stunning life form as I walked in the rainforest. There, on the ground, streamed a single-file line of leaf-cutter ants. Determined workers carried a small green leaf piece on their backs as they marched toward their underground nest. I reveled in nature's cathedral. As a seeker, I asked, how can there not be a God?

2004

At the end of my mother's life, as she lay in bed covered by the imbued grayness of the nursing home, I looked into her eyes; the dancing bright olive color faded, dull. She stared at the ceiling. "What do you see?" I asked.

"God," she said.

2005

I once read these words in the Bible, "You are my beloved Son, in whom I am well pleased." When I replaced "Son" with "Daughter," I touched safety. I had craved my father's love all my life. When he died, I made a list of things I knew about him: He cheated on my mother, his second wife, and his third wife. He enlisted in the Navy and Army. And after his death, I found his birth certificate, which disclosed a different last name from the one we shared while I was growing up. So why had he changed his last name? Both he and God wore mystery masks. To be the beloved of God and my father was always my prayer.

2007

As a child, my belief in God had come quickly. He glowed within me at Sunday School and dwelled inside St. Patrick's Catholic Church, that I walked past on my way home from third grade. And he sparkled in the eyes of the twelve disciple pictures that my grandmother had given me. But as an adult, I wondered who heard my prayers. Could I only be talking to myself? I truly wanted to believe in an omnificent Being who would love and protect me.

2009

After the death and destruction caused by the Arab terrorists on September 11, 2001, I reflected on how a loving God could let this happen. How does one credit God for good but not the bad? At times, I free-floated in a sea of anxiety and fear over life events. One day, I noticed an advertisement on a booklet's front page: Free meditation classes at a local religious center. I thought it might be helpful to learn how to still my mind. Maybe this place could help me understand God. I soon enrolled in the publicized class of "awakening" and began a meditation practice using a mantra with each breath. It aroused a new-to-me inner calmness.

This place of worship was worlds apart from my time at Unity Church just a few years earlier. When I entered their temple on Sundays, my eyes seized upon the stunning sky-blue carpet. The chairs and stage heralded the same shade—the color blue signifying heaven and the god Krishna. Clusters of gold and purple balloons touched the wall and framed the altar. Ignited candles highlighted five large pictures of Ascended Masters that formed a religious cross above the altar. The congregation quietly sang a hymn. They followed the words displayed on a monitor that hung from the ceiling, and their bodies swayed. The ring of three chimes signaled the entrance onto the stage of seven leaders dressed in floor-length white and blue robes. The congregation chanted, "Aum, Peace."

I focused on learning how to meditate and even practiced the center's chakra yoga. Yet after six months, I found myself treading in a pool that longed to regain faith in God. I needed to understand why I must rely on their living guru. Or why I needed to worship the "wisdom and mastery" of their Ascended Masters. I felt an increased sense of unease. Had I wandered into a cult? So, I decided to move on.

2010 UNTIL NOW

I still meditated but now without a mantra. I focused on the breath. One morning, as I sat with my eyes closed, a voice popped into my head with the familiar words, "Please, dear God." Now, why had I thought of that? I asked myself, annoyed. Hadn't I gotten over the God-pleading? It reminded me of the childhood letters I'd written to my father after he moved from San Diego to Los Angeles: "Please, Dear Daddy, can I come to see you this weekend?" How irritating the way this beseeching voice signaled an uncomfortable truth. Deep down, I hadn't gotten over a need, along with a wish, that I might believe in a supreme power—to whom I could turn over responsibilities of my life. (Except, of course, for the things that I wanted to control.)

This awareness conveyed that I needed to relax, remember, and relish all the earth's beauty. I did not require a conception of God (or a big daddy) to protect me. Then, a year after attending the "blue" spiritual temple, I discovered in my neighborhood a Buddhist community. Once again, I asked my friend Grace to come with me to investigate this center. Inside the building, the bare walls held no images or divine beings to worship. Instead, I gazed at a glass-windowed wall. The frosted panes covered the lower half and stair-stepped up toward clear panes. I watched with pleasure as sunlight glowed off the foliage of a green lacy-leafed tree. The teacher sat upon a black cushion on a small platform and led a meditation. Later, a talk. With my eyes closed, I focused on my breath, in and out like the ocean ebbing and flowing.

It is clear, for now, that my search has stilled. I have found my spiritual home. With observation, I breathe in a feeling of contentment. I am no longer that lonely nine-year-old girl who gazed into the sky, wondering if God dwelled there or if her father loved her. I learned I am responsible for my thoughts and actions. There is no one else to blame. I do not walk alone in the garden. On its path I gather the flowers of friendship, happiness, and kindness. I bask in nature's beauty. With palms together, thumbs touching my heart, I bow my head in gratitude.

BETRAYAL

DAVID HARRIS

E ZRA'S NAME POPPED UP on Daniel's phone for the third time that morning. Daniel had no choice but to take the call from his brother. He was likely in bullying mode and would just keep calling. While Daniel was used to Ezra's irrational rants, he was long past trying to steer his brother toward reasoned discussion.

"Mom said you and Devorah would abide by my wishes," Ezra said, dispensing with any greeting. He was sitting in the kitchen of their mother's condo in Nyack, glancing toward the hospital bed in her living room where she had spent the final months of her life. The Hudson River, wide and wind-capped, was visible in the distance.

"I told you both last week, and Rosario will back me up on this," Ezra said. "Mom said it was up to me what to do with her ashes."

Daniel, gazing out the window of his editing studio in Brooklyn, took a small measure of solace that he had come to accept Ezra's personality in all its flawed dimensions. Over the course of their lives, Ezra had bent, fractured, and distorted the truth whenever it suited him. He had never acknowledged this shortcoming nor apologized for it.

"She hadn't been making sense about anything for months, Ezra," Daniel replied. "If that's what she said, it doesn't reflect our mother when her mind and spirit were intact."

"How would you know? You and Devorah abandoned her."

Daniel heard an infant crying in the background.

"You told us she didn't want to see us, Ezra. You wouldn't let us into her place."

Daniel turned toward the bank of monitors he used to produce documentary films. His appearance was standard hipster—a red plaid shirt, black jeans, and a trimmed goatee with hair down over his ears. His deep-set eyes, framed by wire-rimmed glasses, held an innocence not unlike their mother's when she approached middle age. Daniel was working on a film about the use of psychedelics to treat people with emotional disorders. It dawned on him as the narrative took shape that mind-altering drugs might have improved his brother's life.

"I'm going to see our sister later today," Daniel said. "Devorah and I haven't had a chance to talk lately. I want to hear her take."

"It doesn't matter," Ezra said. "Dad fucked up Mom's life twenty-five years ago. I'm not going to let her spend the rest of eternity with him."

•   •   •

Daniel met Devorah later that afternoon at the Grand Army Plaza Greenmarket and they walked together through Prospect Park. It was mid-September and a few oaks and maples had started to fade toward brown and red. He had a love/hate relationship with this time of year—mourning the end of summer yet invigorated by the city's energy in autumn.

"It's not news that he's out of his mind," Devorah said to her brother after they had walked in silence for several hundred yards. "I was hoping the love child he had with Rosario might calm him down, but there's no sign of that."

"Sometimes I think Rosario and Renaldo have made him crazier," Daniel said. "He becomes a parent at fifty with our mom's caretaker and shows no interest in marrying her. Now he's attempting to support all three of them." Devorah agreed that their brother's self-storage business in Newburgh wasn't going to make him rich. Ezra had been waiting five years for that to happen.

The three siblings had been raised by parents who expected great things of their children yet were clueless about how their own values might influence their offsprings' success in life. Before their father, Harry, died during their teen years, he had made a fortune in the mattress business in upstate New York, then lost most of it when he got overconfident and overextended. As young children, ski trips to Aspen and summers on Martha's Vineyard were the norm. Their father always had a new Mercedes coupe in the driveway for himself and a sedan for their mother. Such was their parents' base case for success.

After the mattress business went bust, Harry decided to run for elected office. He squeaked by in a State Assembly race to represent the old Borscht Belt resort towns in the Catskills, Daniel recalled. While Harry was no longer wealthy, he learned how to accumulate power and favors during three terms in Albany. He had just launched a long-shot bid for US senator when a heart attack killed him. The Daily News ran a front-page story that a woman who was not Harry's wife was in the hotel room with him when he died. He had collapsed on top of her. Estelle, visibly grief-stricken, had given no indication to her friends she was surprised.

"Ezra was acting like the older brother I always wanted a couple of years ago," said Devorah. "He was helping me open that boutique in East Hampton. He even loaned me some money."

Ezra had helped their younger sister that much? He had a tendency to go white-knuckle hard with many endeavors, to raise everyone's expectations too high and then view any skepticism as disloyalty. That had been the pattern through any number of ventures, most recently the self-storage business. Devorah, in her growing desperation to get something going in her life as she approached her thirty-fifth birthday, must have cautiously welcomed Ezra's support. Through no fault of either of them, the pandemic had brought it all tumbling down.

"Ezra has been trying to redeem our family's name, at least in his own mind, since Dad died," Daniel said. "The harder he tries, the more elusive it becomes. Making sure Mom's ashes are nowhere near Dad's grave ties into it in some twisted way."

"Mom's summer house on Buzzard's Bay was the only place I think she felt at peace in her later years," he added. Devorah put her hand through her brother's arm as they walked past a carousel.

75

Daniel noticed a young couple embracing under a blanket and oblivious to passersby. He remembered that a few months after Harry died, Estelle's sister told Devorah about an attractive young assistant to the Madison Avenue ad executive in charge of Harry's mattress account. Estelle had said she knew about the woman but mentioned it to no one. She never even mentioned it to Harry. She then told her sister she also knew about the skinny-dipping incident at a pool party one summer with the wife of one of Harry's top salesmen. Shortly after Estelle had been diagnosed with Alzheimer's, she'd volunteered both stories to her daughter.

"Mom used to ask me to remind her about our father," Devorah said, "after her mind started turning into dust. She loved him, regardless of his indiscretions. Ezra ought to know that as well as anyone."

Devorah stopped walking and turned to face Daniel. "I've got an idea. A few weeks ago, I was going through some old boxes and found a safe deposit box key. From the savings bank upstate where we grew up. Mom gave it to me about the time she'd been diagnosed. She couldn't remember what was in it—maybe some family keepsakes. I'm driving up there next week to see some friends."

●   ●   ●

"I found something," Devorah told Daniel when she called him from outside the bank on South Fallsburg's Main Street. "It's a deed to two grave plots at the Hebrew Association Cemetery outside of town. It's dated 1992, the year before Dad died, and it's got both their signatures on it."

"It won't make any difference to Ezra," Daniel said. "He's taking Mom's ashes up to Buzzard's Bay next week. He texted yesterday—didn't bother to call."

"That's the type of stunt our father would have pulled. Ezra's acting more like him the older he gets."

As Devorah spoke, Daniel took out an old family album he kept by his desk and flipped through the pages. The resemblance between their father and Ezra seemed to grow through the years. Whereas Harry grew a graying moustache and sideburns, and sported tinted aviator glasses, Ezra, ironically, had more of a rabbinical appearance. He had faintly

Asiatic eyes and a slight stoop, as if he was about to start praying and davening. But their father had those same eyes, and Ezra's consistent lack of any facial expression when responding to a question was similar. They both had the same side-eye glance that could indicate anything from shy curiosity to thinly veiled scorn.

"Let's talk to Rosario," Devorah said. "She thinks about family in a way that doesn't register with Ezra. She's the mother of a young child."

• • •

"He won't tell me anything," Rosario said to Devorah on the phone. Daniel listened on the speakerphone connection. Rosario's calm voice sounded tired. "He changes the subject. I've asked him several times."

"Could you do me a favor?" Devorah asked. "Daniel and I are planning a memorial service in three weeks in South Fallsburg. Tell him we'd like you both to come and bring the baby."

Silence.

"We've invited some of their old friends. Whether Ezra brings Mom's ashes or not, we're going to remember her and share memories."

"Will you have a rabbi?" Rosario asked finally. "It's the one thing he keeps talking about, finding a rabbi he connects with."

"Devorah told me there's a young one, new to the area," Daniel said. "He's very popular in town."

Again, silence.

"I need to tell you something that I don't think Ezra wants you to know," Rosario said finally. Devorah locked eyes with Daniel. One of them needed to say something.

"Okay," Devorah said.

"During the last few days before your mother died, she had these hallucinations that your father was with her. They were out to dinner, they were having a great time. She kept saying things like 'I love you. Don't leave me. I want to go away with you—just the two of us.'"

"Did Ezra hear it?" Daniel said.

"He did," Rosario said. "He tried to convince her that your father never loved her. Your Mom just laughed. 'Oh Ezra, you've always been the crazy one.'"

• • •

Rosario called Devorah the next day. Devorah put the call on speakerphone so Daniel could hear. Ezra had left for Buzzard's Bay with their mother's ashes. He didn't tell her what he was going to do with them or when he might return. She could not remember a time when Ezra acted so detached from her or their infant son.

Daniel decided to rent a car and drive up. When he and Devorah arrived at the house, Ezra lay on a faded yellow chaise lounge on the wide empty deck with a vodka tonic in one hand, gazing toward the translucent, mirror-smooth bay. He was listening to heavy metal, judging by the sound coming from his AirPods. He didn't hear them approach.

Ezra turned when Daniel stepped onto the deck. His eyes narrowed to the side-eye glance, and then a look of surprise and a grin.

"You know it was a protest, right?"

Daniel and Devorah stared at each other. She looked as mystified as he did.

"January 6th—there's no way that was an insurrection."

"Okay," Daniel said.

"I just want to be clear on that," Ezra added.

"Good to know. I don't think Dad would have agreed with you."

Ezra shook his head slowly, as if he was agreeing and disagreeing in his own mind with what Daniel had said.

"We're taking some of Mom's ashes back to South Fallsburg," Devorah said. "If the three of us can't agree on what to do with them, Daniel and I have come up with a solution."

Ezra got up from the chaise lounge, stumbled on a warped deck plank, and recovered himself before opening the sliding screen door into the house. He walked through the kitchen and into the large living room. Estelle had spent several summers of her twilight years in the room watching TV until she could no longer follow Jeopardy or knit the pink mohair sweater she'd never finished.

Daniel and Devorah followed him as far as the kitchen. Daniel saw what they had come for. He picked up a cardboard box labeled "Cremated Remains."

"We're taking this into the back room to divide it up," he shouted into the living room. "It will take a few minutes and we'll be on our way."

"Don't do that," Ezra replied.

"You don't have a veto," Daniel said. "We're going to have a memorial back home. We will inter some of her ashes there."

Devorah reached down to a cabinet where the Tupperware was kept and put a container on the faded Formica countertop. Daniel opened the box and unfolded the thick brown paper. Devorah pulled out a drawer and retrieved a large soup spoon.

"You shouldn't do that," Ezra said from the doorway.

The ashes were a mixture of fine grey dust and larger pieces of material Daniel assumed were fragments of bone. Devorah's hands shook. Her tight-lipped expression reflected her determination to stay focused on the task at hand.

"I can't let this happen," Ezra said. His speech was slurred and his intonation flat.

Devorah continued to spoon the cremains into the plastic container while Daniel stood between her and Ezra. Ezra started to breathe heavily and turned away. He walked back into the living room. Daniel heard a brief ripping sound, as if a Velcro strap had been undone.

When Ezra returned, he held an automatic pistol in his hand. "Please put the ashes back in the box."

Devorah raised her eyes and glared at Ezra for a moment, swallowed, then went back to what she was doing. She looked both frightened and infuriated.

"We're almost done, Ezra," Daniel said. "You're betraying Mom."

He remembered their father had a fascination with guns. Harry never kept any in the house, but he'd hang out at the local Rod & Gun Club on weekends, borrow a shotgun, and shoot clay pigeons with the locals.

Ezra stared at his siblings, wobbling slightly on his feet. He had the look of someone thinking intently, trying to figure something out, but gave no indication he had found an answer.

Devorah put the lid on the Tupperware container, closed the box containing their mother's ashes, then returned it to the kitchen counter. Daniel nodded at her, and they walked past Ezra, out the screen door and up the path through the overgrown grass to the garage.

Ezra followed them out, raised the gun at them, and then lowered it.

Devorah opened her car door and got in. Daniel turned toward his brother and they stared silently at each other for a moment before Daniel opened the driver's side door and slid behind the wheel. As he drove the car down the gravel driveway, a shot rang out.

A few days later, Daniel received a phone call from the police. Ezra had been found by a neighbor: collapsed on the deck, a bullet in his head. Neither Daniel nor Devorah had heard their brother take his own life.

Shades of Blue

MIERA RAO

Like the ocean it comes in waves over sands of
time. Like the ocean it washes over you and
drenches in dismal shades of blue.

Grief

it is deep—with its ebb and flow with tentacles that
drag you by your ankles to its murky bed below
where there's despair in its desolate dregs that swirl
you in indigo. In its inky depths are questions.

Anger.　　Questions.　　Guilt.　　Questions.

Loneliness

Questions　　　Questions　　and Regret.

Sometimes it is gentle. It rocks you like a baby and
wraps you in a soft blanket where aquamarine
memories cocoon. And you float. Sometimes it is
sapphire. A celebration of life, love, of laughter and
desire. Sometimes in a shade of briny blue where
dawn is twilight where day is night where night is
the color of grief it shows its mercy.

Suddenly

Unexpectedly

it will toss you a line. Toss you from the tempest to
the turquoise tops, and let you catch a breath let you
glimpse the sun and let your world glitter again. In
due course it will release you.

Wash you back to the beach where the sharp pain
loosens its grip. Where the sun will shine and heal.

You will find your smile...

You will laugh...

Grief.

Like the ocean it comes

in waves.

NODDING INTO A GROOVE

ALISHA WILLIS

T HEIRS WAS A RELATIONSHIP of a sort. At the end of her workday, after a quarter mile or so walk away from her Mission Street building in San Francisco, she'd see him cocooned and shivering inside a sleeping bag on Duboce Street, the part just under the Central Freeway overpass. Or he'd have placed his unrolled bag up against the train station's wire fencing. Sometimes he wasn't in these regular spots, but farther down the street, across from the gym. Curled up in one of several v-like niches. She'd grow worried when she didn't see him and once after not seeing him for a week, broke their nonverbal communication and asked after his well-being. He was fine.

Five days a week through rain, wind, heat, and fog they went on like this for three years. Until she got a new job, a new train-to-work-to-train route and knew not to tell him. Theirs wasn't that kind of relationship. They communed with head nods, quick smiles, and occasional grunts of acknowledgment but only that once with words.

Then one evening two years and two job changes later, they re-connected. After a celebratory French feast weighing heavy in her stomach, she had been walking for an hour sidestepping human, tree, and dog detritus, on the way to the Caltrain station when she saw him. Cocooned inside a sleeping bag in his semi-usual spot up against the train station's wire fencing, he was shivering. He looked a little more weathered, his tan face reddened and leathered a bit more by the elements. In joy she rushed him—babbling about not seeing him—and pressed money into his hand. He startled, glanced twice at the twenty, made it disappear, then he looked up at her and nodded. She nodded back, certain he recognized her. In case he didn't, she knew not to ask.

PARTED, NOT SEPARATED

EVELYN LATORRE

A NTONIO AND I FELL IN LOVE when we both were twenty-three and I was serving in the Peace Corps in his country of Peru. In June 1966, at the end of my two-year commitment, I bid a tearful good-bye to friends and colleagues in Abancay, the small Andean town that had been my home since November 1964. For one last time, my roommate Marie and I bumped along the narrow dirt road that wound around the mountains to the ancient Incan capital of Cusco where Antonio lived. There, I'd bid farewell to the dark-eyed university student responsible for the surges of passion I'd felt often over the past year—feelings I'd tried hard to discount.

After the seven-hour drive in a friend's pick-up, and a day in the ancient capital of the Incas, I'd board a plane for Lima to attend a week's debriefing with Peace Corps staff and get some medical tests. Then, it was off to either reunite with my family in Northern California, or travel with Marie to other South American countries. I hadn't yet decided what to do. I only knew that when I returned to the States, I planned to begin graduate studies in social work at the University of Wisconsin, where I'd been accepted for the 1967 fall semester.

The Peace Corps' regional doctor in Cusco had set up a medical exam for me with a physician in Lima to see if my latest stomach discomfort was worms. For the past month I'd spent a couple days in bed because of a strange intestinal irritation.

"Probably nerves," Marie said.

"You're probably sad," Antonio added, "about leaving." He was right about that. We both refused to think it might be something more serious.

On the tarmac of Cusco's international airport, Antonio and I kissed for the last time. My *novio* and I wouldn't see one another again soon—if ever. Though he'd asked me several times to marry him and stay in Peru, I didn't see marriage or living in Peru in my immediate future. Antonio still had at least a year's studies left at his university in Cusco. At this point in his life, he had few marketable skills with which to support himself, let alone a wife. Besides, there was much I still wanted to see and do, so I would continue on my own, travel the world, and attend graduate school.

"Time to leave, Evelyn," said fellow volunteers, as they skirted around Antonio and me on their way to the plane.

I forced myself from the comfort of Antonio's embrace. I'd lost count of the number of times he or I had broken off our relationship since first meeting over lunch at his parents' Abancay home. I'd been drawn to his kindness—and his Latin handsomeness. On the other hand, we had different opinions on many topics like US foreign policy, capitalism, and the value of the work ethic. We'd hashed over personal and world problems during our many hours-long talks sitting side-by-side in Abancay's central plaza.

"You should apply yourself." I looked into his eyes, hoping he understood my meaning. "Plan for the future you want."

Frowning and lowering his eyes, he said, "It wouldn't do any good. Things never work out anyway."

"You're smart! Use your intelligence." I wanted my optimism to be contagious. "You're too fatalistic."

"And you want an ideal man!" He gestured at the people walking in the plaza. "But you'll never find him in reality."

"I know what I want. Adventure and a master's degree—then marriage and a family. Do you even *know* what you want?"

He grinned. "You're what I want. No other girl I've ever met has been so frank about everything."

Several times, when upset with one another, we ended our boyfriend-girlfriend relationship. Days later, in a beautifully phrased letter, Antonio apologized for his angry words. Other times, it would be me writing to say I longed to be with him and had spoken too bluntly. Or we both wrote, and our letters crossed somewhere in mailbags being transported along the winding 130-mile mountain road between his Cusco and my Abancay.

Each time we'd reconcile. Over the sixteen months of our courtship, we were like two magnets that changed poles—attracting one another one month and repelling each other the next. More than once we'd agreed that a life together couldn't happen because he had no way to get to the US and I didn't want to stay in Peru forever.

Regardless of our seemingly different world views, I valued how Antonio encouraged me to seek higher education. He diligently corrected my Spanish. And, we had similar rural upbringings—his on a hacienda in the shadow of the Incan citadel of Machu Picchu, and mine on an in town farm in the southeastern Montana cattle lands. And there were other characteristics that drew me to this slim, broad-shouldered youth with a shock of wavy black hair.

Whenever Antonio encountered a helpless animal or human, he would assist them in getting to their destinations safely—like the blind man he helped up the cathedral stairs. His gentle affection extended to me, too. I'd never before experienced the amount of consideration he showed—about my health, education, and general well-being. Unfortunately, despite all the love we felt for one another, neither of us saw a way forward together.

After our good-bye at the Cusco airport, I held back tears until I took my seat on the plane. From my window seat, I saw Antonio standing alone, shoulders drooping. The DC-4 taxied down the runway. As the plane lifted into the narrow passageway between the surrounding 17,000-foot mountains, the pain of leaving overtook me and I burst into tears. Wet tissues piled up at my feet for most of the two-hour flight to Lima.

In the excitement of seeing the sixty-seven of us who remained from the original group of 102 Peace Corps volunteers trained at Cornell, I almost forgot about my upcoming doctor's appointment. For most of my Peace Corps assignment, I'd been healthy, except for a few colds with coughs. I had lived in Abancay's sunny valley 7,000-foot altitude rather than at Cusco's 12,000 feet, so I'd escaped the respiratory problems that plagued my colleagues at the higher, colder altitudes.

After the past month of nausea and stomach issues, I felt a bit better and considered cancelling the doctor's visit. After all, my stomach malady had not kept me from packing and sending off my four large metal trunks filled with alpaca rugs, colorful local indigenous clothing, and quinoa gifted to me by the girls' club I'd formed. The local items replaced what I'd brought in my trunks from California—a typewriter, a never-used mimeo apparatus, and kitchen equipment. Women in town bought most of the clothes I'd sewn. I had a more emotional attachment to the Peruvian handicrafts and food than to the US apparel and cooking utensils. Money from the sale of the items I sold would finance my future travels. Antonio and I joked that I should pack him inside one of my trunks so he could be with me in California.

On the last day of our Peace Corps group's debriefing in Lima, I walked to the doctor's office. A nurse greeted me with a cup and requested my urine. After delivering the goods, I was ushered into an examining room. Shivering in a thin white gown, I sat on an exam table and listened to muffled voices speaking Spanish on the other side of the door. I couldn't make out what was being said and wondered what was taking so long. Could a case of worms be causing their discussion and my morning bouts of nausea?

The exam room door opened. With a swish the nurse entered and asked me for my blood. She tightened a plastic band around my upper arm then pricked my vein with a needle. I bit my lip and watched blood fill the glass vial.

"*Pobrecita,*" she said, and left the room.

Why would she feel sorry for me? Obviously, the tests had told her something I didn't know. My heart beat fast. I felt like I was twelve and back in Dr. Treat's office thinking I just had a bad sore throat. My Montana pediatrician had ordered blood tests and a spinal tap. Before I knew what was happening, I was diagnosed with rheumatic fever, then hospitalized. My parents and four younger siblings lived sixty miles away from the hospital and were only able to visit me at Christmas. After a month, the doctor finally released me to home bed rest and daily doses of penicillin for five more months.

"That's to prevent permanent heart damage," he told me. "If you don't have a strong heart, you'll never be able to bear children."

"I don't plan on having any," I said, my pre-teen face blazing hot with embarrassment. No one I knew, including myself, was comfortable talking about how a woman came to bear a child.

I'd learned about the "birds and the bees" from the phonograph records that a visiting seminarian played as part of summer catechism classes. I'd gotten a thrill reading about pregnancy in my parents' big medical book, under the covers with a flashlight. No one had explained how often doing "it" might lead to having a baby. At twenty-three, I was still unclear on exactly how much contact it took to become "pg." I could count on one hand the number of times Antonio and I had been intimate.

I'd resisted "going all the way" with Antonio for fourteen of the sixteen months we'd been in a committed relationship as *novios*. Before our first time, he reassured me that he'd "take measures" to prevent anything from happening that neither of us was prepared for. I had no idea what those measures were. Birth control pills were condemned as forbidden fruit at the Catholic college I'd attended. And anyway, I didn't know where to get them. When I was a teenager, Dad had given me a stern warning "not to do it until I was married." Now, there was a real possibility that something was growing inside my body—something that unlike worms, I could never explain to my very religious parents.

After what seemed like hours, the doctor and the nurse reentered the exam room. The nurse laid her hand on my shoulder as the obstetrician gave the pronouncement.

"*Sí, usted está embarazada.*"

I'm pregnant? No, it can't be! My body shuddered. The doctor's words felt like a slap in the face. Sobs I'd been holding back poured out in a torrent. My life was ruined forever, and I was to blame.

"What will you do?" the doctor asked.

I couldn't answer because I didn't know. I was alone and confused, without anyone to comfort me. Turning to my parents was out of the question. They would condemn me for my mortal sin. I'd said good-bye to Antonio. Even Marie was leaving in two days. She'd asked me to travel around South America with her small group, but I'd not yet agreed to go.

"There are measures you can take," the doctor said, looking past me. His words brought me back to reality. I knew he was suggesting I consider an abortion. "I'll give the Peace Corps my diagnosis, and they can help you decide."

The next day was a whirlwind of meetings with Peace Corps staff. They could get me a job in Washington D.C. until the baby was born and I could give it up for adoption. *Maybe that's what I should do.* Then again, there was the option of terminating the pregnancy, which I could not bear to do.

My morning nausea weakened my ability to decide. Should I take the abortion solution the doctor suggested, or the Peace Corps' offer of adoption? Neither choice was palatable. I hated to leave the country without at least informing Antonio, but I didn't know where to reach him. Then too, Peru's phone service was undependable. Mail delivery wasn't much better, but I might find someone leaving for Cusco who could get a letter to him in the next few days. I cried softly as I wrote.

> *Querido Antonio,*
>
> *I am pregnant with your baby. I can't explain how confused I am. Peace Corps people think I should give it up for adoption. I cry whenever I imagine giving it away after carrying it for nine months.*
>
> *I don't want to give you responsibilities you aren't ready to take on . . . that's why I decided to go to California first, then to Washington, D.C. where I'll wait for you. If you don't come, I'll do what I have to. If you come, we'll see. I'm enclosing a form you need to immigrate to the U.S.*
>
> *Love, Evelyn*
>
> *P.S. I still might travel around South America with the others.*

Marie pressed me to commit to leaving with her group. I longed to go but wasn't certain I should. When I didn't give her an answer, she gave me an inquisitive look.

"Evelyn, are you not committing to the tour because of your doctor's appointment?"

I couldn't look at my caring roommate. "I can't go with you because I'm pregnant with Antonio's baby."

"Oh no!" Marie gasped, her eyes widening with realization. She wrapped her arms around me. "I'm so sorry! I should have been there for you. And now I'm on my way to Brazil."

"I'm frightened and not sure what to do," I said, squeezing my empathetic roommate's hand, grateful for her love instead of her judgement. "I found someone going to Cusco who can deliver a letter to Antonio, but I'll likely be back in the States before he gets it."

The next morning, in the hotel room we shared, Marie awakened me.

"There's an urgent phone call from Cusco for you," she said. "It's Antonio."

I grabbed the phone. My heart leapt at the sound of Antonio's voice.

"I called last night," he said, through a scratchy connection, "but you were out. I don't care if you are pregnant or not. I want you to come back and marry me." We had both been denying the idea that pregnancy could be at the root of my stomach problems. Now, he apparently had acknowledged that possibility.

"Yes," I said through tears of love and relief. "I am, and I'll return to marry you as soon as I can book the flight. I love you."

The same day around noon, I was packing when there was a knock at the hotel door. A Peace Corps volunteer from another group said he'd come from Cusco and had a letter for me. I recognized the blue ink of Antonio's typewriter spelling out my name on the envelope. I tore open the envelope and saw the date—June 8, 1966—the day after I'd said good-bye to him at the Cusco airport. My body flooded with warmth at the thought of Antonio writing to me before his phone call and even before receiving my letter.

Querida Evelyn,

You can't know how despondent I am in these moments of almost infinite agony knowing that I can't reach you. Nor can I comprehend how great is my love for you. When you left, it was like a part of me left with you. I was so confused that I could do nothing. I can hardly write, even now, remembering that only a few days ago, I could hold you and kiss you and I was so happy. And now I am so alone I can barely express it in words . . . I would marry you in a minute if you would return. I hope to receive word from you about our ???? very soon.

Yours for eternity,

Antonio

His question marks referred to the baby that he knew only as a faint possibility when I'd kissed him good-bye for what I thought would be the last time. I loved him even more for what he'd said in his phone call: "I don't care if you are pregnant or not. I want you to come back and marry me." And now his letter was poetry to my heart. I was marrying the right man.

Antonio arranged our wedding in six days during which I sewed a wedding dress. We married in an ancient Spanish chapel that stood atop sturdy Inca walls that had survived Cusco's 7.0 earthquakes. The Inca walls proved to be a symbol of our marriage.

My "accidental" pregnancy was the best mistake of my life. It forced the union of a relationship that was headed towards a permanent disconnection. My plan to attend graduate school wasn't abandoned, just delayed for a year.

We've had two sons and six decades of joy, peppered with a few temporary detachments. All of which, through love, we've managed to join back together. Our shot-gun wedding turned into a bullet-proof marriage.

My life, like many, proves the truth of the quote from the American mythologist and writer, Joseph Campbell, "You must give up the life you planned in order to have the life that is waiting for you."

PABLO AND MARIA

BRUCE NEUBURGER

I WAS IN THE IMPERIAL VALLEY for the winter lettuce harvest
when I caught sight of Pablo Ramos on a street in downtown
Mexicali. Pablo's slight build and long dark hair were familiar to me. I
hadn't seen him since the summer harvest season in Salinas. Now,
winter, he was back in his hometown while I was on the road following
la corrida, as farmworkers called the north-south crop circuit.

I caught up with him just as he crossed Madero Street a few hundred
yards from the border station. He was carrying a bulky shoulder bag.

"Whatchya up to?" I asked Pablo.

"I'm heading to a restaurant for *menudo* (tripe soup). And as soon
as I get rid of this little *crudo* (hangover) I'm going to my office." I had
an idea his "little *crudo*" was the prize he'd earned from his previous
night's bout with a bottle of tequila.

"Your office?" I asked. Pablo grinned and took my skeptical tone as
his cue.

"You think I can't have an office? I have to be a big shot to have an
office? Well, it's not only an office—it's one with a view!" I was neither

93

surprised nor put off by his exaggerated tone of indignation.

Suddenly in the mood for spicy tripe soup and the kind of *vacilando*—joking around—I knew Pablo was good for, I tagged along to the restaurant. After the *menudo*, we headed across the border for Calexico and *El Hoyo*, the large lot where farmworkers gathered early mornings on work days to catch their rides on company buses and vans to the fields. Under an overhang between the Farm Labor office and the fence that rimmed the lot, Pablo opened his shoulder bag, took out a portable typewriter and set it down on a rough wooden table.

"So, here you are, my very doubtful friend." Pablo grinned. "My office. All I'm missing is a secretary."

"Okay, but where's this great view you were bragging about?"

He pointed in the direction of the border fence, a brown wooden swath that snaked across the vista.

"A view of a long wooden fence?"

"Not just any fence. Look there," he said, pointing down. Between the wooden fence and *El Hoyo* was a small gorge with bare brown soil. At the bottom of this arroyo was a narrow river running slowly and darkly, with a cap of foam. The foam was so thick in places that it wasn't apparent there was any water under it at all.

"A view of the river, *El Rio Nuevo*," he said. "An office with a river view."

"Looks like *El Rio Feo* to me," I said. Pablo's laugh had his trademark sarcastic edge.

"And it doesn't look anything like new," I added.

"It was new some years ago."

"Why don't they call it *El Viejo Rio Nuevo*?"

He paused to think. "It's not that old. Maybe sixty years or so."

"How does a new river come about like that?"

"Well, after your *gringo* ancestors stole our land, they decided to steal our water from the Rio Colorado that flowed into the Mexican side. But the river got out of control and almost washed them all away. This river was the result of all that. So, you see what your *gringo* ancestors did?"

Pablo, like many *campesinos*, often used the word "gringo." And sometimes they would apologize to me. But to be honest, I never felt offended by it. I once asked Pablo what he meant when he used it. He said it usually just referred to white people from the United States. At other times, when he was angry, it meant arrogant bastards who think they have a God-given right to fuck over the rest of the world. In the first case, it seemed innocent enough. In the second, I shared his sentiments for the arrogant, brutish behavior that America had become infamous for around the world.

When, over the years, I'd asked Mexicanos where the word "gringo" came from I got two versions. Both involved US General Pershing's invasion of Mexico in 1916 in pursuit of Pancho Villa. In one version Pershing's soldiers sang the song, "Green Grow the Lilacs ..." as they marched south. Thus: "Who are they?" "Oh, those are the 'Green Grows.'" In the other version people expressed their anger at the invaders who wore green uniforms by yelling, "Green, go!" as in, "Yankee, go home!"

In either case, the name is associated with invaders who had stolen Mexican land, treated Mexicans as inferiors, and exploited and plundered their resources and people. Given all of that, "gringo" seemed like a pretty benign expletive. If gringo is a pejorative, at least it's a pejorative with historical content—contempt shown for unjust actions and harsh behavior. Which is far different from the racist terms Americans have pinned on just about every non-white, and some white, racial, and ethnic groups. You know what names I mean.

"Don't blame my ancestors," I told Pablo. "My ancestors were Germans. They would never do anything bad like that." It was my turn to laugh sarcastically. "So, somebody started dumping their shit in that river."

"Yah, it's more shit than river now," said Pablo.

It was evident that the small river was the only thing of consequence that stood between the wooden fence on the Mexican side and El Hoyo on the US side. There was just a simple chain-link fence around El Hoyo.

"Too bad the river's so messed up," I said. "This would be an easy place to cross over the border."

Pablo's expression became more serious. "I've seen people crossing wearing nothing but their underwear, with their clothes in plastic bags on their head, wading through the typhoid or whatever's in there. I once saw a group of women in the river turned back by the *migra* with their guns drawn. I'd hate to go within five yards of that stinking mess." Then he could not help himself: "You see all the shit people have to go through to come here!" It was Pablo's favorite humor, laced with irony.

People milled around the farm labor office and the covered area where Pablo and I sat. Farmworkers came to the office to apply for services. Sometimes they would have to fill out applications and Pablo made a few dollars assisting those having trouble navigating the forms. While we were talking, a man came and asked for help. He was maybe sixty. I noticed his thick hands and gnarled fingers. He wore a straw sombrero with a tassel that hung down at the back. He pulled a paper from his shirt pocket and unfolded it carefully next to the typewriter. Pablo picked it up to examine it.

"Let me ask you some questions," Pablo said to the man.

I got up. "Sit here," I said. I told Pablo, "I'll leave you to your office work." And he invited me for dinner at his house in Mexicali. With the memory of his partner Maria's cooking from other meals, I readily agreed. We arranged to meet later in the day.

I'd first met Pablo a few years before in Salinas. We worked together on a D'Arrigo Brothers broccoli crew. This was a piece rate crew and the work was very fast. But it was still possible to talk to someone working next to you. I was still traveling linguistically on Spanish training wheels, but with Pablo I could move at full speed in my native tongue. More than language, we shared a lot of attitudes in common. These were, especially, negative ones towards the company, the growers in general, and a political system we both referred to as imperialism. Pablo and I had absorbed a lot of the rebellious spirit of the times, especially a loathing for the war in Vietnam and a jaundiced view of US democracy.

Cutting vegetables next to Pablo gave me an ear to his personal story. I learned his father had left his mother shortly after he was born and that his mother died when he was around eight. He had an aunt and several uncles in the border area, but he was never close to them and grew up mostly on the streets of Mexicali and Calexico. His first language was Spanish, but he learned English as a child. He had a clever mind and learned to read and write well in both languages. This proved useful.

One day, during the Salinas broccoli harvest, we had worked late. It was deep into Fall and nearly dark by the time we got back to town. We were both very hungry. I gave Pablo a ride home from the Safeway parking lot where the bus let us off, and he invited me to eat at his small cottage on Sanborn Road, an upstairs unit behind a house and not visible from the street.

Pablo was living with Maria, a woman of stocky build, medium height, a wide face and long dark hair. Pablo called her *La India*. They had been living together for a few years, but this was the first year Maria had come north with Pablo. She didn't work in the fields but did laundry and ironing for some working families, mostly out of their small cottage. I thought she must have been bored staying home most of the day in that little place.

There wasn't much furniture in the apartment. But there were pillows on the floor, and we sat on them while throwing down a few shots of tequila. Then Maria came into the living room with the food.

Perhaps it was my hunger or the stimulus of the tequila, but it was a dinner so delicious that the pleasure of it remained with me long after I scooped up the last bits of meat juice and beans in the last piece of tortilla. It was not a fancy meal—thin beefsteak, beans, nopales, rice and handmade tortillas, some jalapeños—but it was fantastic. I don't know how Maria managed to create such a delight with these simple ingredients. But that was the case.

As in nearly all the Mexican households I visited in the years I spent in the fields, and where I was invited to share a meal, the men would sit and be served by a wife or a daughter, a niece, or any other women in the house. Despite feeling uncomfortable with that arrangement, I usually didn't make an issue of it. But being pretty well-acquainted with Pablo, I thought I could say things to him without him taking offense. So, I questioned this arrangement of wife as servant. The tequila made his face a bit flush and his sarcastic laugh louder than normal as he launched a defense by saying that he worked all day, Maria was not working outside the house, so it was only fair that she did the work in the home, including the cooking and serving.

"I know you believe in women's equality," said Pablo, "but there is reality." He took another sip of tequila. "Call it a division of labor—does that make it okay? Ya, women get the short end of the stick. But we men don't have it so great either—us field workers. I know," said Pablo, anticipating a reply I had yet to formulate, "we can't ever be *liberated* unless *everyone* is liberated, but we have to live in the meantime."

He then poured me another tequila and insisted I drink a toast with him "to the liberation of us all from this truly fucked-up world."

Pablo, like most Mexicanos I knew, was bitterly cynical about "*la política*"—especially the governing system in Mexico. There was a deep distrust of political leaders—a belief that anyone who rose to leadership in the system would sell out. People used the phrase "*puro conveniencia*"—pure self-interest, to describe this—the belief that everyone in government was out for themselves. Therefore, however abused most workers felt by the way things were, they saw little hope of finding a way out.

Pablo also had a sadness in him, a tendency to depression, you might say in psychological terms, and he "self-medicated" with occasional but devastating binges of alcohol. More than once he'd disappeared from work and I'd see him on the street, pretty messed up. I scolded him and struggled with him about this, and about how he had things to offer the world. But it was a tough battle to win. Later I learned that this greatly saddened Maria as well.

I met Pablo late in the afternoon, after his "day at the office" and he took me to his Mexicali home, an adobe house in a new *colonia* on the outskirts of the expanding border city. Its thick walls enclosed two rooms, a combination living room and kitchen, and a bedroom off the kitchen. Toilet facilities were in a wooden outhouse.

The living room's cement floor was covered with several layers of rugs. There was a couch against the wall facing the kitchen area and a table underneath a window whose frame was not perfectly set in the wall, leaving a space between the window frame and the adobe surrounding it. A wire came through that space and split in two. Each section led to a different part of the room, where hooks in the ceiling held small fixtures, each with a 60-watt bulb. The house was fairly dark even during the day. But that adobe structure kept homes like this somewhat insulated in the blast-furnace days of summer.

Pablo and I shared another delicious dinner. We drank beer. We spoke about upcoming union elections that had come as part of the state's Agriculture Labor Relations Act. Pablo caught some of the skepticism circulating about the union—rumors of corruption—and this fed his inbred cynicism. Maria remained in the background, busying herself with recharging our supply of warm tortillas and cold beer and clearing the table after we were done eating.

Pablo drank without much pause. By nine o'clock he was semiconscious on the couch. I had no idea where we were in Mexicali and no interest in exploring the area at night. Nor was Pablo in any shape to guide me to my downtown Mexicali hotel. With Maria's assent, I prepared a spot on the floor near the couch.

Maria was putting things away in the little kitchen area, which consisted of a sink, a wooden table, and a stove powered by propane from a large metal tank.

I thanked Maria for the food and said if she persisted in feeding me so well she might never get rid of me.

In our conversation I found out she was from Tabasco in southern Mexico. There she had three children but came north to find work to feed them. Her mother was taking care of her kids. The father of the children was no longer around, and Maria sent money home to help support the children. Pablo sometimes gave her money to send home, and she made money helping people at a laundromat near the *colonia*. She hoped she could bring them up north someday, but not now.

When I told her how I felt uncomfortable with the men always eating and the women always serving them, she laughed. I thought she would think I was crazy, but she understood quite well. She told me that as men go, Pablo was pretty good. Except for his drinking. He was never abusive as others were with women she knew. And even with the restricted life in Mexicali and Salinas, she felt freer now than when she lived in the south in a village where women's lives were tightly proscribed. I said I didn't like the way men treated women, but I understood how society molded them that way.

I told her how I'd had to confront my own instilled male attitudes. I related an incident years before when I worked in a GI anti-war coffeehouse near an army base. How the women who worked in that project were critical of a "division of labor" whereby jobs like cooking and making coffee were left up to the women.

One evening the coffeehouse was filled with GIs who'd come to hear music and relax. The women who were there caught everyone's attention by stopping the music. They played Tammy Wynette's song, "Stand by Your Man." I was groping for words to translate the song title. "*Pararse junto a tu hombre*," the literal translation, didn't do it. So I said, "*Apoyar a su hombre a pesar de su estupidez*" —Support your man no matter how stupid he is. Maria laughed heartily at that.

"Well," I said, "the women were angry at the song and at us men for assuming they'd do the physical work in the coffeehouse—cleaning the dishes—all that. I too was angry. I thought, 'Here we are trying to organize against a brutal war in Vietnam and these women are just nitpicking, looking for things to criticize—raising personal grievances above larger, more important issues!'"

After a time, I told Maria, I realized that my attitude was largely bullshit. Because we opposed some injustices didn't mean we were free from distorted relationships and backward attitudes.

Maria listened patiently to all this. Then she said that she hoped to be able to work and support herself so she could decide about things in her own life. She said she knew women who were mistreated in their relationships but accepted this as their fate and obligation.

I asked Maria about the father of her children. Her face turned somber, and her stocky body slumped. For a moment I thought she was going to fall, and I'd have to catch her. I felt a sense of dread and regret. Why had I opened my mouth? Maria caught herself and turned to me.

"*Lo siento ...*" she said, her eyes welling up.

She'd just told me she was sorry. In that instant I too felt tears cloud my eyes. The sadness in her face and in her voice shook me. I felt foolish to be near tears when it was her torment, not mine.

I didn't push the conversation and Maria did not take it any further. She wiped her face, went into the bedroom, brought out several large, warm blankets. She put one down on the rug in the living room area for me. She took the other and laid it over Pablo who was still asleep on the couch. Pablo stirred, looked around and fell immediately back to sleep. I rolled up in the blanket and tried to sleep.

"*Hasta mañana,*" Maria said.

"*Hasta mañana,*" I repeated from my cocoon.

A THOUSAND YEARS

RICHARD E. MCCALLUM

OUR VILLAGE GLOWS with a blood-red sunset as our mission bells ring. My concerned mother, Chin Ming, calls out, "Lin, time for mass."

The responsibility for my younger sister became mine when I turned seventeen. "Hurry! Upon dark, the insurgents will emerge with the quiet skill of a tiger."

"Pray for our safety," she says. Birds chirp, whistle, and flutter.

"If danger approaches," I tell her, "the winged ones will sound the first alarm."

"Có thể bạn sống một ngàn năm." My younger sister wishes me a long life.

We pass by the temple where our neighbors have gathered. Chanting resounds. The mantras passed down through generations provide background accompaniment to the incense, and a mood of solemnity and reverence pervades. The people attending the temple are not sympathetic toward Catholics and resist the government and US forces. We walk without talking through their sector.

Arriving at our parish, we linger to watch the sunset. Christian hymns sung within welcome our arrival. "*Un beau coucher de soleil.*" With pride, I demonstrate my ability to speak French.

A nun stops before entering and interprets my remark, "a beautiful sunset," in English. The priests and nuns of our order attended seminaries in France. "It's almost noon in Paris," she adds, knowing I wish to improve my ability to speak English as well.

After the service, my best friend and I hurry along the path, my sister now safely with our mother. "Remember just a few years ago," Sun says, "all the children played hide-and-seek together?"

"Yes, it's too dangerous for us now."

"Sad. We had many good times."

Out of safety concerns, Sun and I walk without speaking again, until we reach our dwellings. She departs, chiming the same colloquialism my sister had, "*Có thể bạn sống một ngàn năm.*"

"Yes," I say to myself in English, "may we both live a thousand years."

·   ·   ·

After the harvest season, the South Vietnamese military sets up a recruiting station in my town square. Young men, including my brother, line up to join our forces. Parents from the village socialize and mingle in the bustling center. The family dog follows me as I visit with my friends. Helicopters flying above drop pamphlets. Flags flap from the turbulence. American tanks, armored vehicles, and armaments display the power of the joint forces and impress onlookers.

Politicians take turns speaking from the podiums. "Join the struggle to keep our country free from foreign dictatorships." "Protect property rights." "Receive high pay, bonuses offered." "Save your religious freedom." "Send money to help your families."

Then a loud whistle pierces my ears. I look up. White smoke streams from a projectile overhead. My dog yelps. A nearby blast knocks me over. Chaos and destruction enter my peaceful world through fire, smoke, and screams. Machine gun bursts shatter structures and rip through bodies. The war has come to us.

"Jesus, have mercy on my soul. Protect my family." My fingers grip my crucifix necklace, providing a moment of comfort and hope.

Stumbling to my feet, my ears ringing, I choke on smoke and am blinded by soot. When my eyes clear, the sights horrify: a bloodied arm on the ground—attached to nothing—a body without a head—a man on fire runs among us panicked survivors. He trips and falls atop the slain.

Another explosion hurls me face down in the mud. My soul prepares to leave my body as my dirt-filled mouth prays. "Dear God, forgive me for my sins. I was sometimes mean to my sister, but I love her." My dog finds me; he licks me, whines and growls, and tugs at my wrist. He guides me out of harm's way.

The attack leaves our hamlet in ruins; chickens and pigs lie dead on the ground. Forlorn and mournful, my father, mother, and sister huddle over the remains of my grandmother. My poor *bà nội*! News of my brother's death arrives. In a matter of minutes my life has been shattered.

My family discusses if I should leave our village and move to my uncle's city. To make decisions in the mist of unimaginable tragedy confuses me, but few alternative options come to mind. As I journey from the smoldering ruins of my life, I can't help but wonder what lies ahead.

•   •   •

My uncle has heard nothing from my family since I left them. We fear the worst has happened. I shed ten thousand tears. My earth rotates around the sun many times. My new life unfolds.

In a joint-forces hospital, where I am now employed, a cultural affairs officer announces, "Please allow me to introduce US Navy Medical Corpsman . . ."

When Howard appears on stage, my girlfriend, Bian, squeezes my hand tightly. With a teasing and suggestive voice, she whispers, "Handsome in his uniform."

". . . Howard Washington, the first African American assigned to the Combined Action Program, CAP, will perform a puppet show with Lin Minh, one of our medical staff employees."

Bian waves her hand flirtatiously, and I slap it away. She embarrasses me. Howard waves to us all: US and Vietnamese soldiers, civilians, and staff. Everyone claps, and his friends call out, "Go, Howard." I feign a jealous look that makes Bian laugh, but then Howard looks directly at me and smiles. My heart melts and I flutter my hand over my heart for him to see.

"We have all benefited from Howard's volunteer effort," the CAP officer says, "dispensing medicines, treating patients, and his participation in improving relations with the local population."

The master of ceremonies steps back and beckons me to the stage. "For the final act of our show, Howard joins Lin Minh to present the Asian creation story."

A surge of excitement lifts me out of my chair. My moment to be with Howard performing arrives. Bian laughs and taps my arm, "Tell him you love him and want to have his babies." My heart speeds up and my body warms as I soar to his side.

"Throughout these last months," the host remarks, "you may have heard these two speaking in each other's languages and making everything around them sound as though it were talking." He contorts his face to express wonderment.

The spectators laugh. My smile hides my fear. In Vietnamese I whisper to Howard, "I cannot remember a word of English!"

He murmurs into my ear, "I love you."

"*Anh Yêu Em*, Howa'd," I respond in imitation of his words.

"In exchange for Lin teaching Vietnamese to Howard," the MC continues, "Howard taught Lin ventriloquism. Together, they will demonstrate their ability both to translate and to project their voices to make it sound like the puppets speak."

We pick up our puppets, dressed like ancient gods, as an interpreter repeats the officer's speech in Vietnamese. Red round light beams illuminate the backdrop. In front of the floodlit screen, we position ourselves.

Calmed by Howard, I address the audience, "Our puppet show depicts my country's folklore as told in Pangu's creation myth."

In Vietnamese, Howard repeats the phrase and I smile as we hold our decorative puppets in our laps and the screen displays images of a tumultuous universe. As I begin to tell the myth, my fears and insecurities evaporate in the magic of the moment.

Howard locks his eyes on mine, and I feel his love for me without him having to say anything. We bow at the end of our lines, and the audience, on its feet, applauds. I float through the crowd of smiling faces as I step off the stage. My dream of us being together has come true.

•   •   •

Howard deploys on medivac evacuation missions over the year as the war rages. I worry for his safety, but each time he returns, our hearts fill with love. In the hospital ward following his most recent three-month deployment, we get a chance to spend time together. I try to hide my medical condition but it's hard to control its symptoms. My light brown skin pales, I gag, and run to the sink. Howard, concerned, notices my distress, and pulls me close. He wraps his arms around me and assures me that everything will be all right.

Crying, I push him away. "Leave me alone." My self-conflicts confuse me; I am a good Catholic girl, and I knew Howard and I should have waited for marriage. Also, I am terrified he will leave me and not want our baby.

"What's wrong? Are you sick?"

"Yes. You go."

"I'll help."

Shaking off his attempt to hug me, I say, "Please leave me." His image in the mirror shows profound concern. A handful of water on my face calms me down. Howard hugs me from behind. The sound of my sobs echo.

"Please, Lin, what is it? How can I help?"

His need to console me interferes with my privacy, making me feel smothered.

"Oh, my god! You're pregnant?"

The expression on my face matches the look women give men when they figure out something that would have been obvious to any woman.

"But it's been three months since . . . why didn't you tell me?"

"My girlfriends all say you will leave me when you go. Lots of Vietnamese girls with abandoned American children." Tremors twitch on my face as I watch Howard's eyes for the unmasked moment of his true feelings before he can conceal them.

"I love you, Lin."

I do not detect falsehood in his gaze. "I love you too, Howa'd."

Rather than make up in the washroom, where I've just been sick, we move out into the hallway. As Howard hugs me, he says, "We can't go on as if nothing happened. We'll get married in an allied country,

105

then the authorities will have no choice but to allow me to see you, and you'll be able to come to the States as my wife."

"How will we get there?"

"We'll fly. We'll only go for a day."

"I love you, Howa'd." I flush with relief over his non-judgement and commitment.

"I love you too. Don't worry, we'll do it. Please trust me."

"No one believes me, Howa'd. Everyone says you will leave me if you know about the child."

"I'll never leave you. Never. I love you."

"*Có thể bạn sống một ngàn năm.*"

•　　　•　　　•

Five months pregnant, I step cautiously down the stairway as the colossal jet unloads its passengers. In the customs lines, disorder presses on us from all sides as Howard struggles with my baggage and I try to protect my inflated belly. Despite being pushed, shoved, battered, and exhausted, we finally reach the official.

Howard and I are scrutinized by a customs agent, who checks our papers and declares in English, "Pregnant Vietnamese not permitted entrance."

"What?" I question in shock.

The man repeats, "No allow. No have baby here."

"We're only staying one day to get married," Howard states.

The officer says, "I call American MP."

The agent blows a whistle and Howard grabs me and begins breaking through the lines. I attempt to help. Howard loses control when he sees them hitting me and starts swinging wildly. The MPs come running and beat us both with clubs, not sparing my pregnant belly.

•　　　•　　　•

Several months after returning to Vietnam, I give birth to a baby boy, whom I name Lực, Luke in English. Howard calls me after six months of separation. "Lin, I'm on a navy helicopter aircraft carrier."

"Howa'd, you in Vietnam?"

"No, off the coast."

"You not in America?"

"No, I requested to stay here rather than go back to the States so I can work on getting you out."

"Why they let you?" We aren't even married.

"They are shorthanded with the medical staff."

"We hear rumors of Vietnamese families being evacuated by Americans."

"Operation Baby Lift is the name of the program. Every couple of hours, flights arrive with swarms of Vietnamese American children fleeing with their mothers. Ask the hospital staff about catching a plane for you and our baby."

"Howa'd, we terrified. The airports blocked . . . riots rage . . . looting everywhere. I live in the hospital, and we shelter in the basement. The brave doctors and staff offer what assistance they can. The Vietnamese and American officers fled."

"You must get to the airport and try to get on a plane out."

"I need fellow workers here to help me with Lực. They, in turn, depend upon me to aid with their children. We work together and pray for each other. Leaving would be abandonment."

"Lin, tanks are moving into your area. No time to stay. THEY WILL KILL OUR BABY! Get out, get out, in any way you can."

"I . . . I cannot leave my friends. Howa'd, I scared for them, for me, our son, and you. What should I do?"

"Go, go, go. I am sending money; pay everyone and anyone to help you get out."

●　　　●　　　●

Within a short period of time, the opposition forces enter the capital, and my country dissolves. Rumors spread about the victors killing interracial babies as the days and nights pass in frightful isolation. One day I hear the unique throbbing of large US medivac helicopters approaching. We rush out with the families.

Howard yells at me, "GET ON THE CHOPPER. NOW, LIN! We will shield you!"

With the strength of a python, I squeeze Lực to my chest, and rush through the whirlwind of debris towards the helicopter's open hatch.

The binging sound of bullets hitting the helicopter sounds like hail. The armed men on the helicopter provide protective counter-defense with gunfire, smoke bombs, and rocket launchers. Time slows down as the distance between me and Howard decreases, and I lose hope of closing the gap. With one last heroic leap, I pass off our precious baby into Howard's waiting open arms. He spins and passes the baby to a medivac. Howard reaches to help me, but I must aid my comrades. Young children crawl on the ground amongst the bodies of their mothers and hospital staff. Howard and I race to save the ones we can reach. The chopper lifts off as Howard forces me aboard.

Children cry. Mothers scream. Men yell orders. And the thudding of the rotors deafens everyone. Howard, our child, and I huddle together. I kiss him, he kisses me, we both kiss our baby.

"You came back for me and our Lực. You risked your life for us."

"I will never leave you, Lin, never abandon him."

My heart pounds with love, tears blind me, and I choke on sobs, "Howa'd, *Có thể bạn sống một ngàn năm.*"

"Lin, may we live a thousand years together."

You Can Go Now

NANCI WOODY

JULIE WATCHED on her computer screen as nurses checked her son's ventilator. She longed to climb into the hospital bed with him, wrap her arms around his pitifully thin body. She couldn't bear to see him suffer any longer, wanted to put her cool face next to his fevered one and whisper, "You can go now. Don't worry about us." But because of the virus, she was forced to be where her son was not.

Davey, born with asthma, knew the ICU well, had stayed there many times in his young life, but always with his parents by his side. Now, unthinkable as it was, he had to suffer alone. Julie witnessed her son take his last breath on Facetime. Her tears flowed unceasingly.

Brad, working late, arrived home too late, aggrieved. Julie comforted him, made the arrangements for their only son's burial and memorial service.

A year later, the image of Davey, as white as the hospital sheets he lay on, would not leave Julie's mind. A searing, ever-present ache replaced the numbness, making it painful to be touched. She slept alone in the guest bedroom, her loss filling her consciousness.

When Brad's dreams became unbearable, he reached for Julie, but awoke with empty arms, bereft. Every night, his heart broke again at the loss of his son and his wife.

Driving home after a visit with their grief counselor, Julie found herself jerked into the present when Brad suddenly stepped hard on the brakes. Her seatbelt tight against her chest, she spotted a doe leaping to the side of the road.

"Thank God you didn't hit her," she cried.

Brad accelerated, but almost immediately again jammed on the brakes. Too late. The car rocked with the impact; Julie heard a sickening thud. Her scream pierced the still night air.

She jerked open the door, knelt by the front of the car, and put her hands on the warm, furry neck. "She had a fawn, Brad. Look what you've done," she sobbed. Julie pressed her ear to the fawn's chest, trying to find a heartbeat. "I think he's dead."

"I'm sorry, Jule . . ." he began. "We hit him pretty hard. Come. Help me move him." They each grabbed a front leg and pulled, the fawn's neck flopping backwards.

Julie spotted the doe they had barely missed, standing in an oak grove nearby. "Look, Brad. She's here. She knows." Tears streaming down her cheeks, she held out her hands to the doe, beckoning. "Don't worry about us."

Brad's hand pressed her arm. "Julie. Get control of yourself. I couldn't help it."

She recoiled from his touch, knelt again. The fawn's leg twitched. "Did you see that?"

"He's hurt bad, Jule. You stay here with him. I'll be right back."

"Tell me you're not getting a gun."

"You don't want him to suffer. Do you?"

"I don't want him to die. That's what I don't want."

"Okay. I'm leaving now. I'll be right back."

He pulled onto the lane, leaving Julie kneeling by the fawn, stroking his neck. Unwanted thoughts filled her mind. Davey as a young boy, joyful, riding his new bike down this same lane. Her mother, who died suddenly just months before her son. Her high school friend who, with no explanation, drove her car into the river. Her nine-year-old self, arms tight around her collie's neck, a bullet hole in his side.

The doe ventured ever closer, watching, waiting. Brad's headlights illuminated the fawn. He pulled to the side of the road, parked the car, reached for his gun.

Julie sat upright, whispered to the fawn. "You can go now."

The fawn's front legs jerked a little. He tried to raise his head, laid it down again, and then, with what seemed to Julie a valiant effort, he stood, wobbly, weak, then stronger, then stronger yet, until his mother was beside him, nudging him. When she knew the time was right, the deer leapt into the woods, her fawn close behind.

Brad dropped the gun, took Julie's hands, helped her stand. She didn't resist when he pulled her close, stroked her hair. Her heart poured out its grief onto his chest.

"How I've missed you," he whispered.

Julie put her arms around her husband, clasped her hands behind his back, held him tight.

"Bittersweet as it is, Jule, we still have each other. Let's go home now."

TO MY MOTHER
ON HER TENTH BIRTHDAY

ANNE MARIE WENZEL

– *after Joanna Ingham's "To my mother, aged 10"*

You will not always be the timid girl,
huddled with your siblings next door,
your parents fighting in the kitchen.
There will be lovers. There will be
fancy meals and censored letters,
your husband in his uniform,
that winged pin. There will be children.
There will be a divorce, but it will not
take everything from you. You will learn
of your strength and resolve, a turtle's back
bone and spine. You will not always
feel inadequate. There will be men
who rely on you in offices, who beseech
you for your service. There will be
operations, lumps stripped from your breasts,
scars and new diets. There will be
grandchildren, and you will care for them;
there will be celebrations—and a garden

To my mother on her tenth birthday

that bestows flowers. You will at times
be alone. You will not be the homemaker
you wanted to be. But you'll
find your own path—instead of travel,
a home you love. You will sit and read and learn.
Don't worry. You will come to understand
your sinew. And I am here, awaiting
the heritage you will gift to me.

WHAT COLOR IS MY EMPTY NEST?

KORIE PELKA

EVERY PARENT KNOWS the time will come when their precious babies will leave the nest. They will grow up and go to college or move out and into adulthood, searching for their own identity and purpose.

I assured myself I would be the epitome of grace when this time arrived. I'd be cool. Hip. I'd welcome this exciting transition, eager to see the beautiful adults my children would become in this big wide world.

I'd prepared from a financial sense with college expenses planned and handled. I'd prepared from a career sense, ready to take on a larger role that required more time away from home. From a social sense, I'd planned to eagerly fill my time with new activities and travel. I even thought I'd prepared emotionally.

Boy, was I wrong.

Now, my emotional angst didn't show itself with a crying and gnashing of teeth. I didn't cling to my sons and sob before driving away from their dorm room—although I wanted to. I didn't hound them with phone calls or text messages. I thought I had the situation under control. Then the time arrived to redo their bedroom, the heart center of my home.

This room had evolved over the years from nursery to bedroom for my older and then my younger son. Any parent knows this room. It's where you rocked your fevered child through the night. Where you tiptoed through the Lego replica of the local zoo and read that dang Tweety Bird book till you had to hide it. This room had seen fights and tears and hugs—and laughter that made you fall down on the floor. It's where you sang softly and rubbed backs and offered prayers each night to guide your children when you weren't around.

With both sons now in college, it was time for those petitions to their guardian angels to kick into high gear. Meanwhile, I was left alone in a room full of memories.

I needed an action plan, a plan to paint this room so that it would be, well and truly, an adult room. The current state of the walls, washable eggshell with faded outlines of sports posters, was in desperate need of a refresh. I had a gallon of paint my youngest son had picked out before he left for college. While not thrilled with the color, I set about painting the room in anticipation of his return. When his plans changed and he decided to live elsewhere, I was faced with the prospect of living with a room that was now so dark and depressing only Ozzy Osbourne would love it. I came to think of this color as "Goth Purple" and it had to go.

So, off I went to my local paint store for a new gallon of paint.

The next color, I decided, would be a happy blue. I spent the following weekend covering up the dark purple with my new color. Now this blue, when viewed in full daylight, was so bright my eyes hurt ... and so "happy," only an outrageous clown could pull off wearing it. I hated its forced happiness. Clown blue had to go.

I returned to the paint store.

This time I was in a better emotional space, having at least accepted the choice of blue as my palette. I envisioned a calm and soothing room. I chose a wonderful blue: neither too light nor too deep with a vibrant tone. After another weekend of painting, I stepped back to look at the final result. Oh, no! The color didn't look quite right. When I put the swatch up to the wall, the two didn't match! The store had mixed the paint three shades lighter than the one I wanted.

Back to the store I went for the right color. It was, as you would expect, free of charge but truthfully, I think they would have done anything to make sure this crazy woman was happy.

About this time in the process, my friends started calling. They worried the paint fumes had made me go crazy, suggesting, not so subtly, that I should be dating not painting. One even threatened to come over for much-needed "paint intervention," conjuring up images of her gently asking me to "put down the brush, Ko, and step away from the can."

While I didn't need intervention, I did need time. In those long hours of rolling and brushing, I'd thought about the years I'd spent in this room. Memories had flooded my eyes while emotions filled my heart. I'd listened to podcasts and playlists and heard echoes of laughter bounce off those silly walls. And sometimes I'd just listened to my own silence.

I spent my fourth and final weekend painting what I had now decided was my yoga and meditation room. The operative word there is "my." This remains the heart center of the house and it's now *my* heart center for this stage of my life. I've spent hours in downward dog and practicing crow stand, meditating and journaling. Sometimes, when things are tough, I lie on the floor and try to remember how to breathe. I now start every morning in this room, opening the window to hear the laughter of children walking to school, their young voices floating into my heart center, reminding me that the cycle of life continues in such a beautiful way.

Letting go of my children was the hardest thing I've ever done as a parent. Cognitively, I knew that if I did my job right, they would become wonderful, awesome adults that made their own impact on the world. They wouldn't need me anymore, at least not in the same way. That's what success looks like. Emotionally, that acceptance took time. I could no longer control their actions or their choices but by God, I was going to control the color of that dang room! I'd just needed a month of weekends with a paintbrush in my hand to come to that place in my heart.

A RENDEZVOUS WITH TIME

LUCRETIA LEONG

ON A BLUSTERY SPRING DAY, I watch as the wind whips the tops of the eucalyptus trees that line my street. The scene reminds me of an angry cat clawing at a row of feather dusters. Unfortunately, these trees that give my town its quiet charm will soon be replaced by a sturdier breed. Historic storms have relentlessly pummeled Northern California, uprooting and ripping up these delicate, majestic beings. The fact that their time is coming to an end triggers thoughts about how my own is running out. My days, months, and years race ahead like Ben Hur's golden chariot, but instead of Charlton Heston at the helm, the reins are held by Father Time. If only he would slow down so I could tend to my unfinished plans before they slip through my fingers.

Time flowed more slowly when I was young. As a seven-year-old in Hawaii, I spent every school day staring at the clock with its unmoving hands, waiting for the recess and end-of-day bells. At ten years of age, the hour spent at holy mass stretched out like a medieval torture rack. Back then, time stood in the way of life. I couldn't wait to run from church to Chang's grocery store to fill my mouth with a gooey Big Hunk bar. At fifteen, I longed for my sweet sixteenth birthday, complete with a handsome beau and my driver's license in hand. Before I was eighteen,

I saw myself as irrelevant since I had no right to vote, and at twenty-one I thirsted for something more potent than Coca-Cola. Youthful anticipation and impatience have a way of keeping one's gaze transfixed on the horizon.

As an adult, I was trapped in the vortex of time. I embarked on my teaching career, got married, and tried my hand at the usual homemaking pastimes, like cooking and crafts. I experimented with *pakalolo* (Hawaiian for marijuana), took Lamaze classes, and gave birth to two rambunctious boys. In my mid-thirties, Father Time whipped forward with increased speed, taking me "over the hill."

I divorced in my forties, and in my fifties my sons graduated from college. Soon I was sixty, and the owner of a precious miniature dachshund named Palehua. She filled my retirement years with comfort and love. I brought her with me from Hawaii to live in California. The old anticipation of youth returned as I looked forward to seeing my devoted companion whenever I returned home. She was always there waiting for me at the door. We went almost everywhere together, to the point that I saw her not as a pet, but as my true friend. But alas, a dog's life is measured in a different time warp and our days together were over too soon.

The clock on the mantelpiece of life never stopped ticking and the years rumbled beneath me like an earthquake. Old age cascaded down upon me with no mercy.

"Stop!" I cried out to Father Time, the one responsible for all this destruction. "Slow down, please." But he continued to plow ahead. My metabolism, on the other hand, slowed to a crawl, leaving an expansive paunch in my belly and a sparse, thinning head of hair.

"Hey!" I shouted once more, but Father Time continued to barrel ahead at full speed, sprinkling wrinkles on my face, multiplying the crevices on my knees, and bequeathing me with a turkey neck. During the height of the pandemic, my hands even started to resemble that lurid Chinese delicacy: chicken feet. I became so alarmed by the sight of them that I immediately stopped using hand sanitizers. COVID be damned!

I have toyed with the idea of having plastic surgery to regain my youthful glow. But what good would it do? Deep inside, I would still be the same person who has to listen to her old bones creak and moan each morning. Modern medicine cannot stop the sun's march across the sky, unlike the Hawaiian demigod Maui, who once lassoed the sun so his mother Hina would have more time to dry her *tapa* cloths.

I'm haunted by the feeling that I'm hurtling toward my final demise. I still need to relish my grandchildren while they are young. I need more time to fulfill my life's ambitions. I need to write, draw, and paint more so I can call myself a true artist. I need to lose weight and fix my hunched posture.

But Father Time never heeds my words, just like my two offspring who don't listen to me anymore. Where once they hung on my every word, as I spoke like the Pope *ex cathedra* on all matters, my iconic stature has long lost its luster. My grown-up sons now believe they possess more knowledge, skills, and competence than their once great, clever mother. I miss the adulation of my dear Palehua, who saw me as the greatest being alive.

I can feel my arthritic hands losing their grip on the sands of time. Perhaps I should take some refuge in this lovely spring day, with its lush, rain-filled green grass. My canopy of eucalyptus trees won't be around much longer. The sun is warming the air and the wind has eased, swaying the treetops like Martha Graham's lithe dancers. I need to sit down so I can recalibrate and settle myself. Just as I start to get comfortable, I hear what sounds like a stampede. I look up and see Father Time speeding by on his chariot. Startled, my attempts at serenity dissipate immediately.

"Can't you stand still for a moment?" I yell with frustration.

Surprisingly, he slows, and lowers his reins. Turning to me, with an almost imperceptible smile, he says, "My dear, *the moment* is all you have." The smile vanishes as he turns to go.

"Wait!" I blurt out desperately. He pauses and glances back at me. "I remember there were some moments in my life when you actually stood still. Like when I was a kid and went sliding down grassy hills on makeshift sleds made of flattened cardboard boxes. It was so much fun. I lost track of time then."

His hands impatiently tap on the reins. I look into his gray, deep-set eyes.

"What about when I was in the delivery room? Twice. The pain was unbearable, and I told the doctor 'I wanna go home.' But when my sons were born, you stood still for those miraculous few moments."

"Or how about when my mother died, and I sat beside her bed as the memories flooded over me?" As I placed my hand on my mother's hands for the last time, images flashed through my mind. I saw old sepia photographs of her as a youth. First as a lonely, three-year-old ragamuffin, then as the eighteen-year-old beauty she had blossomed into. Transporting myself to my college days, I reminisced about our walks at dusk, with the soothing trade winds caressing our faces after a hot, Hawaiian day. My mother often eased my troubles. Then I saw her standing in the nursery, proudly showing me how to carry my first newborn child. When my sons were older, she always shielded her youngest grandson from my ire. "Those last moments I had with my mother expanded into a timeless ocean of love, regret, and grief," I say softly.

Father Time's eyes squint off into the distance in the direction of the setting sun. "I did nothing different for you then. I have already stayed too long," he says as he picks up the reins again.

"Just go then. I'll figure it out," as I wave him on.

He leaves in a flash, his form fading into the horizon. The world rushes back in. I hear the light rustling of the eucalyptus and feel the cool wind on my face. I remember my mother. I remember my darling little Palehua. I think about my caring sons. It occurs to me that the finite quality of time is what gives these memories their preciousness. Instead of being trodden down by the steeds of time, I must find a way to ride upon them.

Is There a Teacher in the House?

SUE BARIZON

I N AUGUST OF 2020, my husband, Steve, and I stood shoulder to shoulder alongside our son and daughter-in-law, waiting for their computer to boot up. It was five-year-old James' first day of kindergarten, and we were positioned around their kitchen table to meet his teacher, Ms. Valentine, and his soon-to-be-classmates. We were an anxious audience waiting for our intro to Zoom, distance learning, and the new normal.

All week, the family including his ten-year-old sister, Sophia, had coached James on the joys of being a kindergartener. He and his mother had walked Sophia to Parkside Elementary School every morning since he was a baby. James appeared resigned to the inevitable. But, that was before the quarantine. So, what was he doing sitting on Mommy's lap staring at a computer on his first day of school? Ms. Valentine, a middle-aged woman with a warm smile that made her look younger than her years, magically appeared in the upper left-hand corner of the screen. We watched intently as she introduced the gallery of five-year-olds, one by one, like the opening credits of a Brady Bunch episode. But, instead of smiling faces greeting each other in familial harmony, James saw a mosaic of dazed and confused strangers just like him. When Ms. Valentine called his name, the ensuing meltdown of primal screams and flailing limbs was the stuff CPS (Child Protective Services) reports are made of. The first of the red flags had been waved. We were about to embark on a one-way trip to Crazy Town via the public school system.

•   •   •

We were on "day 23" of distance learning. I knew because Ms. Valentine had pulled out the linear calendar each morning to show us. Steve and I, pushing seventy, had never seen a linear calendar until last month. We'd never experienced Zoom, Chromebooks, or quarantine pods, but ready or not, here we were. Our son and daughter-in-law—considered essential workers by virtue of his job in hazardous waste disposal and hers in the family's auto repair business—left for work each morning, entrusted us with the grandkids all day. We assumed our age and titles, Nonni and Nonno, would be a disclaimer so others would not expect much from grandparents whose kindergarten days had included taking naps and eating paste. As the household's primary co-educator, I had to switch from doting grandparent to stern teacher to oblivious student so often I'd taken to referring to myself in the third person.

"Nonni says to unmute yourself before you speak."

"Nonni will set the timer for the small group meeting."

"Nonni will give you a time out if you roll your eyes at her one more time."

Distance learning had become one long, out-of-body experience.

Ms. Valentine was on to me from the start. I was careful to sit next to James, just off camera, to make sure he kept up with the class. I pressed unmute for him, corrected his pencil grip, and fed him answers to questions like, "How many legs does a centipede have?" After the first week, Ms. Valentine suggested that my helicopter helping was not part of typical classroom instruction.

"The learning is in the struggle," she said.

I knew that, but I'd seen Julian's mom doing it too! My bad.

Ms. Valentine acquiesced to my offer to observe class from another room with the camera on but my audio muted.

Sophia, our fourth-grade "ten-ager," embraced her Zoom sessions with all the gusto of a contestant on "Are You Smarter than a 5th grader?" It was a relief to know our self-starter with the sunny smile and natural inclination toward learning preferred to be on her own . . . until her computer froze, or she got hungry, thirsty, cold, needed a tissue, or sensed that her little brother was getting a bigger piece of the Nonni/Nonno pie. Steve and I thought we were pretty good with computers until . . . we weren't. Mercifully our tech-savvy son and daughter-in-law were just a frantic phone call away. We were two months into troubleshooting—their internet service versus the school's server versus computer glitches versus teacher error versus one of our senior moments—before tech issues finally settled down.

Our sanity had depended on keeping the grandkids focused and on schedule. All distractions were a threat to order. Exit Otto, the family's new Boston terrier puppy, whose contribution to morning mayhem was to leave a wake of disemboweled stuffed animals. He was relegated to spending his days with Mommy at the shop. Early on, I'd been forced to flex my in-house principal muscles and ban Nonno from sight during classroom instruction. His carryings-on as Monster Man and Human Jungle Gym during recess breaks made it impossible to rein the kids back into their seats on time before classes resumed. One day, I intercepted him about to deliver one of his stealth, rapid-fire, head-kissing attacks on Sophia. She had been live on camera, the leader of a mindfulness exercise. For his own protection, I relegated him to "go-fer" status: he set timers for music class and PE, made smoothies, ran for coffee, picked up lunch orders, and took photos for posterity. He also became my most devoted cheerleader.

"You're doing great, Nonni."

•   •   •

At 7:30 a.m., "Good Morning" greetings between me and my daughter-in-law were reduced to a no-frills set of one-liners initiated by whomever was on their second cup of coffee.

"Did you get the email?"

"What email?"

Although we each received the same barrage of communications from the school district, principal, PTA, and teachers, it took two of us to decipher and keep track of them.

"School's re-opening mid-May." My daughter-in-law sounded cautiously confident.

"Define re-opening." I was wary, the school system had become a fickle master.

I needed clarity before Steve and I popped opened the champagne. School officials had been working on the re-opening recipe all year, and left us unsatiated with promises of early January, mid-March, and April 1st. When those had fallen through, they'd offered a hybrid version of school: three days online/two days on-campus. The news was tempting but like my Italian grandmother used to say, "It's the aroma without the meat."

"The teachers are pushing for May 3rd," I broke the news to my husband.

He pinched himself. "I just want to go back to being good ol' Nonno, again."

Was it possible to go from indispensable to obsolete with the ping of an incoming email? I'd be happy to retire Drill Sargent Nonni for my Old School Nonni ways, where a whole number is a whole number, not some fancy-schmancy "integer." Would the new normal abandon the term "asynchronous" for its pretentious tone and bewildering pronunciation? (Sophia was soooo tired of sounding it out for Nonni.). I wanted to go back to what's easy. I'd remind Sophia to "carry the one" and James that "double ees," say their name. I feared the jig was up on my wannabe teacher ways, but was afraid to say, "the jig is up." It probably wouldn't be politically correct.

What if I was held accountable? I meant well, initially, making up schedules to mimic the pre-quarantine school routine, including a snack time, recess, and lunch. Now, the schedules mocked me, taped to the kitchen wall with their penciled scars of canceled classes and revised timetables. Snack time had morphed into lunch. Banning Nonno and the grandkids from soccer drills in the garage had been essential—the washer and dryer were dented enough already.

There was that wretched day when I had to call a timeout and shuttle Sophia to Mommy's work. She'd pushed the edge of the Nonni envelope with a snarky attitude that would've brought the Kardashian sisters to their knees. Mommy had our backs and summoned Sophia to spend the afternoon with her in the auto repair shop's cold, cramped office. The next day, I overheard her teacher prompting the fourth-graders to share one thing they were most grateful for during shelter-in-place. Sophia responded, "My grandparents distance learning me and my little brother."

"Each child learns at his own level," Ms. Valentine would reassure.

Eventually, she told us, James would remember to press the red dot at the bottom of the screen to unmute. That was no news to me. I'd worked in a high school counseling office for twenty years.

"Don't worry," I told my husband, "By the time he's a senior, he'll learn to unmute."

I took comfort when I saw James was not the only one who yawned into the camera or looked everywhere but at the screen. I was thankful he wasn't given to eyeball close-ups or empty chair disappearances. No matter what the subject, when called upon our avid dinosaur buff could be relied on to work a Jurassic theme into every answer. One day, he overheard Nonno and me wondering if he was the only one in his small group session for whom English was not a second language. He motioned me over and whispered in my ear, "I speak dinosaur."

From my vantage point at the kitchen counter, I stood at the computer and watched as Ms. Valentine monitored more than twenty angelic faces with the expertise of an air traffic controller.

"Now everyone, turn your paper over and write your name on the back."

"Aww Cynthia, are you having a bad morning?"

"Bernard, are you writing your name? Hold your paper up higher so I can see."

"Please use a tissue, Arney."

To me, it felt counter-intuitive to teach James the sounds a letter makes before knowing the letter's name. I finally caught on but wondered when James would. We weren't quite ready for counting by twos, but it appeared smarty-pants Julian was the way he rattled on, ". . . 42, 44, 46, 48, 50."

When I asked Nonno if he ever thought kindergarten could be so tough, he just shook his head. "I wish I'd had a teacher like Ms. Valentine." This from a man who, as a boy, once locked himself in the school bathroom to keep from having to recite his multiplication tables in front of Miss Bethunia's class.

. . .

When the May 3rd news broke, we were blinded by the light at the end of the distance-learning tunnel. We'd worked five days a week with two grade levels on a multitude of subjects—without the use of drugs or alcohol, despite subsisting on the crusts of leftover PB&J sandwiches and the last lump of mac 'n' cheese. By the end of the day, our brains were mush. At home, we'd reward ourselves with a bowl of ice cream and a high-five as we passed each other in the hall for separate timeouts to binge-watch HGTV and Cobra Kai. Could we wean ourselves away from this window into how another generation lives and learns?

. . .

Now, I'm worried that FOMO (Fear Of Missing Out) will set in. I admit enjoying the online PE classes and the hysterics that followed, as Sophia helped Nonni up off the floor from her yoga pose. Overhearing little Ellie's dad's day trading during his daughter's rendition of Pledge to the Earth, made me curious about how Roku stocks are doing. I hope I can count on my granddaughter to catch me up on her Zearn Math lessons. How else will I learn to differentiate a square from a rhombus? What about the little girl who innocently repeated her mother's derogatory remark regarding a prominent political figure? It elicited enough cheering from parents listening in to prompt a district-wide reprimand to "Keep politics out of the classroom."

Coincidentally, the reopening of school coincides with Teacher Appreciation Week. The mug I purchased back in January for Ms. Valentine reads, "Teaching is the art of shaping young minds, without losing your own." Steve and I discuss the inadequacies of such well-meaning gifts. What's the going rate for her extra one-on-one Zoom tutoring with James on Thursday afternoons? How much for her thoughtfully assembling extra materials for me to pick up from the school secretary? Can we place a value on the confidence-building we witnessed online and since James finally joined his classmates in person?

What about us? Is this where we get off? How will the kids look back on our role in this nationwide academic hiccup?

"Remember when Nonni helped get you through school during the Pandemic of 2020?"

"Was that after you got the vaccine and I asked you to keep wearing your mask because you had coffee breath?"

But we're not teachers, we're grandparents, and the hair-pulling frustrations of the last eight months have already begun to subside. The other day, Steve was left with a lump in his throat when James abruptly stopped some serious LEGO building to come face to face and declare, "Nonno, you are my BEST friend." On their first day back at school, we were careful to stand on the sidelines, in the shadows, so as to not infringe on Sophia's mini reunions with her friends. She caught a glimpse of us, broke out of line and ran with opened arms and that sunny smile, squealing, "NONNIS!"

My husband contemplates the woefully inadequate mug in his hand. I remind him of an excerpt from an article I once read: "... people believe that teaching should be its own reward and teachers are such 'giving' people, and want to help make the world a better place ..." It's how we delude ourselves: the compensation is adequate because maternal instincts are their own rewards.

"Maybe we should fill the mug with hundred-dollar bills," he teases. "Better yet, how about a blank check?"

I take the mug from his hand and pat his shoulder.

"Let's just write her into the will."

WHERE THERE'S SMOKE

EVA BARROWS

T HELMA'S HEAD JERKED BACK as she awakened to a beeping
sound. She sat at the card table where she ate her meals. She had
wanted to get off her feet for the few minutes it took to bake a batch of
sugar cookies. *Beep beep beep* ... that was the smoke alarm! Startled, she
pushed herself up out of the vinyl-backed chair. She had rested too long.

"Be quiet, you darn thing." Thelma shook a kitchen rag in the alarm's
direction. Would she be able to save the batch? She wanted to share a few
cookies with Macy, the little girl next door. Macy was the cutest thing.

Thelma grabbed her potholders and opened the oven door. Thick
black smoke poured out, hitting Thelma in the eyes and stopping up her
throat. Her eyes watered. She couldn't see through her glasses' thick
lenses. Coughing wracked her body. She couldn't grab the cookie sheet.
Thelma closed the oven door and backed away.

Her heart rate leaped. What should she do next? Thelma heard her son
Alan's voice inside of her head. Snippets from their recent conversation
circled through her mind. "What are you going to do, Ma, when something
bad happens? Are you going to be able to take care of yourself?"

"Of course, I'm going to be able to take care of myself," she'd replied. "I took care of you and your sisters all those years."

"But you're older now, Ma. I think it's time for someone to take care of you."

"I'm fine," she had said. He'd given her a sideways look that meant he'd be bringing the subject up again soon.

Now the black smoke streamed out from around the oven door. The smoke alarm continued to tell the world Thelma was burning something.

Wait a minute, hadn't the apartment management installed a fire extinguisher in her kitchen just a week ago? Thelma yanked open the cabinet under the sink. She bent down to reach it but a familiar shocking pain surged up her spine. Her lower back screamed at her. She scrunched her face, sucked in her stomach and willed her body to move. She grabbed the heavy red canister, setting it on the kitchen counter.

Before she could pull the black plastic ring from the nozzle, a knock came at the door.

"Oh, what do they want?" Thelma left the extinguisher on her counter, smoke still billowing from the oven, to answer the door.

She opened the door just wide enough to stick her head into the hallway. A young man she didn't know balanced himself on a one-wheeled hoverboard. The hallway lights grew dim behind a growing smoky haze.

"Hi," the man said. "We're trying to locate the source of the smoky smell in the hallway. Is anything burning in your apartment?"

"Oh, no, not here," Thelma answered. The smoke alarm and clouded room behind her told another story.

"Are you sure everything is okay?" The man put his hand up to her door frame. Was he catching himself from losing his balance or sneaking glances inside her apartment? "I can hear your alarm going off, and the smoke's thicker at this end of the hall."

"Oh, that thing is just sensitive. It goes off when someone lights a cigarette outside." She laughed nervously at her attempted joke. "Gotta go. Thanks for checking." She closed the door on the guy. He knocked again, but she did her best to ignore him, rushing back to the kitchen.

She pulled the ring from the extinguisher and pulled back the trigger. A stream of white retardant flew from the canister's hose. Thelma armed herself in oven mitts and again opened the oven door. She held the extinguisher under her arm, pulled the trigger a second time and aimed the stream into the oven while sickly sweet smoke pooled into the kitchen.

"Take that and that!" she said as if in an action-adventure movie. She hit the cookie remains, the burnt tray and both oven racks. She squirted the bottom of the oven and the crumbs that had settled there. The oven stopped smoking, yet the apartment was full of the stuff. Thelma set the canister down.

Just then, her cell phone buzzed alive inside her apron pocket. The caller ID flashed her son's name.

"Hi, Alan," she said, a note of guilt seeping into her tone.

"Hey, Ma, are you okay? I just got this text message from your apartment management that they are trying to locate the source of a fire at your building."

"I'm fine, sweetie," Thelma said. "Nothing's wrong here. I'm not sure what's going on." She stared at the black gooey mess she'd made of her oven.

"Oh, good! Glad you're okay. You might want to go outside until they figure out where the fire is."

"Yes, good idea. I'll get my things together and go outside."

"Okay, be careful. I'll check on you again in an hour."

As Thelma slid the phone back into her pocket, someone knocked at the door again, this time so hard the door shook in its frame.

"Fire Department," a deep baritone voice called. "Open up!"

Thelma scrunched her shoulders and hung her head like a child who'd just been caught with her hand in the cookie jar. She opened her door a few inches.

"Yes?" she said.

"Ma'am, we're trying to locate the source of a fire," a seven-foot-tall beefcake of a man towered in her doorway. His eyes scanned her apartment. "Ma'am, will you step aside and permit me to enter the premises?"

He clicked the side of his radiophone and talked into it, "This is Williams. I think I've located the source of the smoke. Entering apartment unit 210."

Thelma opened up her door. Now someone would see she'd made a mess of things. It took the hulking man just two steps to arrive inside her kitchen. He thrust his gloved hand into the oven and pulled out the cookie sheet. He set it on the stovetop and clicked the oven's knob to the off position. *Oh yeah, turn the oven off.* Something she definitely should have done a while ago.

"Let's get some windows opened up in here," Williams said. He walked through her living room and slid back the porch's sliding door. She went around to the bedroom and opened the window there. Williams lifted his tree-trunk arm to effortlessly pull the ceiling fan's chain, setting it to full blast.

"All right, tell you what we'll do, Ma'am. Follow me outside, and we'll get you set up out there while this place airs out." Williams picked up Thelma's card table chair and motioned for her to follow him. He set the chair down under a tree on the lawn, and she sat down dejected. Thelma watched as the firemen packed up their truck and talked with the guy on the one-wheeled hoverboard and a couple other concerned residents.

Floor fans whirred in the hallway, pushing the smoky air out. The entrance doors were all propped open to help with the circulation. Little Macy bounced out of the side door where Thelma was, her mom following.

"It smells weird in there!" Macy said, dancing up to Thelma.

"Yes, it's smoky," Thelma said, putting out her hand for Macy to grab as she passed by.

"Smok-y?" Macy stopped mid-twirl to look at Thelma with quizzical brown eyes.

"Smoke happens when something burns."

"Is it okay?" Macy asked.

"Everything is fine," Thelma said, bringing her hand back to rest on her lap.

When Thelma got the all-clear to go back inside her apartment, she looked up and down the hall to make sure no one watched her return to the site of the incident. She slinked inside and gave the middle finger to the now silent smoke alarm.

She resigned herself to cleaning up the oven. The blobs of burnt cookies stared at her. She took the tray over to the trashcan and sloughed off the remains. At the sink, she examined the black streaks stuck to the blackened tray. The tray was beyond the magic of Palmolive dish soap, so she tossed it too.

How lucky, the cookies and the tray were the only things that had burned. It began to dawn on her that things could have been so much worse. Macy's question, *Is it okay?* ran through her head.

The buzz of a text from Alan vibrated against her hip. *Is everything alright, Ma?* it read.

This time, she wasn't sure it was.

ODE TO AUTUMN

JO CARPIGNANO

When Autumn chill announces season's end
let's not blame Winter for this transformation
Cold winds are harbinger of Autumn's finest fare
in rich wines, sweet jellies, apple pies
'Tis then, as though seduced by Winter's chill,
that Autumn celebrates—releasing gaudy leaves
into a frenzied flight across the fallow fields
Torn from weak anchor to their branches, leaves swirl
in swarms, as if announcing they're now free to fly
A flock of color in pursuit of phantom butterflies
And speak of beauty?
Gaze upon those naked trees bereft of leaves
eagerly anticipating kiss of winter snow
are they not perfect in their graceful symmetry?
So why should we bemoan
the shortened days and longer nights
when extended darkness means more time
to savor Autumn's bountiful delights

HAZE

HEATHER E. FOLSOM

T HE SKY TURNED ORANGE and we didn't know what to do.
The day was a work day. I was working from home, on chat with a dozen or so colleagues, on video calls with a few more. In the six months since the pandemic began, we hadn't met in person. The strangeness of this had faded. I felt as if we were all present, all the time, together in a world that didn't exist.

Can you get a photo? someone asked on chat.

The reply came fast. *Image sensor's screwed up. Sky keeps coming out blue.*

That's not blue! Another reply.

A few seconds' pause. *My phone thinks reality doesn't exist.*

California had been burning for weeks. The air tasted of smoke. A thin scrim of ash dusted every outdoor surface. The ash rose in eddies when the wind blew. And now—when I looked out the window, the sky was orange. I'd never seen anything like it. It might have been pretty if it weren't so terrifying.

What's it like in San Francisco?

Typing. *Looks fake. You?*

The distances between us seemed immense, but we all still lived commute distance to the office. Our homes were scattered like satellites around San Francisco Bay. We were close enough to see the same sky.

It's creepy. Like a horror movie.

There's ash floating down. Squint, it looks like snow!

We had that yesterday in San Jose.

I miss Tahoe.

After a while the line between speaking and writing blurs. As I read their texts, in my mind I heard my team's voices: sarcastic, incredulous, pragmatic, the flash of an accent, a characteristic turn of phrase.

Can you get a photo?

Phone camera keeps looking like the sky is blue.

IT'S NOT BLUE

At eleven a.m. the birds stopped singing. The sky blurred down from burnt orange to dark sepia. I squinted to look across the street. The room I worked in, normally bright with daylight, grew dark. I couldn't see the keyboard or notebook in front of me. I turned on the overhead lights.

This is weird.

Seems wrong to work on a spreadsheet when everything is like this.

I can't focus.

Literally or metaphorically?

It's the end of the world, who cares?

If it's the end of the world I am literally lighting this spreadsheet on fire.

LOL

We worked in the tech industry. We all had high-end phones, built to make every photo beautiful. Our phones expected blue overhead, or at worst pale gray, and had the processing power to make it happen. The deep burnt toffee of the sky we saw came out instead as brilliant, sparkling, everyday blue.

Try the brightness setting.

This automated image post-processing is bullshit! Should be a way to turn it off.

I'll ask a guy I know who's got a real camera.

I kept sneaking glances out the window. Could it really be orange? Was it still like that?

By now it was two p.m. on a summer day. Shadowed trees stood silhouetted against the dark sepia sky. I blinked and rubbed my eyes. Nothing changed. Adding to the eeriness, the street outside was empty. No cars moved. No one walked their dog. I hadn't noticed how much I noticed the birds, until they weren't there to hear or see.

This is happening, right? I'm not imagining things?

Oh this is real. This is all real.

Could I trick my phone by focusing first on something blue indoors? Years earlier, I'd painted the wall next to the window a deep bright aqua. This might convince the phone's image sensor it had found blue. I held focus on the aqua wall, the orange-sky window in the background, and quickly snapped the photo.

Success! The sky the camera hadn't focused on looked orange in the photograph, just as it did when I looked outside.

I sent the photo out on chat.

Oh damn.

Ok.

Oh hell.

Yes.

Since then, years have passed.

I speak of fire season now as if it is routine.

The team has scattered, but every so often we message one another:

Do you remember?

Replies come slowly, but we do reply.

That was like nothing else.

You hope.

Yeah. I hope.

I have the photo still: shadowed aqua walls, dark-glowing burnt orange sky.

The sky looks just as orange as I remember.

I have the photograph. I know it happened.

THE ICE CAVE

HARLAN SUITS

L ATE IN THE DAY, the ice cave near camp glows from within. Echoes of afternoon light seep through its translucent walls. The ice, melt-polished, tinged with green, still glistens from the day's heat. On my nose and cheeks, the chill of night approaches.

I am alone on the glacier. Don, Bill, and Kanchi left early this morning for one last attempt to find a way through the icefall. They are somewhere up there in the maze of crevasses that guard the mountain's upper slopes. They plan to return in a few days, and if things look promising, we'll pack up our camp and move it higher.

I decided to stay behind. To me, their quest is hopeless. On our last attempt, we didn't get far, the plain of fractured ice extending beyond for more than a mile. Because of drought, the layer of snow on the lower glacier has melted away, exposing every fissure, every pit in the icefall. There are only four of us, and we would need an army of Sherpas working for weeks to bridge all those crevasses.

I go back to the tent, put on my down jacket and pants, and return to the entrance of the cave. How magnificent. What human could devise such sculpture? Curved crystalline walls like heavy jade, massive, but on the left side pocked with melt-windows, where the cobalt sky peeks through. As the sun sinks further, dark green shadows bloom in the cave's deeper recesses. I notice a laminar pattern in the ice—faint parallel lines, each marking the edge of a layer of snow that fell to Earth long ago, before being pressed and purified into glacial ice.

I'd like to enter the cave and fully immerse myself in other-worldly beauty. But for all its icy solidity, the cave looks unstable, the massive roof supported by walls of varying thicknesses. Why should I, by entering, add unnecessary risk to our already risky journey up the mountain? Earlier in the day, I heard the ice underfoot creaking, then a loud crashing noise nearby. A tower of ice must have toppled over. In recent years, the glacier retreats, the ice wasting away, sometimes violently. Only a fool would tempt fate by entering a structure that seems on the verge of collapse.

But isn't that what we're doing up here, tempting fate? This mountain has never been climbed in winter. Such a project would be a hard, bitterly cold task even for seasoned Himalayan climbers, so why are we here, a ragtag group of amateurs sprinkled with a few strong veterans? One reason is that Tim, our trip leader down at basecamp, arranged all the logistics and offered a bargain price. The opportunity was hard to resist. I suppose the prospects of success were slim all along, but sometimes, I have found, climbers get lucky. The weather stays calm, the chemistry of the group gels, and we discover in ourselves unexpected reserves of strength. Sometimes. This mountain is not particularly steep. It's just high and cold, and as we have now discovered, girded by a daunting sea of crevasses.

I'm getting hungry. I fire up the stove and melt chunks of ice for water, then drop a foil food pouch into the boiling pot. A muffled sound pierces the silence. A human voice? Or just another groan from the shifting ice?

"Hey, Harlan, we're back." I turn toward the icefall and see my three friends shamble into camp. Tired, faces flushed, they cast off their heavy packs. They did not get far up the glacier. "There were too many crevasses," Bill confirms. They crossed a few shallower fissures by descending to the bottom and climbing up the other side—slow, laborious work. In one crevasse, a wall of ice nearby collapsed abruptly, a close call. Before long, they reached the lip of an immense crack, the depths shading ominously into darkness. There was no way to cross the break, and at both ends, other deep fissures hemmed them in.

Our climb up the mountain is over. The fact I could see it coming tempers my disappointment. That huge sea of fractured ice remains impenetrable. Nature has spoken.

After dinner, the others retreat to their tents. I look up at the arctic-white summits above the icefall. They retain their mystery, their god-like inscrutability. We must leave to others the job to bridge the gap between here and there. Far to the south, fog rolls up the deep river canyon that drains this range of snowy giants. The villages down there appear dark and damp, but up here, the golden sun kisses the high ridge to the west. We are alone in a cold, wild world, a paradise of harsh beauty.

By sunset, my feet and hands grow cold. Nearby, my thick down sleeping bag beckons. I will sleep well tonight. The burden of risk has lifted. The way down the mountain is little more than a long, strenuous hike. We dreamed big. We did all we could under the circumstances, but now it's time to go home. Just above our camp, the glacier creaks again, a living thing.

In the tent, I pull the top of my sleeping bag around my face and cinch it down. I still feel the presence of the ice cave nearby. It slumbers, shrouded in darkness. The cave will collapse soon—maybe tomorrow, maybe in a few weeks. Fragments will melt and recombine with the ice beneath it or be buried under the first winter storm. After we leave, no one will see the cave again. It will exist as a memory only, but even as the glacier continues to decline, other wonders will sprout up randomly here in the years to come and on other glaciers on high mountains everywhere.

That's nature's way, its cycle of rebirth. Not perfect renewal but transformation. Everything beautiful always turns into something else.

THE FIGHT

BRUCE NEUBURGER

I T WAS JUST PAST SEVEN in the evening when Fritz returned home to his Munich apartment building on Trogerstrasse. A summer-solstice sun was still bright, and the air was pleasantly warm. As Fritz shut the door to the street behind him, his neighbor Ludwig Eiber appeared in the doorway of his ground floor apartment and beckoned him inside.

Eiber closed his front door and turned to Fritz. "Your father told me that you are leaving for America soon. Congratulations. When are you going?"

"In about a month. I'm making my arrangements."

"God, so good," Eiber said, putting a hand to Fritz's shoulder. "I was so glad your poor sister got away. How is she?"

"Fine," said Fritz. "Having a hard time with her English but managing."

"I guess you'll be seeing her?"

"Yah, if all goes well." Fritz sighed. "I have to prepare myself—learn to dry dishes."

"I don't understand," said Eiber.

"Nor I," said Fritz. He laughed. "My sister writes me, 'you need to learn to dry the dishes. Men dry the dishes in America.'"

"I guess there are worse things." Eiber chuckled. Then, his face took on a more serious look. "Your father told me they're putting you through hell."

"Not so dramatic." Fritz shrugged. "I just have to leave nearly everything I own here in Germany and then pay an exorbitant tax on the few meager things I'm allowed to bring with me."

"Those liars and lunkheads—or I should say—our *overlords*—how skillful they've become at the art of looting. Especially when it comes to Jewish properties."

Fritz nodded. "We just got word that Thormann and Dannhäuser will soon become an *Aryan* sports shoe company."

"Where you've worked for the last, what, thirteen years!" Eiber closed his eyes and let out a sound of disgust. "Such crap! But before this gets too somber Fritz, let's sit. I want to enjoy a moment with you." Eiber led Fritz to a dining table where a pile of jackets, pants and other clothing items were stacked. An ironing board next to the table held an upright iron. The scent of steam hung in the air. "Forgive the mess, Fritz." Eiber laughed. "Welcome to the after-hours life of the tailor."

The sound of a Wagner operatic piece wafted into the room from a shiny brown Volksempfänger radio across the room. Eiber went over and turned down the volume.

Eiber shrugged. "Love the music. Not so fond of the man."

"Sounds like music to iron by," Fritz said with a broad smile.

"You've got that right. You should see me when I get in rhythm." And Eiber mimed the movement of an iron with flourishing sweeps of his hand.

Fritz clapped in appreciation.

Eiber walked to the table and pushed a stack of pressed pants closer to a wall to make room. He motioned for Fritz to sit. "Can I get you a beer?"

"Yah, of course." Fritz sat at the newly cleared section of the table. "Where's Berta?"

"Out doing chores. That's what she said. I think she just wanted to get away from this place. Can't blame her. It's not so fun when your work life takes over your home life." As Eiber spoke he opened a door and disappeared into the kitchen. A short while later he returned with two open bottles of Gunzenhausen.

Ludwig Eiber, in his mid-forties, stood slightly taller than Fritz, with a thin face, thick eyebrows and a neatly trimmed mustache. He combed his light brown hair straight back, revealing a receding hair line that still held its own. While Eiber was fifteen years older than Fritz, he'd retained much of the athletic build he'd developed through sports activities in his youth.

He and his wife Berta lived in the apartment nearest the front of the building and the storefront where the Eibers had their small tailor shop. A door from the living room of their apartment led to the shop. During business hours Ludwig Eiber, his wife, and several employees worked sizing, sewing, and pressing clothes.

Tonight Eiber wore a crisp white long-sleeve shirt and neatly pressed slacks. All that was missing from his normal work attire was a silk bow tie and a grey frock coat. He'd cultivated the habit of dressing up, even at work in his shop. As Eiber would say to anyone who commented on his formal appearance at work, "No one wants to patronize a shabby looking tailor."

Fritz regarded keeping up a good appearance as an essential element of his job as a traveling shoe salesman. It was clothing that had brought the two neighbors together in the first place. Fritz, who spent much of his time on the road in cities all over Germany, often sent clothes home to be cleaned and pressed. His mother, Anna, brought her son's shirts and pants to Eiber's shop for those services.

Eiber took a sip from his beer. "It's been a while since we've talked, Fritz. I want to know what's been going on with you. I hope we can make time for that before you leave the country. But," Eiber's voice took on a more serious tone, "I want to remind you of something immediate—the match."

"Oh, yah, yah," said Fritz. "The Schmeling and Louis fight—I've been thinking about it, too."

"Well," said Eiber, "it's very early tomorrow morning. You're welcome to come here and listen to it."

Fritz nodded. "Yes, thanks, that would be good."

"You know where my sympathies lie. And I think that we might be in for a pleasant surprise. If you know what I mean."

Fritz nodded.

"I've learned some things about Louis." Eiber took several sips of beer. "He may have lost last time, but I think this fight will be different."

Fritz felt a sudden surge of excitement. "I've heard that Louis has prepared himself better this time."

"The *swine* certainly hate him, and they're all puffed up about *their* boy Schmeling! And, you know," Eiber leaned in toward Fritz as though sharing a secret, "Hitler's people have never gotten over what happened with that fellow Owens. Don't you think so? So, we might have something to look forward to."

Fritz grinned, recalling how two years before, in 1936, shortly after Fritz's family moved to the Trogerstrasse apartment, he and Eiber had engaged in long conversations about sports. They were both engrossed in the summer Olympic games in Berlin that year. And when the Black US athlete Jesse Owens stunned the country and the world with his four gold metal victories, defeating some of Hitler's favorite athletes, Fritz and Eiber found themselves exulting. It created an emotional bond that still warmed their friendship.

Eiber's words about the coming boxing match roused Fritz's enthusiasm. But he was reserved by nature. In the five years since Hitler's rise to power, Fritz had developed a habit of carefully measuring his words in conversation with anyone outside his family circle. It was a survival skill he'd had to learn as a Jewish traveling salesman in Germany in the 1930s. "We'll be able to hear the fight here at 3:00 in the morning, just as it's going on at the stadium in New York! That's quite something," Fritz said marveling at such long-distance communication.

"And I think the whole world will be listening," said Eiber. "But it's better you listen to the fight here and not in your apartment. You can never tell with these idiots around here."

Fritz knew what Eiber meant. Everyone had to be careful about what they said, and what they listened to in Germany. This was true ten times over for Jews. And Fritz was wary of the neighbors on either side of his apartment. Herr Hack and Herr Kandl made no secret of their enthusiasm for the Nazi regime, nor of their hostility to Jews. As a result, Fritz and his family had become very cautious when listening to the radio in their apartment.

Eiber got up to walk Fritz to the door. "Come a few minutes before the match. I'm probably going to sleep for a while, but I'll be up for the broadcast."

"I'll be here."

"Invite your father, too. And Fritz, I'll leave the door open, so you don't have to knock. No reason to give the snitches any cud to chew on."

•　　　•　　　•

Fritz arrived at Eiber's door around quarter to three in the morning. He went in the apartment without knocking as Eiber had requested. He came with a pot of hot tea and a dish of Hamantaschen cookies his mother made for the occasion.

"Excellent," said Eiber. "And your father?"

"Asleep," said Fritz. "I didn't want to wake him."

As he entered the apartment Fritz heard the voice of German broadcast commentator, Arno Hellmis. It was nearly 9 p.m. in New York and Hellmis, a devoted national socialist and a regular writer for the Nazi Party paper *Der Völkischer Beobachter*, was describing the scene at Yankee stadium where 70,000 people had come to watch the fight.

Hellmis recounted the first fight between the two boxers that had taken place two years before in 1936. He was profuse with praise for the "mastery" the German fighter, Max Schmeling, had demonstrated in defeating the younger and favored "American negro" boxer, Joe Louis, in that previous match. Hellmis emphasized how Schmeling had sussed out Louis' weaknesses and employed his "superior intelligence" to overcome Louis' physical advantages. Schmeling outlasted Louis in their first fight because at every turn Schmeling's "Aryan instincts" prevailed. "Schmeling had a will as hard as Krupp steel," Hellmis asserted. "And he carried an autographed photo of the Fuehrer wherever he went!"

"Just shut up," Eiber hissed at his radio as he took a bite of a cookie. "Nazi blabber is so tiresome."

The cheers from the stadium crowd could be heard as the names of the fighters were announced.

Fritz felt a knot in his stomach. He put down his cup of tea and sat forward on his cushioned chair.

At the sound of the bell for the first round the German announcer described the boxers approaching each other at the center of the ring. As the first punches were exchanged, Hellmis sounded confident, even cocky.

"Maxie (Hellmis used the diminutive for his admired fighter) throws a right." Then, "Maxie takes a right." And then "Maxie backs up and hits back."

But just past the first minute of the round, Hellmis' voice began to change. Louis was landing punches that Schmeling could not return. The announcer's cockiness morphed into something akin to hysteria. Fritz and Eiber looked at each other in mutual astonishment.

By a minute and a half into the fight Louis had Schmeling up against the ropes and was pounding him so hard, and so frequently, that Hellmis began screaming. Then Schmeling went down and Hellmis implored, "Maxie, *steh auf! steh auf!* Get up! Get up!" Then, with relief, "Maxie is back on his feet." But shortly, Schmeling went down again. This time Hellmis was screeching, "Get up! Get up!"

After that little else was intelligible.

Fritz was on the far edge of his seat, stunned by the confusion in the announcer's voice, and its implication. "Sounds like Krupp steel might be melting," he said to the delight of his friend.

Barely two minutes into the fight and Hellmis' voice went silent.

From what they could make out, Schmeling was on the canvas and was not getting up.

Eiber pounded his fist on the table and looked up at the ceiling with an exuberant whisper, "wunderbar!"

Suddenly the radio station cut away from the fight scene, and after an odd silence came a terse announcement that the broadcast had ended.

"Well, we'll never hear another word about that fight." Eiber said, sarcastically.

"Can you imagine," said Fritz, "the expressions on some faces around here? I would very much like to see that right now."

Fritz was referring to the man whose picture poor Max supposedly carried with him at all times: The man, Hitler, whose Munich apartment was just a few blocks up the street from where Eiber and Fritz had been listening to the fight.

Fritz and Eiber both laughed, while, at the same time, motioning to each other to keep their voices down.

"Our Fuhrer are you furious?" Eiber whispered happily. Eiber walked over to Fritz and put his hand on his friend's shoulder. "This fight is a good going away present to you my dear Fritz."

Fritz had to wipe away tears as he stood up. "Danke," he said, "to you, for your support, and for that Louis fellow."

Eiber had his hand on Fritz's shoulder as they walked to the apartment door. "If you ever see that Black fellow over there in America, thank him for me." Eiber's watery eyes belied his own emotions. "And please tell him, and the people over there, not all of us Germans are Nazi pigs."

Halfway around the world, in Harlem, and in other sections of New York and in other cities in the US, people were dancing and shouting in the streets, unaware that their joy was shared by some Germans at that same moment.

OFF TO THE
OSTRICH RACES

MARGARET NALBACH

"HUH! Well, will you look at that!" I pointed beyond our windshield. "What? What are you talking about?" My husband Rob was dealing with the Saturday morning traffic as we headed out of town.

"There's a billboard ahead announcing 'Ostrich Races' the first Saturday of each month at the Fairgrounds."

"Yeah? That sounds interesting." Rob glanced to his right. "The turnoff is in two stops. Wanna go?" He signaled to change lanes. "How come we didn't know about this?"

"Ha! You're the driver," I snorted. "And how fast are we going?"

"Point taken" he muttered, then slowed.

We were having an "Anything Goes on the Road" day. A free day when we hopped into the car to try something new and different. No agendas. No meetings. Cell phones off. And this was the first Saturday of the month.

Soon we parked, exited the car, then donned our baseball caps and sunglasses. We started across the half-empty parking lot. Guess we were early. It was then I saw a tall, thin man with jet-black hair slicked back Elvis-style. Having just arrived, and heading towards the racetrack was

155

Phil Barker, who we often privately referred to as our home-grown Elvis impersonator. Wearing a yellow-and-black checkered jacket, yellow shirt and black bolo tie, he was hard to miss. My eyes hurt. Well, at least his pants were black. I really needed the sunglasses.

"Fast-talking Phil" was a local well-known personality, an auctioneer and used car salesman, known for his quick wit. He supported and announced many local school sports and fund-raising events, delighting everyone with his humor and wardrobe.

He spotted us immediately and came over. "Hey, there! It's been a while since I've seen y'all. Pro'bly the last time was at your son's last baseball game just before he graduated. Have y'all come to see the races? It's quite a show."

"Hey back, Phil." Rob said. "Good to see you too. Is this one of your gigs?"

Phil smiled broadly. "Yep. And folks, you're in for a real treat. This here group of farmers started these ostrich races a few years back, and the competition is fierce. They race up to six birds in teams of two. Today's special as it's the first race of virgins."

"Virgins?" My eyes opened wide.

"Ha. Right. Well, today's the start of a new season, so we've birds who have not raced before."

"How big are the crowds? Do you get a decent turnout?"

"We get a good crowd. Some first-time folks like you; a few who are friends of the farmers, and some hear 'bout the races by word of mouth, social media or the billboard and come to watch the fun. Big enough to keep us going on a reg'lar basis. Hey, y'all need to meet these here farmers. Afterwards, we usually hang around for lunch at Lola's coffee shop. Yer welcome to join us."

We walked over to a group of large animal transport trucks and Phil introduced us to a few of the bird farmers, each wearing colored t-shirts with their farm-brand logos.

"Gotta run; they need me at the announcers' booth." Phil said, leaving us to get acquainted with the friendly farmers.

We watched while the farmers unloaded their flocks from the rigs, removed the socks hooding large eyes and head-tops, then tried to tie matching logo-colored ribbons around the necks of their birds. Tall, strong, squirming birds, dancing around, who were cranky and oh my goodness, incredibly smelly.

"Welcome" said one of the farmers, with a squirming and swishing bird on a kind of leash, "to the dinosaur bird zoo!"

"What? Are we in a Jurassic zone?" laughed Rob.

"Oh, that's our inside joke," the farmer said. "I heard Phil invite you to join us after the races. We'll tell you about these birds then. Yeah, they're amazing survivors. But don't get too close. If they don't know you, you might be kicked. And their kick is lethal."

Duly warned, we kept well away.

One farmer groaned. "Ribbons are the only way we can tell them apart, especially in a large flock. It's not as if they had any distinguishing feather features. Although I swear, I'd dye some of their feathers if I could get them to hold still long enough."

Other farmers burst out laughing. "Yeah, good luck with that!" one yelled.

Rob and I grinned at each other. We'd hit the jackpot for an "anything goes" day.

•   •   •

By mid-morning the racetrack bustled with activity. The starting gates, the same type of gates used for horse-racing, were set up at one end of the track where the farmers led their birds.

And, oh, the birds were not happy, squawking and hissing, dancing a two-step, and trying to kick. After being confined to a very small space on the trucks and freed from the head socks, the ostriches now made the farmers struggle to keep them from bolting. It took two farmers to lead each tall bird into a racing gate. Wings flapped and feathers shook. Glad it wasn't me dealing with these fine feathered creatures.

We walked on over to the bleachers and saw plenty of empty seats. Since the seats were old and worn, most of the spectators stood behind the wood railing separating the bleachers from the track. Sitting on splinters is not anyone's favorite activity. Viewers happily munched and crunched away on chips and other food from the snack bar.

Tap-tap-tap was heard over the loudspeakers, then a blowing into the microphone. "Testing. One. Two. Three. Can you hear me?" That must have been a joke because Phil never had problems being heard. Ever.

"Ladies and gentlemen." Phil's voice was loud and clear. "Welcome to the Ostrich Races. Not your usual, hum drum horse-racing event, folks, these here birds are young, and raring to go. Hang on to your hats and get ready for a real treat. Today we have virgin birds ready for their first race! These lovelies are new to the racing world so anything can happen, and pro'bly will.

"Here is our bird line-up for race number one. In gates one and two we have. 'Feathers Frank' wearing a natty green collar, along with 'Flirty Frieda' sporting a lovely green boa. That's gates one and two, folks."

Green T-shirted spectators in the crowd responded "Go Frank! Go Frieda!"

"In gates three and four we have 'Roaming Robby' with a scarlet ribbon, accompanied by 'Rita Rouge' sporting a red flower lei."

Not to be outdone by the "green" group, fans of the "R" duo blew horns and waved red pompons, which made the birds jump and squirm.

"Gates five and six have 'Peter Pluma' wearing a purple tie-dye necktie, along with his racing partner 'Patty Petunia,' finishing off the set with a matching purple and pink tie-dye kerchief."

Not to be outdone by the green and red cheerleader outfits, supporters of the purple pair wore purple and yellow tie-dyed T-shirts along with purple hats with yellow ponytails.

The cheering crowd was making the birds more nervous.

"Let's have a round of cheers for these awesome birds, folks. Thank you, thank you, thank you very much," drawled Phil.

Now, that sounded just like Phil, coming up with funny, creative names and descriptions. I suspected he made them up on the fly. Why not? Listening to the crowd cheering plus the carrying-on by Phil, I laughed with Rob. Obviously, Phil was in his element. How did he do this so well?

The crowd loved it and the roar from the fans made a real ruckus.

"Hey, y'all. Let's get reeeaady to raaccceeee! Gentlemen, are your birds ready to run?"

With a wave from the farmers, Fast Talking Phil started.

"Okay folks, here we go! On your mark! Get set!"

Riiiiinnnnnnnngg.

The gates opened.

158

Startled by the bell and freed from the gates, the birds bolted. Feathers Frank and Roaming Robby headed straight towards the farmers waving at them from the first bend of the track, hissing and snarling as they ran. Boy, they were mad.

Phil tried to keep up.

"Folks, look at these birds run. Feathers Frank and Roaming Robby have taken the lead in just a few strides, not wasting any time they're headed directly to the finish line. Catching up with them should be . . .

"Well now, here comes Peter Pluma but he's not doing much of anything, just strolling along, looking around. Is he stopping to smell the flowers? Sorry, birdy, but the garden show is next week. Oh, there he goes, but now he's trying to get away from his farmer who is chasing him. Oh, oh, he's changed direction to follow the ladies. Ah-ha, a ladies kinda guy.

"But what's happen' with the ladies?"

Flirty Frieda and Rita Rouge had bolted out of the gates and now eyed the crowd behind the fence.

"It looks like the ladies are interested in you folks by the fence. Oh, oh, our lady birds are eyeing your snacks! Frieda and Rita are headed straight for the fence. Look out!"

The farmers, alarmed at the possibility of the spectators being subjected to their bird's ire, ran onto the track. They waved their arms to try and redirect the hens' attention back to the race. Unaccustomed to the farmers running towards them, but not wanting to miss a snack, the hens stretched their legs and dashed directly toward the spectators.

Seeing a good thing and not to be left out, Patty veered and was right behind Frieda and Rita. Peter turned to follow Patty. Watching the farmers try to redirect the birds and getting into the spirit, spectators started yelling and waving their arms, as well as the pompons. Startled, the hens turned around and ran smack dab into Peter. Bouncing back, tripping over each other, they fell into a tangled heap.

Legs up, tails down, wings spread in a glorious pile of fluff.

Feathers flew, hisses spewed out as the farmers tried to sort out the chaos. The crowd roared. Tears were streaming down my face and my ribs hurt from laughing, and Rob was right there with me.

"Ah. Ah. Ah. Ah-Choo!" I started sneezing. Rob started sneezing. A slight breeze had wafted over the racetrack and blew an aroma of ostrich along with feathers, dust, and dander our way which set us off. We were not alone. A chorus of sneezes came from the other spectators as well.

"Whoops." We heard Phil say then "Ah. Ah. Ah. Choo." Nor was he immune. "Well, now, it looks like we have these lovely lady birds getting a bit too close and personal. Ah. Ah. Ah. Choo. Hey, Peter Pluma is running away in the opposite direction. Is this too much for him? Ah. Ah. Ah. Choo." Phil was barely able to continue, sneezing and sniffling.

Startled by the jumbled mass of wings and legs, hissing hens, farmers waving their arms, and the pile of feathers, Peter managed to free himself and ran willy-nilly, zig-zagging his way back to the starting gates.

Out of the crowd came a yell, "Hey, that's the wrong way!" which set anyone who wasn't sneezing, laughing harder.

"Yes, ladies and gentlemen, it looks like we'll have to rename Peter to Wrong Way Willy." Phil announced.

Finally untangled, with wings flapping, the hens ran in circles around the yelling, arm- waving farmers. How useless was that? The birds ignored all waves and other signals.

"Ladies and gentlemen, while we were watching the flighty feathered fiasco, we had a winner! Annnnd, the winner is Roaming Robby! How did he miss all the hullabaloo going on? Well, congratulations to Robby for crossing the finish line a knee and toe length ahead of Feathers Frank.

"Now, here comes Rita Rouge in third place. How did she get over there so fast? She must have slid out from under the feathery mess and chased after her mate, Roaming Robby, thinking she needed to rein him in."

Oh, my. The first race over and there were more to come. This was too irresistible. Rob and I looked at each other and simultaneously pulled out our mobile phones to record the next races. I wondered how we could post this on our social media sites.

When the races were over, and muscles in our sides aching from laughter, we headed out to Lola's coffee shop. As we walked in, Lola took one look at us, then asked "Have you two been at the racetrack?"

"Yes, Ma'am. Sure have," replied Rob with a big smile on his face.

"In the backroom dining room, please."

"Special treatment?" I asked.

"You betcha. We have a special buffet set up just for the farmers and their guests."

"Wow. Such a deal! Why is that?"

"Well, after a few times of the ostrich guys taking over a bunch of tables, we had some issues with other customers and the wait staff. No one wanted to be near them. While it's better now because the guys change clothes before they come, the 'essence of ostrich' fragrance is still a bit too much. With a buffet, we can set up ahead of time and everyone can help themselves. We keep track of the buffet, but there's minimal contact. We also have the fans blowing. They help keep the room aired out."

Savoring the smell of coffee over the distinct bird aroma and seeing the luncheon buffet, we found seats and went about helping ourselves to lunch. While we were eating and talking with the farmers, we learned a lot about the birds.

Native to sub-Saharan Africa, ostriches are the tallest and largest of all birds. Some species can grow up to 9 feet tall. To me it looked like their height was all in the neck, like giraffes. The farmers agreed that they have a great time racing them because, once they get going, the birds can run over forty miles per hour and their stride can reach over fifteen feet. Great competition between the different farms. As an added benefit, they started a co-op where they sell not only the fine feathers, but there are other product lines: ostrich oil, soap, and even a fine grade of meat.

"Ostrich meat?" asked Rob. "Does it taste like chicken?"

"Ha. No, it's more like filet mignon," one farmer responded. "Some of the local butchers carry it as a specialty item, like rabbit. Or you can buy frozen meat available at the co-op."

Suffice it to say, we will never look at an ostrich the same way again. I think it will be some time before I make a meal from one of them, however.

On the drive home I was lost in thought when Rob looked over. "Whatcha think'n' 'bout? Painting an ostrich? Or a new story?"

"Just wondering how well I could write a story using ostriches. They have a sneer that might be hard to capture from the photos. Hmm, I wonder what they'd look like if I put glasses on them?"

I barely heard his laughter added with "and she's off and running!"

THE PALO ALTO
POOP PATROL

MICKIE WINKLER

THE ENTREPRENEURIAL, Silicon Valley spirit has overtaken me. My friends here churn out new ideas and new enterprises—and, oh yes, get rich. But what about me? What is my special calling? What was I brought into this world to do? Ladies and gentlemen, that search appears over.

As my fellow residents know, Palo Alto Code 6.20.045 states:

Dog defecation to be removed by owners.

It is unlawful for any person owning or having control or custody of any dog to permit the animal to defecate upon the public property of this city or upon the private property of another unless the person immediately removes the feces and properly disposes of it.

That law has inspired me to become the founder of the Palo Alto Poop Patrol.

So what is it that I, as the founder of the Palo Alto Poop Patrol, do? Do I issue fines? No! When I surreptitiously film a law-breaking, dog-

The Palo Alto Poop Patrol

pooping dog and its owner, I don't issue fines. I do accept bribes. Are poopetrators happy to ante up? No! But they would rather pay me than have to pay a dog-pooping fine in court. And they will ante up even more when I offer to delete my videos of them—with their dogs and the unpicked-up poop—and to not post them on all social media sites.

I've expanded my business to include disposable doggie diapers, fashionably designed for male dogs, female dogs, and LGBTQ dogs in a variety of dog-matching colors.

Most offending owners immediately invest in my disposable doggie diapers which I always carry with me on patrol. Doggie diapers protect dog owners from having to publicly pick up the putrid poop—which is obviously why they are trying to evade Palo Alto's public-poop law.

As for me, I am one proud—and getting ever richer—Silicon-Valley success. And I hope that whenever you see a dog pooping, you will think of me.

IF I LET IT . . .
(An ode to the pandemic)

IDA J. LEWENSTEIN

My room
Could be a tomb
Filled with gloom and doom
If I let it . . .

It could also be my stage
Where I could express
Love or even RAGE
If I let it . . .

It could be my favorite spot
To peel back time and
Reminisce a lot
If I let it . . .

And last but not least—
It could become my Camelot
Where good things happen and
Bad things do not.
If I let it . . .

STAGE NAMES

SCOTT BEST

I T WAS TOKYO, it was cherry blossom season, and it's entirely possible I was dreaming. I'd a few hours between customer meetings and set off to explore the East Gardens of the Imperial Palace, one of the better places in Tokyo to see the annual *sakura* blossoms. It's an unusual public park for a national capital, as it's situated within a walled fortress moated off from the rest of the city. A handful of bridges lead inward to its sculpted paths—greens, fuchsias, lavenders, meticulously arranged, dappled in perfect shadow—and I wandered there, maneuvering between groups of students, tourists, and weary salarymen seeking a moment's solace from the nearby banking district. As usual, I felt both surrounded and isolated, an unimportant foreigner, the center of my own attention.

I find the city both impersonal and compelling for many reasons. For one, my name has too few vowels to work correctly in Japanese, so when introducing myself I necessarily become someone else by adding extra syllables to my name, a surprisingly comfortable adoption of a slightly-not-me identity.

The street signs are another reason. Twenty years ago, people tell me, there were no English road signs or shop names in major cities like Tokyo. But as the city prepared for hosting the Olympics in 2020, all were updated to a combination of English, Kanji, and Hiragana. It is this lettering, of all things, which reminds me of dreaming: the closer I examine the details of something within a dream, the faster those details change, the faster the text swirls. My subconscious cannot seem to supply written language quickly enough, and thus it's become a fail-safe test to answer the occasional "wait, is this a dream?" moment. It always works . . . except when I'm in Japan.

And finally, there are the city's fabled trains, as orderly and intensely anonymous as a locker room. Onboard, I try to fit in, doing whatever I can to disappear: I stare out the window, I flip through my phone's social media apps, I detach like a ghost. The ebb and flow of the passengers are as calm, enduring, and indifferent to me as beach-front tides.

But after a few days, the whole of Tokyo can feel like a permanent train-ride experience, as if the pervasive train culture has mated with the introverted Japanese culture, creating a sensation that I'm being completely ignored, in the most polite way possible. I have felt it before, how easy it would be to slip under the surface here where detached ghosts are traditionally welcome. I am so far from home, I fear it would take but a moment's inattention to forever not find my way back.

•　　　•　　　•

That night, after the last of the afternoon meetings, my Japanese colleagues guided my American team into the *Roppongi* neighborhood. Where they brought us wasn't exactly a bar, nor exactly a brothel. It was a hostess club—a *kyabakura*, a clumsy Japanese mimic of "cabaret club."

I remember the place being slightly warmer than necessary, a tight maze of several well-appointed rooms, every other corner a mirrored inset of halogen-lit shelves crowded with bottles: auburn whiskey, emerald-green vermouth, painted-ceramic *sake*. The walls there are indistinct, concealed by arbitrary decorations of Asian-themed statuettes, silk tapestries, and red velour, making the overall size of each room difficult to gauge. Beige leather sectional couches that surround low tables of ebony wood define small, independent islands of seating for each group of customers. Perky conversations bounce around the room, riding on the background of familiar music coming from the high-end, unmistakably auto-tuned karaoke system.

A high-end *kyabakura* like this one requires a reservation—you'll request a table for your group of four or six or however many you're traveling with. The security staff confirms your reservation and sizes you up while you wait outside beneath their security cameras. After buzzing you in from the street, Linda, the *mamasan* owner of this one, will greet you in the foyer then usher you to your table, orchestrating four or five young women in her wake who'll join your group for the evening. The young women who work there—the *kyabajo* cabaret girls—all have carefully-chosen stage names when Americans visit: Stephanie, Allison, Jessica.

At the table, one can expect a decanter of decent whiskey, an antique silver tray of American cigarettes, and an iPad linked to the surround-sound audio. The women wear slightly ill-fitting evening gowns and sport four-inch heels that some struggle with on the plush carpeting. What stands out the most to me, however, is how few of the women are Japanese, or even Asian. There are few immigrant workers anywhere in Tokyo—street sweepers, cab drivers, and even office-tower janitorial staff are almost exclusively native Japanese. But at Linda's hostess club, the women confide they're émigrés from places where Linda herself used to live: Russia, Ukraine, Belarus, perhaps Estonia if you believe all their stories.

You'll find Linda strong and certain in the way only a five-foot tall, sixty-year-old business owner in a foreign city of fourteen million people can be. She is fair-haired, wild-eyed, plump, and firm: an artillery shell of a woman. But there is wisdom there too; whatever difficulties and complications she's overcome in her life, she exudes an easygoing, serene perspective, perhaps simply by knowing nothing here this evening will be remotely difficult or complicated.

That night with my colleagues, Linda and I were both several whiskeys along when she and I finally spoke more than polite superficials. We chatted about her business, her strange path to living in Tokyo, what she loved most about her third husband and least about her second. Before too long, she had me describing what I found most compelling about the women in my life.

169

"Humor?" Linda asked incredulously. Her eyes weren't on me as she spoke; her attention was with the women who moved among my coworkers. She gave silent direction to one, inclining her head just so, swirling a finger like she was mixing a drink. "What of boobs? Of ass? Of legs?"

"All three, ideally attached," I said. "But I only fall for the funny ones. The ones who can surprise me."

"How many times have you fallen?"

"Just twice," I said. "A girl back in college and my wife now."

"And they both surprised you?"

"Their thinking could always sneak up on me."

As she motioned her swirly finger towards a fair-headed waif sitting across from us, the bracelet Linda wore up near the elbow slipped to her wrist, as if for emphasis. "This one is Catherine; she enjoys surprising me."

I looked up and caught Catherine's eye. She sat cross-legged next to one of my coworkers, as close as she could without sitting in his lap. She wore an angular seafoam-green dress and an ankle bracelet flashed just above her gold heels. Pale with sad eyes, she radiated a vagabond's grit, as if she had not long ago traveled a great distance, her quiet sadness suggesting not everyone survived the journey. I noticed her hand, stroking my coworker's thigh, while he loudly and obliviously argued with the others about the next karaoke song. Holding my gaze, she paused to squeeze his knee and graced a sideways bank-robber's smile at me.

I sipped my whiskey and turned back to Linda. "I am so far from home."

•   •   •

Years before my career required travel to Japan, when I first moved to California, I worked for a semiconductor company which'd been part of Silicon Valley ever since it started calling itself that. The company was well known for hiring dozens of new college-grads every year, and in the late '80s I was part of one year's batch. My coworkers and I were all unattached guys, with similar caliber engineering degrees and social awkwardness. We also had similar never-seen-this-before salaries, and so a group of six or eight of us hung out together pretty much every night.

In the span of a year or two, we must've visited nearly all of the bars, dance clubs, and concert venues on the peninsula. For every new place, we'd learn of another we'd have to try next. Ostensibly, we socialized as a team of coworkers, but in truth we were each simultaneously running our own private life experiment: *Do I like it here? Am I going to stay with this company, with this career, with this whole Californian situation?* We ended up with different answers, but back then we were pretty much an every-night group.

One night, my work friends and I drove up to San Francisco for a burlesque performance at the O'Farrell Theatre. I found the show through the weekly "Pink Pages," a now-discontinued section of a major San Francisco newspaper. The Pink Pages advertised the bands at every nightclub, the films at every movie house and—if one kept reading to the very back—the porn stars at every adult theatre.

This particular advertisement caught my attention because I knew the star performer: she was my college girlfriend's older sister. I'd spent three of my four undergraduate years inseparable from this girlfriend—the one I found myself telling *mamasan* Linda about twenty years later—and spent no small amount of time with her family during summer breaks and over the Christmas holidays. Over those years, her oddly-famous sister and I became friends. Her career choice was treated with a very matter-of-fact, so-that-happened attitude by both her and her family. When I first met her, she was in sweatpants and a T-shirt, lying on the living room couch, watching a black-and-white movie on TV. I think she'd either just been napping or was headed into one. She paid wearied attention to the movie, blinking slowly, as if trying to decipher what the bygone characters were all carrying on about, but only with sleepy half-interest.

My work friends and I had been to the city several times before to visit mainstream music venues and a couple of Irish pubs, which suited us. In contrast, the O'Farrell Theatre was a vintage cliché of adult cinema: lit only by a few weak floor-lights and the exit signs, it smelled of sweat and cigarettes. Its dingy movie-theatre seats hid a sticky floor which hinted darkly at the biological. The room could seat a couple-hundred if full, but there were hardly a dozen or so other guys tonight besides my friends and myself.

The main stage was mostly dark and empty, with a crimson curtain and a lonely microphone withering under a fixed spotlight. A series of young women took turns parading grandly from the side stage, stripping with various degrees of allure their outfits of feathered boas, G-strings, push-up bras, fishnet stockings, garters, pasties, tassels. Each routine lasted a few minutes, and then, naked, they exited offstage, leaving behind their slight, individualized stage-litter. A small group of men, including my coworkers, cheered their approval from the first few rows of the theatre, while several other men silently observed in darkened, sinister isolation several rows back. I sat at the very back, the last row, close to the lobby exit. I wanted to see my friend, but I didn't want to see her *that* well.

"What are you doing all the way back here?" a nearby voice asked.

I turned quickly, and there she was, sitting just a few seats away at the end of the aisle. I hadn't noticed before, but several of the performing girls were walking around the darkened theater, soliciting any isolated theatre-goers with personal visits and momentary companionship.

I leaned forward into a stray light column so she could see my face. "I guess I didn't want to embarrass anyone, A___," I said, addressing her by name.

The shock on her face was immediate and genuine. In one continuous motion she jumped to her feet, turned to run out of the theater, remembered she was the obligated star, spun around, and zipped right back into her chair again. She looked around quickly to see if anyone else had caught the whole panicked maneuver.

"How ... What ..." she started, closed her eyes, raised her hands, and caught her breath. She inhaled slowly, deliberately, pressing her hands down towards her lap as she exhaled. "Okay, wow. *Totally* wasn't expecting to see you."

"I should have called or something, but I had no idea how to reach you. I, umm, brought some co-workers with me," I said, motioning to the goofballs near the front of the stage who were waving around dollar bills at the current performer.

"They look like they're enjoying themselves."

"Yep. They're harmless, and—"

"Don't call me that."

"Hmm?"

172

"My name. A___. Don't call me that. Not here."

"Oh, right. Sorry."

She stood up. "I'm on in a few. Please stay and watch; I'm trying something new and want your opinion. Find me in the lobby after."

"Gotcha. Will do."

She waved goodbye to me—a rapid, clandestine hand movement—and then fled down the theater aisle.

●　　　●　　　●

I'll spare you the details of the "something new" part of her show, but let's just leave it with this: some sex-toys utilize batteries not just for vibration, but for illumination as well. And if the light is bright enough, the human body, while not transparent, can be surprisingly translucent.

I retreated to the lobby after her performance, and she soon emerged from a passageway for the talent. She'd thrown on a floor-length puffy winter coat over her reassembled stage costume, and she smiled nervously, possibly for my benefit.

"So, did you like the show?"

"I did," I lied, because I didn't. It turns out, watching my almost-sister-in-law strip-tease fell outside of my erogenous zone. But you know, until you know, who knows?

"And the light show?" she asked.

"That was ... that worked. I can see why you're the main act, if that's the right word."

She smiled. "The headliner."

"Right, yes. And, sorry again I surprised you earlier, but I'm glad I got to see you."

She hugged me then. "I was surprised to hear my real name," she said. "I never use that name when I'm working."

"My bad."

"I need to go," she said. "I've got ... I've got to go undress."

I couldn't help but chuckle at how much sense that made. "Quick thing," I said. "How's your sister? Is she still ... happy? With what's his name?"

Her smile wandered off, and she leaned her head sideways. And then her genuine sympathy stabbed my heart like a spotlight. "She's good. They're still together."

"Ah."

She frowned softly, understanding the whole point of my visit even before I did. She was so kind and compassionate with my humiliation in that moment, naked and on stage. "You really miss her, don't you?"

"Yes," I said, fading. "Yes, I do."

•   •   •

It's been a year since the Tokyo trip and well-more than twenty since the San Francisco one. Today I'm on the Caltrain line, three stops into my twelve-stop commute. It's a two-level car, and I always try to find a seat in the top section, where seats are arranged in single file, making it even more effective than sunglasses for avoiding onboard eye contact.

The commuter train is an old, utilitarian diesel wreck built back in a time when the comfort of passengers on public transportation was as pertinent as that of cargo. It roars and lurches to start, and once moving, it's all thundering certainty and no grace. Like most passengers, I'm politely disconnected, absorbed, my body just a static placeholder to be reunited with my absent consciousness once the experience ends.

This morning, I'm gazing out the milky, plastic window, the music on my earbuds fortifying my isolation from the train's agonizing shrieks when braking. I watch as the train pulls up to the platform—not my stop—while awaiting passengers group and regroup into organic clumps, trying to anticipate where the carriage doors will eventually stop and receive them.

As I'm watching the platform, I suddenly notice a young woman hurrying towards the train. Actually, no, she's not hurrying: that's what catches my attention. She's walking with a certain, measured stride, as if she knows the exact number of seconds it will take to procure a ticket from the vending machine and step onto the train before the doors close, and she's got a comfortable margin of three seconds like she always has, so why hurry? She has a satchel over one shoulder, she's wearing red-rimmed, mirror-shade sunglasses, and she's drawing deeply from a cigarette. I notice her neck and chest are adorned with several silver necklaces that all bounce rhythmically with her stride.

I find myself drawn to her as she secures a ticket from a vending machine and turns to board the train. At that very instant, however, her path is crossed by an old man. He's shabbily dressed—a dirty T-shirt, baggy jeans more brown than blue—his tattooed arm clenching a bulging trash bag, his gray hair as wild as the train's diesel exhaust. My attention shifts from the vagrant to the woman and back to the vagrant; I become convinced they're going to collide. He's about to stumble into her, and the doors will close, and she'll miss her train. Wherever she was going, whatever she was going to do, she's going to be late. Maybe too late. He's going to ruin everything.

But at the instant their paths intersect, instead of colliding, she casually removes the cigarette from her mouth, flips it around filter first, and hands it to the old man who deftly receives it, right in stride. She exhales as he inhales, and she then nimbly boards the train. I lose sight of the young woman, never to see her again, but I watch the old man as he turns away from the train and shuffles down the platform, enjoying the gift of his morning smoke.

I turn from the window, startled, blinking. I was so wrong ... the tragedy imagined; my certainty as fragile as a dream. And like a dream, the characters, plot, and set pieces now hurry offstage, dodging the glare of my awakening. A dream of ... of what? ... of me? With the college girl? I didn't become this way because she left me—she left me because I've always been this way. So lightweight a thing! How seamlessly it fits.

A BIG DAY FOR BILLY

JO CARPIGNANO

W HEN MY NEPHEW BILLY'S slow physical development was diagnosed as Duchene's Muscular Dystrophy, the prognosis was dire: *progressive muscle deterioration, and life expectancy beyond age twenty-five, rare.* The prediction stabbed straight into my heart. Billy! Our precious four-year-old, Billy! He now had an entire lifetime to live before reaching twenty.

I clutched my cell phone tighter. I'd sit down before relistening to my sister Toni's message. Maybe I'd heard something wrong. But the only thing I'd missed was that she'd waited four weeks to report the devastating news. I felt like my eyes would bleed tears. I needed to call Toni, but I'd have to calm down before I talked to my sister. I turned to Google for more information on Duchene's.

A slew of decisions faced Toni and her husband Ron: choices about Billy's medical care, his education, his playmates, and his future. How were they going to cope with all of this by themselves? Surely, these necessary questions had already occurred to them. How many others hadn't?

As Billy's recently widowed Aunt Joan, what could I do to help? How should I help? I loved that little boy and was prepared to do whatever I could for him, and for those responsible for his care. What if Toni and Ron wouldn't want me to get involved? They might consider any offer to help as questioning their competence or, perhaps, think of it as interference.

What the Hell! I needed to know where I stood on this, or I'd go out of my mind.

I dialed my sister's cell number and asked how she was holding up.

"I'm sorry I didn't notify you sooner," she said. "I just couldn't talk about it earlier."

"How are you and Ron managing now?"

"Doing the best we can, I suppose. We consulted another specialist last week, and the answers were the same."

"I'm sorry, Sis. I was wondering if—if I could talk to you about how I might be of help with this?"

"I think I know just about all I want to know about Duchene's Dystrophy right now," Toni said, her voice brisk.

It was clear that my sister really didn't want to talk about the subject. After a long pause, I had a brilliant idea.

"Hey, how about I meet you and Billy at the park tomorrow? With a picnic lunch, maybe?"

Getting out of the house might be a welcome change from the stress of medical appointments. Also, it would give us a chance to talk more freely if Billy were busy playing in a sandbox.

Toni hesitated, then agreed, "But only if you make peanut butter and banana sandwiches," she added.

"My God, Toni, are you still addicted to those Elvis favorites?"

"It's not just me, Billy is addicted too," she said, and I heard a little smile in her voice. "San Bruno playground a good place for you?"

"Fine with me. It's a deal then. What time?"

"We can get there about 11:30, that okay?"

"Sure, that's a perfect time. What about cookies or fruit for dessert?"

"Billy loves grapes. You know, those big yellow ones that don't have any seeds. I like them too."

"Done! I'll get busy right away." I had found *something* useful to do. A wave of relief washed through me.

San Bruno Park was about halfway between my house in San Francisco, and where Toni lived in San Carlos. It would be good to see Billy interact with kids, for a change. No one in our family had children Billy's age, so I'd only seen him with grown-ups. He had the whole family of adults charmed with his good looks and easy smile.

•   •   •

The next morning, Toni and Billy arrived at San Bruno City Park Playground promptly at 11:30. I waved when I saw the Lexus turn in from Crystal Springs Road. Toni parked a couple of yards from the picnic table I'd selected.

"Auntie Joan! Auntie Joan!" Billy shouted joyfully as he scrambled out of the car. "Look at my hat. It's the one you gave me. I like it, I like it. Gonna wear it every day!"

"Well, good, Billy. I'm glad you like it," I said as I hugged him.

"Mom, can I go play now?" Billy asked, turning to his mother for permission.

"Sure, kiddo. Just don't get to digging in the dirt before we eat lunch, okay?"

Was Toni's concern about Billy's susceptibility to infection, or just keeping hands clean before lunch? We spread out the tablecloth, laid sandwiches on paper plates, and tucked napkins under them. I'd brought orange juice for Billy, and a thermos of hot coffee for Toni and me. The table prepared, we sat and watched Billy play awkwardly with a couple of younger kids on the "kiddie-go-round." He appeared to look in the direction of the slides a few times, but stayed where he was.

Billy came back to us and begged for a push on the swings, and I volunteered. With Billy firmly seated, I pulled the swing back, and held him suspended until he squealed for me to let go. Then I pushed him higher and higher, until he squealed again. I glanced at Toni, concerned about possible overexcitement, but she smiled her permission and approval.

"Enough on the swing now, Billy, I think it's time for lunch," I said at last, growing tired from my own exertion.

Seated at the table we enjoyed the sandwiches, drinks, and grapes.

"This is really good," Billy said through a mouthful of peanut butter and banana sandwich.

"Wait 'til you swallow, Billy," Toni cautioned. "Talking with food in your mouth is not such a good idea. When you talk after swallowing, we can hear you better."

Might Billy's condition make him subject to choking? I needed to learn so much–if allowed to help.

After lunch, Billy's shoulders sagged, and his eyelids drooped. "Ready for your nap, kiddo?" his mother asked.

Billy nodded reluctantly, and followed Toni to the car where he lay down on the back seat and tucked a pillow under his head. Toni threw a small blanket over him.

"Sweet dreams," I heard Toni whisper, closing the door and checking that the window was slightly open. She smiled on her way back to the table, seeming to relax now that her fragile child was settled safely. She sat down with a sigh.

"Well, Toni, what shall we do now? Can we talk about Billy, or just sit and enjoy our coffee?"

"I'm really okay now, Joan, we can talk about Billy if you like. I was in a bad mood yesterday. Sorry I was short with you."

I shook my head. "Don't apologize, Sis. What you said gave me a clear message about how you were feeling."

"Then, let's get on with it," Toni said, clenching her hands and placing them firmly in her lap. "Let's talk about Billy."

She stared at her clenched hands for a moment, then turned her head to address me.

"It's awful, Jo ... about the worse thing for a parent ... when something like this happens to your child ... and there's nothing you can do about it. Especially when you can't stop it, you can't change it, and you can't make it better. So, you need to learn to live with it. And it's hard ... so damned hard," she added bitterly, as tears began to well.

"I'm so sorry, but there are some of us who can help. I think I can make it a little easier for you if you let me. You just need to tell me how."

"I know you want to help. But you can't make this go away, and you can't make it any easier to bear." She looked at me with raised eyebrows. "But there *is* something you *can* do."

"Let's have it," I said. "I'll do my best, I promise. Just tell me." I brushed a strand of hair away from her face.

"It won't be easy, and you'll be sorry you asked," she warned.

"Let's have it!"

"Well … you know how Mom and Dad are about medical problems. They go ballistic with questions, and suggestions, and remedies … doctors to see, and places to go for better answers. And I just can't face all that right now. I don't want the struggle of reassuring them that we've done all that can be done. Mom and Dad won't accept it without a big argument, and long discussions. I dread the thought of going through that with them."

Toni knitted her eyebrows and said, "Can you fight that battle for me? I know it's a lot to ask, and it's not really your responsibility. Ron keeps reminding me that it's my job. But, if you could step in, it would relieve me of an enormous load right now."

"Hey, that's not a big deal for me. I had plenty of practice with them before Jack died. I know just what you mean. Consider that load off your shoulders and onto mine."

At least I'd found one way to be useful. Never knowing when to leave well enough alone, I pursued a nagging question about Billy's play habits. I had noted his awkward movements and saw how he kept looking at the children playing on the slides.

"When Billy was playing today, he kept glancing at the slides, but he never went over to them."

Toni nodded and said that she too had been aware of that behavior. "He knows he can't climb the stairs, so he stays away from the slides, and I think he'd really love sliding down."

"Then he already knows that he can't do things that other kids do?"

"Oh yes, very much aware. Younger children in the playground are doing many things he can't do. Sometimes he tries to play tag with them but can't keep up. He wants to jump off of curbs, but knows he'll fall if he tries. It breaks my heart to watch him trying and failing."

She crossed her arms against her chest, then cleared her throat. "I don't know whether to encourage him to keep trying, or explain that no matter how hard he tries, it won't get easier. I don't know what to tell him."

"Mo-om?" The sound of Billy's voice from the car interrupted our conversation. Billy Boy was awake from his nap, and ready to tackle the world that still baffled him.

181

Toni led him from the car and brought him back to the picnic table for a glass of juice. Billy climbed into my lap with a boost from his mother. As I held him close to me, his soft body still warm from the nap, I kissed the top of his curly head three times.

Billy giggled. "That tickles, Auntie Joan."

"Is that so," I teased. "If you think that tickles, how about this," I said, nibbling at his neck.

"Stop, stop!" He laughed and struggled to escape.

I did stop, afraid that he might choke on his juice if I continued. How would I ever be able to judge how much would be *too much* of anything I did with my precious nephew? I looked at Toni, but she only smiled.

After the juice and another cookie, Billy slid off my lap, and headed back to the kiddie-go-round.

"Hold on young fellah'," I said, "how about going on the slide? You haven't had a turn on that yet, have you?"

I glanced at Toni, who had a look of shocked disbelief on her face.

She spoke between clenched teeth, in a horrified whisper, "I just told you about stairs, Joan!"

Too late, I realized that I should have talked to her before offering the choice to Billy. I answered carefully, aware that Billy was listening too.

"I know Billy has trouble on stairs. But I can lift him one step at a time to the top, and you can catch him at the bottom. I thought it might be fun for us to do something together, don't you think?"

Taking a deep breath, and looking directly at Billy, Toni asked, "Well, Billy, do you think your Auntie Jo is just being silly? . . . or . . . what?"

"No, Mommy, not silly. Let's go on the slide."

I had no right to offer Billy this adventure without his mother being comfortable with it. I needed to offer her a way out of this.

"Well, you know, it is getting kinda late, Billy. Maybe we can come back another day for the slide."

Billy's face fell, then he looked to his mother for the decision. "Not too late, Auntie Jo! Ple-e-ase Mom?"

Then turning to me, Toni asked, "You sure you can do this?"

I nodded. "I'm sure. I've done it many times with kindergarten kids. Never dropped one of them," I boasted. But what if something went wrong this time?

Toni hesitated, then relented. "Well, Billy, I guess the worst that can happen is that you'll tumble into the sand when you get to the bottom."

Hand in hand, Billy and I walked to the foot of the steps attached to the slide. Billy was so excited he could hardly contain himself.

"Hurry, hurry!" he shouted, pulling on my arm that held his hand.

"No, we're not going to hurry, Billy, we're going to go very slow. You need to listen to my directions and make me some promises. Can you promise to hold on tight to the railing when we go up the stairs? You have to hold on with both hands, and you can't let go until we get to the top, okay?"

"Okay!" Billy said, breathless, and eager to start.

"Tell me what you're going to do with your hands," I asked.

"Hold tight!"

"And, when are you going to let go?"

"At the top."

"Great! Now I'm going to tell you what to do with your feet. Are you listening?'

"Yes!"

Then I told Billy about keeping his feet and legs together, very straight and very strong.

"I know it's a lot to remember, but I'll be right here to remind you if you forget. And better ask your mother if she's ready at the bottom of the slide, Billy."

"You ready, Mommy?"

"I'm ready, baby," Toni shouted, a slight quaver in her voice.

"Here we come," I said, lifting Billy easily onto the first step.

"Hold both rails tight with both hands, and keep feet together," I reminded him, as we negotiated the second step.

As we climbed higher, Billy looked down.

"Hold tight, and look *up, up, up!*" I said.

And, so we proceeded, one stair at a time. I lifted my little nephew at each step to the top of the mini slide. At the top, I had him sit and put his legs together.

Toni, waiting at the bottom of the slide, clapped her hands in relief when she saw Billy safely seated at the top.

"It's all yours now, Billy. Scoot yourself off the seat, put your hands in your lap, keep your feet together, and slide down all by yourself."

He pushed off and squealed happily all the way down, where his mother caught him in a big bear-hug.

"The best ride! Do it again!" Billy demanded.

And we did it twice more, then I got tired. Anyhow, it was time to pack to the car, go home, and tell Ron all about Billy's big day at the park.

Then the realization hit me. My discussion with Toni as Billy had napped, and the excitement Billy felt doing something his mother believed too difficult, were my contributions today. I smiled. This day at the park had proven significant for all of us.

WEIRD TO THE THIRD POWER

LAUREL ANNE HILL

I WATCH CARLO ENTER the passcode for the library's main door. A minute later we're inside and the alarm's off. My long-time buddy, a locksmith, knows his way around our home town's security systems. The beam from his flashlight wavers. Bet he has the jitters too. I glance toward the nearest security camera. Still deactivated.

Oh, man. Two law-abiding old farts shouldn't need to case a ladies' room in the middle of the night. But every 786 days, me and Carlo have no choice. All because I'm a frigging lousy sorcerer.

"Something extra weird's brewing," Carlo says. "Even my teeth tingle."

"Maybe this time he's in there."

"Wish this place was still a vacant lot." Carlo smooths his nitrile gloves.

"I wish a lot of things." Such as that day with Wil the Whacker fifty years ago never happened.

Just picturing those thugs tattooing my name on Wil's two-hundred-pound fresh corpse still makes my stomach churn. A real sorcerer would have made both Wil and his killers go poof for good. Instead, Wil's vanishing act

185

was only temporary and murderer self-elimination by accidental overdose took thirty years.

"It's 3 a.m. already," Carlo says. "Let's keep moving."

We walk down the corridor, past the water fountain. The beam of his flashlight illuminates the ladies' room door. If Wil waits on the spot where I once made him vanish, he'll be a skeleton by now, his bony hand clutching strands of my black hair. Only some of the false evidence planted by his murderers.

"You ready?" I say.

"Sure." Carlo takes a deep breath and exhales hard.

I ease open the lavatory door. A faint odor of wet wool emanates from the darkened rest room. Carlo flinches.

"Tell me that's not pomade," he says.

"That's not pomade." My forearms prickle. "It's fifty-year-old lanolin pomade."

Back in the day, all the young punks over-greased their hair with that shit. Did Wil's remains return in better condition than expected?

I flip the light switch. A fluorescent tube flickers and hums. A guy's desert boot attached to a horizontal leg pokes from under the side of the nearest stall. A thick ankle. More than a skeleton's bone hides underneath that sock.

"Dammit," Carlo says, about the worst cuss word he's used for ages.

Carlo advances to the stall's open doorway, hums the theme song from "The Twilight Zone." I inch closer. No doubt about it. The body slumped next to the toilet comprises the bloodied but otherwise pristine remains of Wil the Whacker—yesteryear's hit man extraordinaire.

Rigor mortis hasn't even started. After five decades! No whiff of shit, either. Bet that tattoo of my name hidden under his black shirtsleeve remains in perfect condition. Guess Father Time's got no clout in the mystical fourth dimension. Talk about weird multiplied by a factor of ten to the third power.

I glance down at the paunch protruding over my leather belt. Not fair that my once-trim frame never escaped the onslaught of passing seasons. No wonder Shauna, the steamy, twenty-something blonde from apartment 4B, always limits our chance encounters in the garage to a short chat and a smile.

That library book about medieval magic, the one I read as a teen, contained only one complete ancient spell. I never conjured up the billowing orange smoke and purple lightshow I was supposed to—just a half-hearted yellow haze. I shrug and focus on the bullet-studded body in front of me. Lean against the wall. The back of my balding head touches the cool tile. Great, I'm leaving my DNA calling card. Am I paranoid? Yup. Ten years ago I did a DUI. Bet the police still keep my record on file.

"Okay." Carlo shoves his gloved hands into the pockets of his cargo pants. "What does the amazing Mr. Magic Squares suggest we do with Wil now?"

"For starters," I say, checking my old Casio watch. At three-fifteen in the morning, I don't need snide remarks. "Let's move him out of here."

"To the men's room?"

"To my truck."

Good thing I have an aluminum shell on the bed of my pickup. Oh, hell! I never bought that just-in-case tarp. Will garbage sacks work? If Wil's corpse could sit straight up and laugh, it would.

Carlo props open the bathroom door while I maneuver Wil out of the stall. The body outweighs me by at least twenty pounds, and my years as a longshoreman ruined my back. I remain stronger than Carlo, though. Me and him improvise a knees-and-shoulders carry. My lumbar spine screams "no." My fear of rotting in jail or cowering in some fourth dimension tells my back to shut up. I bang my knuckles on the door jamb. Really too bad this library isn't still a vacant lot.

Fifty years ago, toting Wil with Carlo's help through the dandelions was more manageable, but only from a lift-and-grunt standpoint. The entire while, our friendly neighborhood gang leader pointed the barrel of his Beretta semi-automatic at my terrified seventeen-year-old brain. Still, that was then, and I have now to face.

Me and Carlo shove Wil into the back of my pickup. Carlo does a timed reset of the security system, then locks the library. At least we won't have to snoop around this building anymore. Hope I zap open a more convenient garbage chute to the fourth dimension. Our clandestine game of "Is Wil Back?" will soon have a new set of rules.

"You have an HP this time?" Carlo shoots an uncomfortable glance toward my truck, parked near his Chevy.

I mumble.

Carlo wants to make sure I can open and close another portal. Calculate how often it might unlock itself in the future. With luck, the new dimensional door won't do its first automatic open sesame for fifty years. Or I conjure enough purple flashes and orange smoke so Wil vanishes forever. Oh, yeah. Dream on, Nick. I pull my slide rule from my jacket's inner pocket.

"Give me a break," Carlo says.

"This is part of the magic."

"We're doomed."

I shut the rear of my pickup truck. Can't see the body through the shell's window. Good.

"I'm on call after breakfast." Carlo says. He does emergency vacation coverage for his old company.

"Ice and a roll of garbage sacks." I rap on the tailgate. "Could you handle that beforehand?"

"Yeah."

"Cool," I say. "I'll need more ice at noon."

"You got to be kidding." His upper teeth crunch his lower lip.

"You'll think of something."

With luck, he will. I can't afford to bungle this vanishing act or have someone smell the body. I don't have a back-up plan.

● ● ●

Latitudes, longitudes, logarithms, and magnetic flux densities smirk at me from the sloppy pile of binder paper on my kitchen table. Wil the Whacker's statistics do likewise, each figure displayed in scientific notation and multiplied by the third power of ten to boost my spell's strength. I pour more black coffee down my gullet. Almost noon. In my garage, will anyone walk by my truck and sniff the wrong fragrance?

The aroma of eucalyptus wafts through the open window. Today's hotter than usual. How much breeze will tonight bring? Better recheck my temperature fudge factor.

Maybe in an hour I'll be ready to add the first numbers to my Wil the Whacker magic square. Plenty of magic square calculations in my nightmares about him. I should have practiced the real thing more often.

188

The basic two-dimensional magic square looks something like a BINGO card without letters. Every such square has one magic number: the sum of its rows, columns or diagonals. Change each number in the square by a constant and the square stays magic. I derive my constants from the identity of my target. In Wil's case, his Social Security number and date of birth, plus his personal measurements adjusted for atmospheric conditions.

My special square has four dimensions instead of two. Except for Wil, I've only used it to eliminate cockroaches—and no more than twice with other people around. I still recall the big wide "O" of Carlo's mouth fifty-two years ago. All those cockroaches in my kitchen vanished, along with the toilet plunger Carlo used to herd them. Carlo freaked, despite the fact we've been friends since third grade. Then the local street gang, a motley collection of hoods in their late teens and early twenties, decided to dispose of its own cockroach: Wil the Whacker.

I brew another pot of coffee. Where can Carlo and me stash Wil if my current numbers game fails? To dig a six-foot-deep hole in dry adobe soil, I'll have to rent a Saint Bernard or a team of huskies.

A text from Carlo arrives. He's on his way with more ice, but won't be back until two-thirty tomorrow morning.

Carlo's my buddy, despite the fact he leaked my cockroach-disposal secret to the local version of a drug lord when we were teens. Hell, lots of kids do stupid things. I pour more caffeinated mud and chew on an acid reducer. A shot of Johnnie Walker would taste better.

"Thanks," I text.

Getting Wil out of my pickup—even with Carlo's help will be another six-ibuprofen affair. Will I need to leave Wil in place? If so, my entire truck might disappear, if the magic still works at all. High-voltage lines could screw things up. Or shifts in the earth's magnetic field. My mystical slot machine might produce three lemons instead of a payoff.

• • •

The alarm on my wristwatch beeps. Two-sixteen Saturday morning. Over twelve hours since Carlo's midday delivery of ice. I sit straight up in my easy chair, my back like a frayed cable on a hoist. Regardless, it's time to hustle my butt out of the prep room and onto the stage.

Keys, pen, incantation: all rest in my pocket. I pick up my construction-paper square. One more number needed—in the blank space, a sorcerer's equivalent of a safety on a gun. As a young punk, I couldn't imagine beyond three dimensions. A couple hours ago, I stapled dimension number four in the same lame flopping-on-top position as before. Don't push Lady Luck.

I take the back stairs to the garage of the apartment house. One parking spot remains empty: 4B. Shauna the heartthrob's usually home by now. Maybe she has an all-nighter. I sigh. Long ago, my own "salad days" gave way to post-dessert indigestion.

Regardless, the time's arrived for serious hocus pocus. If Carlo doesn't show soon, I'll have to perform the rite alone.

I open the rear of my pickup truck. The stench of feces slams my nostrils. Wil's opened his tailgate too. The dimension without time only delayed post-mortem eventualities. Rigor mortis ought to set in soon.

I add the final number to my magic square, tuck the contraption under garbage-sack plastic and down the front of Wil's half-open shirt, then lock the truck. The stink persists. Despite the ice me and Carlo piled on top of Wil, Mother Nature refuses to be fooled. I didn't foresee this consequence any better than I made Wil's corpse disappear forever. My temples throb. What else can go wrong?

An automatic garage door and engine's growl answer my question. Shauna drives down the entry ramp. Yup, here come two headlights. I raise the hood of my pickup truck and pretend to tinker. When Shauna pulls into her parking space, I slam my hood shut.

"Have a problem?" Shauna says. She climbs out of her red Miata.

"Just a loose wire." I get a whiff of her sexy perfume.

"I'm pretty good with cars." Shauna smiles, her dimples showing even in the garage's dim light. The ends of her shoulder-length black hair curl in wisps. "Want me to be sure that wire's connected?"

Shauna's dress drapes her curves. Any other time I'd do cartwheels to stand near her. Not that she has any romantic interest in me. Life gets lonely, that's all.

"Maybe this weekend," I say. "I'm expecting a buddy to drop by tonight."

Another volley of Eau de Bowels wafts up my nasal passages. Shauna gives me a funny look. Well, better she thinks I'm a senile old fart than a body disposal service.

"Yeah." She clutches her shoulder bag. "Sure. This weekend."

She backs away, her legs wobbling on her high-heeled tootsies. No alcohol on her breath. Why's she so unsteady? I follow the line of her wide-eyed stare to the back of my pickup. There's the side of Wil's face, dark plastic edging his neckline. Fuck! His cheek presses against the rear window of my pickup's shell, like he tried to sit up but ran out of space. All the jokes about corpses sitting up are just that: jokes. Things like this don't happen. Except to me.

"I . . . I promise I won't say anything." Shauna eyes me like I'm the proprietor of the Bates Motel in that Hitchcock movie.

"This isn't what you think." I step toward her.

"Please. Don't hurt me." Her hands fumble with her shoulder-bag purse.

"I'd never hurt you," I exclaim.

"Nick," Carlo's voice calls.

Carlo rounds the curve, walking down the entry ramp. His black shirt and jeans blend with the night.

"Sorry, I'm late," Carlo says. Ten feet away from me, he comes to an abrupt halt. "What the hell?"

I open my mouth to explain the situation, then catch movement in my peripheral vision. Shauna stands beside my pickup truck. One of her hands points a pistol at me. The other hand taps the screen of her cell phone.

"If either of you move," she says. "I'll shoot."

Shauna holds the gun like she knows what to do with it. Had some guy in the apartment house once mentioned she did target practice for fun? Regardless, any minute I'll hear a siren. Handcuffs will follow. Forget the fact that Wil might have a fifty-year-old driver's license in his pants pocket. Hard to explain a corpse stinking up my pickup truck to the men in blue.

I must do my spell. Now. Even though my truck might vanish along with Wil. Even though Shauna and I stand close enough to disappear too. Carlo might be clear.

"Stay where you are," I announce. "I've something to say."

"Go ahead," Shauna says, her voice uneven. "Don't try anything cute."

This isn't a good time to reach into my pocket, even to retrieve the folded piece of paper containing my script. Can I pull this off? My hands turn cold and my forehead, hot.

"My extreme gratitude to Ahmad al-Buni," I say.

Carlo knows what I mean. Shauna scrunches her eyes, like I thanked a terrorist instead of the ancient Arab mathematician who'd worked with magic squares and claimed they had mystical properties.

"W-I-L-B-E-R-T-A-V-E-R-Y," I say. "Y-R-E-V-A-T-R-E-B-L-I-W."

My eyes close. I concentrate on Wil the Whacker. I mustn't think of the pickup, Carlo, or Shauna. So why do I keep visualizing Carlo's face staring through my vehicle's window and Shauna seated at the wheel? Sort of like *Ghostbusters*, and trying not to think of marshmallows.

I recite a string of memorized numbers: latitude, longitude, and magnetic flux density. My voice falters. If I say something wrong, I'll have to start over.

"You're creeping me out," Shauna says.

A siren wails in the distance. Will she shoot? If so, she'll have to explain a second dead body to the cops. I repeat the numbers. Two times, then two more. Hope I didn't get something wrong. Three repeats to go.

"Shut up," Shauna hollers.

"I've got my phone camera on," Carlo says. "If you shoot Nick, the police will know you murdered an unarmed man."

Good old Carlo. I repeat the string of numbers two more times.

The siren blasts my ears. The police car has to be at the top of the entry gate to this garage. Another siren warbles, farther away than the first.

I recite the final numbers. Now I'll spell out Wil's name.

"W-I-L-B-U-R-T."

Oh, no! I used Wilburt instead of Wilbert. This won't work right. No time to repeat the entire incantation. I finish the best I can.

Light blazes through my lowered eyelids. Shauna screams. Carlo hollers something worse than dammit. My eyes pop open. Purple hues streak through the air like electric arcs, outlining my pickup truck, Shauna, Carlo, and those parts of me I can see. This isn't like before. Billows of orange smoke pulse like giant hearts, as brilliant as that old spell book had described. Wow! Have I made the real sorcerer grade? Who the crap cares? The magic dimension prepares to slurp up all of us for good.

The smoke clears. The purple lightshow ends. Only a black and gray blur remains. My eyes can't focus. The headlights of John Q. Law sail around the curve, the usual warnings to drop guns and raise hands blaring out of a speaker. The three heads on one cop merge into one.

Shauna keeps screeching, shaking and stomping—clutching a toilet plunger instead of her pistol. Cockroaches crawl on her head and hands. They scurry up and down her arms like her limbs were insect freeways at rush hour. Carlo's bare-chested and shoeless. All that remains of my pickup truck and its contents is a drive train and tires. Cockroaches—surely from my kitchen fifty-two years ago—rain from a dark splotch in the air high above my rear tires. One cop snaps pictures with his cell phone. Carlo plunks himself on the deck and laughs like crazy. Talk about weird multiplied by ten to the third power. May Ahmad al-Buni be praised!

I raise my hands to keep the officers happy. Wil the Whacker's gone at last. Frigging hallelujah. Son of a bitch. No way will that bastard return.

FLIGHT 904

DOUG BAIRD

CAPTAIN JAMES SITS at the controls while scanning the night sky through the cockpit windows. "Yeah, I have two small kids. Oh my, they're a lot of work." He grins. "They just get in there and steal your heart, though. It's as if they know things we don't."

"They do know things we don't," his younger copilot, Ricardo, says, keeping one eye on the flight instruments. "They're smarter than we are, like they're from another planet. Sort of integrating into the human race."

"Oh, they're smart all right." The captain recalls his young son playing in the back yard with his handmade aircraft. "They're a handful, but a bundle of joy."

A knock at the cabin door interrupts their conversation and a flight attendant enters with coffee. "Looks like a quiet night," she says. "Just what we want. Most passengers are asleep. Say, you talking about anything interesting?"

"Not really, Gayle," the captain says with a smirk. "I'm just telling Ricardo what to do if I need to leave the airplane, for a bathroom break. He's picking things up pretty fast, though."

"Hey," Ricardo says. "I've flown off carriers in the Navy, and I've been flying commercially for over four years. I'm a copilot, remember? The guy in the right-hand seat."

Alone, the pilots continue their banter about the captain's kids into the long, routine cross-country flight, cruising at 35,000 feet in a crystal-clear black sky. Captain James never tires of seeing the universe of stars through the front portals, infinite space sprawling in every direction over a circuit board of lights streaming slowly beneath the plane.

Suddenly a pulsating, yellow ball of light becomes visible in the near distance. It appears to be moving directly toward their aircraft. The Collision Avoidance System sets off multiple buzzers and flashing panel lights.

"Holy crap!" Jolted in his seat, the captain spills his coffee as he grabs for the control wheel. "Where did *that* come from?"

"I don't know—it just appeared." Ricardo turns toward the radar screen. "It's an object closing fast on our coordinates. No transponder signal from another aircraft. Too high for a drone. Doesn't track like a missile. Shaped like an orb. It's getting closer, Captain!"

"Quick, get on the radio to Dallas ATC and confirm they see this, too."

The reply is immediate. "*Uh, Flight Niner Zero Four, this is Dallas Air Traffic Control. We copy your coordinates. That is affirmative. We are tracking an object in your airspace that just showed up on radar. It's on a collision course with you. Speed is 550 knots. And its movement is erratic.*"

"Dallas—do you know of any other flight traffic near our coordinates—over?"

"*Flight Niner Zero Four, we have no information of other aircraft or missiles in your area.*"

"Tell Dallas if it continues heading our way I'm gonna have to change course!"

Ricardo points to the radar display. "Look—the orb has stopped midair and is now on the same course we're on, maintaining a distance of 2,500 feet in front of the aircraft. It looks like it's matching our airspeed, Captain. You can't change direction like that in our atmosphere."

"I can *not* explain this one," the captain says. "It's not traversing like an aircraft. Look, its movement is sudden and irregular—you see that?

I'm going to activate the seat-belt sign, reduce our speed, and take us down to 20,000 feet. Get Gayle and Michael in here and explain we need to calm the passengers and let the other flight attendants know we're going to be maneuvering."

After informing the crew, Ricardo calls Dallas to report their unscheduled change in course and altitude. He looks nervously at the captain when Dallas confirms that the orb adjusted its coordinates to remain on course in front of them, traveling at the same velocity.

"Captain, it's almost like we're following the orb, or actually, that the orb is leading our aircraft." The attendants entering the cockpit are frozen in fear at their first sight of the orb.

The two pilots remain silent for a few moments, the captain remembering a similar experience from a past flight. With the flight attendants returning to the main cabin, he says, "Look at that. When I turn to port, it follows our flight path. When I turn to starboard, it continues to align with our aircraft." He takes a quick look at the flight controls. "Okay, we're not going to shake this object. It's obviously intelligent and matching our heading. We should be ready to take evasive maneuvers if it starts to come closer."

"Captain—it *is* getting closer: 2,000 feet, uh, now at 1,000 feet." They can see it as a bright yellowish orb with a pulsating glow, now moving slightly to port then to starboard like a ship's nautical motion, as it continues to match the airspeed of the plane. Ricardo stares out the portal window. "Is the orb sending a signal? Is it attempting to communicate with us?"

The light then becomes even brighter. "I'm going to pitch us to starboard if it moves any closer!" the captain says.

But before he can flinch, the orb accelerates right at the aircraft and just over the top of the fuselage, lighting up the interior of the cockpit like it was hit by a search light. They both gasp. There is no sound except the jet engines in the background, keeping the plane on course at 20,000 feet.

"I felt that," Ricardo says.

"So did I. Like something passed right through me."

"It lit us up like the sun!" Ricardo sounds disoriented. "Did it hit us?"

"Quick—get focused!" the captain insists. "Check the instruments. What's our status?" Looking out into the sky, "Feels like I still have control of the aircraft."

"We're okay. We seem to be good on our flight path, airspeed, altitude, fuel, and uh, cabin pressure." Ricardo takes a deep breath as he looks over at the captain. "I don't believe what just happened. That could have been a midair collision."

"I agree. It was *so* close. When that burst of light passed just over us, everything started to move very slowly for me. I had the sensation that I was not in the airplane, as if I was outside looking at the orb zoom over our aircraft. Then when it was behind the plane, I saw it abruptly shoot into the sky at a ninety-degree angle. There was absolutely no sound. I've never seen anything move like that. It felt more like a full minute had elapsed as it flew by." The captain returns his attention to the cockpit. "Any sightings on radar? Where is it? Is it gone?"

"I've got nothing." Ricardo turns to the captain. "I've heard stories about these things. Other pilots, military and commercial, have confessed them to me. More of them than I care to admit. These objects—they just show up, suddenly, then disappear. I never thought I'd see one."

"I have. Only this time it's hard for me to act indifferent about the fly-by. It came right at us."

After their encounter with the UFO, Ricardo insists the captain report the incident.

"I disagree. I've heard many pilots often receive negative responses after they reveal their stories; some of them I know have even lost their assignments. Let's just handle it like they did at the beginning of *Close Encounters* and say we don't want to report it."

"But that was a near miss, Captain. It was absolutely frightening. If that orb passed any closer, as fast as it was going, it would have hit us for sure, or at least grazed the fuselage." Ricardo is still a bit in shock.

The captain leans back in his pilot chair. His response is almost under his breath. "The orb wasn't intending to hit us. It was very careful in its flight path. It wanted to get our attention, and it sure got mine. I'm just not sure I'm ready to go on the record about these sightings, and risk my career talking about . . . flying objects."

"How about we report this one together?" Ricardo suggests. "We both saw it. Dallas ATC tracked it. There are probably passengers who saw it. I mean, what will you say to your kids when you get home? What if they ask, 'Daddy, did you have a good flight last night?' Perhaps they would understand—you know, the light in the sky. I was serious about them knowing things we don't." He leans in closer. "Captain, this was *way too* significant for us to ignore or forget."

Relieved his crew and passengers had survived this event, including himself, the captain considers what he would say to his kids, with all their questions. Should he ignore this incident like he has in the past? Can he stop denying what he has seen as a veteran pilot? Realizing the extreme danger to an airline full of passengers, and all the other pilots with similar experiences, he then slowly turns to Ricardo.

"Maybe I shouldn't wait for my next encounter to report these sightings."

MY MAW 1957

PATRICIA MCCOMBS

DEAR GRANDCHILDREN,
I write this letter to answer all your questions about what life was like when I was a little girl. The first story is about letter writing. I can see your frowns in my mind. Writing letters out by hand is a lot of work. Yes, I know you'd prefer to hear all about how we went to the bathroom back then.

I can almost hear your giggles rolling over the miles. We didn't have phones, internet, or Facebook. Writing a letter was the fastest way to talk to someone, especially if they lived outside our bicycle range. I'm sorry for you that you may never learn cursive writing. It makes long letter writing so much easier.

Our family was considered poor when I was a little girl growing up in the foothills of the Appalachia Mountain range. Haleyville, Alabama was a very small town. Almost everyone knew everyone else. I was the oldest of five children. We knew we were poor. We had to know because everyone had a place based upon how much money their family had.

One of the times Daddy lost his job, we lost our home and had to move in with his mother. That would be my Maw. Her name was Maude, but we called her Maw. When we lived with her it was the simplest of times. She was a character; with long gray hair she wore coiled on top of her head. All her teeth were gone, but she always had a smile for us kids. She wore home-made bonnets to protect herself from the sun when she gardened.

Maw lived in a one-room house, and she would say she had everything she needed. There was a wood-burning stove to cook on and keep warm in the winter. For reading and sewing at night, there was a light bulb hanging from the middle of the ceiling. No other source of electricity was needed because nothing electrical was owned. A feather mattress for sleeping occupied one fourth of the room. Me and my brothers and sister used to love to climb onto that soft mattress and jump and finally settle down to cuddle with Maw for the night. Mommy and Daddy slept in the lean-to attached to the outside of the house. Sleeping in a lean-to is like camping outside in a tent. Daddy loved it because it reminded him of his youth. Mommy hated sleeping there, "with all the varmints."

Maw's yard was nice with all the flowers she planted around the vegetable garden. Now I'm getting ready to answer your questions about how we took a bath, with no bathroom and no indoor water. First, I love to tell the story about how Maw took her bath. It was the most fun and took almost a whole day.

Maw took a soaking bath once a year. The other times, she would wash the same way we did. She always smelled like the earth and her garden. At one end of her yard, she had a hand pump for pumping water from the ground. A big tub was right beside the pump for taking her yearly bath. In that part of Alabama, the water sprang from the ground soft and clear. It was a private area because the kudzu grew quickly all around the tub and up the trees.

She put the word through her sons for other granddaughters to come and help. She'd pick a time during late fall, usually during cotton-picking time when we'd be out of school. As soon as the others arrived, she'd put us to work. After the older girls built an outdoor fire under the big black kettle, we would draw buckets of water to heat in the kettle. Pumping the water was hard work and we'd all have sore arms afterwards. We washed out the big tub, filled it halfway with cold water, and then started the chore of bringing back the hot water. After the tub was filled, we'd help her take off her well-worn dirty cotton dress and help her into the tub. As she sank into the warm water, she'd say, "Lordy, lordy, lordy." That was her way of letting go of the cares of the day. Using the lye soap she made in her big kettle, we carefully lathered her hair and scrubbed her back. She never minded our water fights and squeals and giggles. I think we got cleaned too. The best part of the day was after Maw was rinsed, dried, and her other dress put on, we would get to take turns braiding her hair. She'd serve us home-made biscuits, strawberry jam that she'd canned herself, and sweet tea for dinner. At dinner, she'd raise her mason jar of water, look at us, and say, "Thankee."

We were exhausted and happily chatted about how easy it was for our baths. We'd just take a cloth out to the pump and wash the best we knew how. Our baths were required every Saturday night because Mommy insisted on our going to church on Sunday morning.

After cotton-picking time, most mornings Maw would help get us ready for school. It was hard to wear shoes after so many weeks of being barefoot. Shoes were only for school and church. We weren't required to go to school, but we loved the bus ride and the many recesses we got at school. We just had to be sure to avoid the mayor's and lawyer's kids. They could do whatever they wanted, even beat us up, and we weren't allowed to fight back. We never had homework. Maw insisted that no child needed school past eighth grade. Daddy had to quit school after second grade to work and make money for the family. He insisted that all his children would get high school diplomas.

Maw taught me how to make quilts. She was always sewing something. On her little porch, sitting in her swinging chair, she'd have me sit on the floor and hand her pieces of fabric. She'd point a gnarled hand and say, "That'n thar." Poor people didn't have a lot to eat—mostly vegetables grown in the yard. What they could afford was flour. White flour sold in beautifully printed cotton sacks. We'd save the sacks for making dresses. When the dresses had so many holes, they couldn't be patched, the good pieces were saved for making quilts. When enough pieces were sewn together, we'd set up the quilting frame. I was fascinated.

Maw's one-room house didn't have room for a quilting frame, but she'd had one of her sons rig up a pulley system. The frame stayed on the ceiling until quilting time. She'd gently lower each corner by rope until the frame was at the correct height for her barrel stool. We'd stretch one layer over the frame and then layer old newspaper over the fabric. Nothing was wasted.

You probably have no idea what a newspaper is. It's just like it sounds. The news from around the world and local towns was printed on paper. The paper was left on doorsteps every morning. Maw couldn't afford the newspaper, so a friend down the street would save them for her. Every word was carefully read before being stacked up to use as kindling for the wood stove or quilting material.

We'd put another pieced-together layer of fabric over the newspaper and sewn all the layers together with a needle and thread. Maw never complained about my haphazard sewing.

Every day, Maw would check the sky for storms. We knew we were safe from harmful storms when Maw remarked, "Lordy." But when she said, "LORDY!" and moved quickly to grab her stick matches and her kerosene lamp, we knew we were headed to the pit. The pit was a big hole in the ground, far away from the outhouse, six feet deep and six feet wide. It had steep stairs, and benches lined the dirt walls. The roof was pieces of tin laden with lots of dirt to keep it down. Weeds grew on top. The door looked like it was laying on the ground. It was hard to open. Not that any of us kids would try to open it. We were afraid of the pit.

Maw moved quickly. She braced one old, laced shoe on the side and heaved. The door caught the wind and flew open. Next, she would carefully light a match and throw it down into the pit. One by one, she would make us go down into the dark pit. We were shaking, but we went. She'd follow us down, lugging the heavy door closed behind her. The light of the match had gone out and we were sitting in the dark, shaking and cold. After she sat down, she'd light the old kerosene lamp. Then, she'd stand up and shine the light all around.

Trembling and frightened, we wanted to know what she was doing, but mostly where our Mommy was. She'd settle in with a sigh and after a while, she'd answer our questions. The lit matches were meant to scare the animals and bugs living there.

We knew Maw and Mommy didn't like each other. It was still a shock to hear Maw say, "You chillen knows yourn Mama'd 'fer to die in a tornado than sully her pretty self in the pit."

We couldn't help but let the tears fall worried about Mommy, but we were more concerned about where all the animals had gone.

Maw would then launch into a scary story about snakes, especially copperheads. We'd jump up and head for the stairs. We knew all about how copperheads would chase a person just for the fun of it. We couldn't budge the heavy door. About that time, Maw would start one of her horror stories about tornadoes. Haleyville was in the tornado alley of Alabama. We'd inch back to our seat on the bench.

"Mussa been 'bout 'en yearn back." Maw had trouble with saying t's because she had no teeth. Mommy would always remind us of Maw's lack of teeth when she wanted us to brush ours.

In her story, the sky had turned green like the green of spring grass. She would pause remembering. The wind was so strong she and her sons could barely open the door to the pit but finally made it in and stayed all night in the pit with the wind howling overhead like a freight train. In the morning they had trouble getting the door open because of all the branches and debris covering the door. The rain was still coming down, but they looked all around to see the damage. Maw's house was fine, but houses across the street were gone and so was a chicken coop. Come to find out, the coop and all the chickens had set down about a mile away.

"Why, Maw?" we asked.

"Only the Lord Almighty knows how it happened." She thought for a moment as if she were wondering if she should tell us the next story. I think she figured it'd scare us enough to keep us coming back to the storm pit.

"You know old Aunt Donny over there 'cross the road. Her daughter, Lula, refused to git in the pit. The whole house done fell down. We found Lula's body under them sticks. Got hit in the haid, she did. Lula had a baby, 'bout nearly a year old."

We held our breaths, wide-eyed, not wanting to hear about a dead baby but yearning to hear all the same. She told us about how people came running and tore the boards apart but couldn't find Lula's baby.

All together we screamed, "No BABY?"

Maw said about two weeks later that word had spread about a baby found across the tracks on someone's porch. "God Almighty, we sure wished that baby could talk."

We were shaking our heads, relieved at the story of the baby, when there was a pounding on the door. "You kids come on outta that nasty place." Mommy yelled.

Maw climbed the steps and peeked out.

"You scared old woman, scaring them kids half to death, there ain't no storm," Mommy yelled.

We climbed out to gentle rain. We were all a little disappointed not to hear another story, but happy to be out of the earthy, damp, and smelly place. Later, after Mommy had fed us, and nestled with us on the feather mattress, I asked her, "Maw told us the story about the baby. The one the storm took away. Was that true?"

"I reckon it was," Mommy said softly as she pulled all of us closer for strong hugs before kissing us good night and going to her bed next to Daddy.

Not long after that night, Daddy got a good job, driving a big truck. We moved into a house with a toilet and running cold water. Mommy said the water came from town, not the ground. We never spent another storm in the storm pit no matter how severe the sky.

And we would still spend time at Maw's from time to time; Mommy wouldn't pass up the free babysitting, but we never spent the night cuddled on her old feather mattress again. We would get some more lessons on how to use a chamber pot without sitting on it, because it was a little tippy. Maw would show us how to spread our legs over the pot while standing up. We enjoyed watching her use the bathroom in the middle of the room.

Maw died peacefully in her sleep at the good age of 85, never having gone to school, but wealthy in the knowledge of how to live a simple life and be happy.

So, my cherished grandchildren, I'm so pleased to live my late years in a home with running hot water and an indoor toilet. I'm pleased you live in an affluent neighborhood on the peninsula of the San Francisco Bay; that you have all your hearts' desires. I pray a big earthquake doesn't hit in your lifetime, but if it does, you now have some knowledge to live simply.

Love, Nana

WASHING THE DISHES

LISA MELTZER PENN

WHEN DINNER WAS OVER, my mother scrubbed the remnants of lasagna noodles and cheese from each plate before standing it upright in the bottom rack of the dishwasher. While she attacked the sink, I cleared the last of the water glasses and silverware from the dining table. I had breezed in for the weekend during my last semester at college. It had been several months, though school was only an hour and a half away.

"The lasagna was good," I said. She'd made it special for me, one of my favorites, while my culinary-challenged father dined on leftover chicken.

My mother frowned and looked away. "You won't visit us anymore now that you don't have to." And as she focused her efforts even more intently on the sink, soapy forks and knives populated the silverware caddy. The remaining dishes lined up in solidarity.

Caught off guard, I watched droplets of water run down each dish. "Why do you wash them before you put them in the dishwasher?" I managed finally. "Isn't the dishwasher supposed to do the work?"

She didn't answer. My mother was nothing if not efficient, and the stainless-steel sink was emptied and the counters sponged down before I could take another stab at formulating my real thought.

"Anyways, it's not true," I said as she sprinkled Comet cleanser on the stainless steel and scrubbed it clean as well. "I'll want to come home."

Until I had said this out loud, I didn't know for sure I meant it. I would be out on my own soon, working, making my own money, not being financed by my parents anymore, not living under their rules. Not that their rules had stopped me asserting my rights before. But always undercover, in secret. I had never done anything obvious in their presence. If a boyfriend came home with me, he was assigned his own bedroom down the hall. If I went to dance parties all night at school or skipped a class, I didn't mention it. It was don't ask, don't tell.

The pasta pot and saucepan balanced against each other on the drying rack, reflecting each other in their gleaming surfaces. By morning they would be dry without any help from me. But something urged me not to wait. I tugged the dishtowel off the oven door, picked up the saucepan, and started wiping it dry. Had this occurred to me sooner, my mother and I could have worked in unison, in tandem. But her work was already finished.

"Well," she said, turning to me, and I was surprised to see her eyes scrunching up with tears. My mother was a no-nonsense person. PTA president, School Board president, raising four kids. She got things done. I'd almost never seen her cry, though I knew from the rare times it happened in my presence that once she got started it was hard to rein in, no longer in her control.

So I averted my eyes and pretended not to notice, frantically trying to think of something else to say. But then she wiped her eyes and said, "That's good to know." And I let out a breath and leaned in to her. My shoulder brushed her shoulder with a soft rustle, her heat matching my own. We were reflections of each other. I opened the cabinet where all the pots and pans went, replaced the saucepan and big pot in their designated spots, then closed the wooden door.

MINESTRONE WARS

SUE BARIZON

I SKIPPED HOME FROM SCHOOL on that hazy autumn day in late October 1962. The weather was in my favor, still warm but crisp around the edges. Back then, we referred to this unseasonal bonus lingering past Labor Day, deep into fall, as *Indian Summer*. It meant I wouldn't have to wear a sweater or a jacket over my outfit tonight. The anticipation of spending an evening, unfettered in my Dutch girl costume, spurred me on to skipping higher and faster. When I landed on the sidewalk in front of my house, I jerked to a stop. Did I see what I thought I saw?

"White smoke!"

The lofty stream loomed from behind the grape stake fence in our backyard. I opened my nostrils wide, like our dog, Tiny Tim, when he nuzzled our knees at dinner for scraps.

"Oh no, Papa, not tonight," I prayed, "not on Halloween!"

In our neighborhood, steam coming from the Capella patio meant our father was practicing his personal commandments. The patio was his place of worship or as my big sister, Elena, liked to call it, The Church of the Gastronomic Misconception.

Most Italian families in our San Francisco suburb had two kitchens: the spotless one that came with the house, and the makeshift one set up in a basement, garage, or back porch. The idea was not to stink up the plastic-covered living room furniture and draperies with the garlic-laden steam from sauce pots simmering on a hot stove all day.

Eight years earlier, when we moved from San Francisco into our newly built ranch style house in the suburbs, our resourceful father had seen the potential in its u-shape. With one phone call and a case of Old Crow, a retired stone mason from "the old country" was brought in to brick up the end of the patio. The result was a monstrosity of a brick BBQ. It took another case of whiskey and a Fourth of July weekend for Papa and his neighborhood buddies to pour the concrete floor. To top it off, Papa installed a flat roof of semi-transparent, green-tinted, corrugated fiberglass, rendering the patio a sweatbox in the summer and an icebox in the winter.

Papa was a garbageman by trade. He worked packing garbage in San Francisco's North Beach for what was then called The Scavengers Protective Association, and scavenge he did for his patio kitchen. "Finds" from a plethora of restaurants on his Fisherman's Wharf route included a bank of kitchen cabinets with an abrasive, industrial finish, a row of institutional Formica countertops, and a pitted porcelain sink from Alioto's restaurant. A neglected rectangle of inch thick marble filched from the back alley at Ghirardelli Square was mounted to the patio wall. It served as an altar for Papa's six-burner stove top, and the electric cheese grater he built from a discarded lawn mower motor.

To my ten-year-old senses, Papa's patio was a culinary limbo. Here, all the old-world smells of our food-crazed ancestors commingled with the ghosts of family feasts past. Braids of garlic bulbs hung from the patio's crossbeams next to salamis, blood sausages, and the shriveled bodies of dried cod fish sacrificed for Papa's "baccala" (fish stew). The air was heavy with the musty smell of his homemade wine fermenting to vinegar. Wild mushrooms dried on wooden frames covered with chicken wire. A twenty-pound wheel of Parmesan cheese sweated on the butcher block waiting for the grater.

Foul-smelling foodstuffs were relegated to the patio refrigerator. I habitually held my breath before opening the door to survey the macabre inventory of head cheese—a confusing name for a non-dairy cold cut made from a pig's head boiled down to a gelatinous mass and molded into a loaf. There were slabs of marinating ribs, anchovies suspended in olive oil, calf's tongue, pickled pigs' feet, and a stinky cheese imported from Sardinia complete with maggots intact. I referred to the refrigerator as *The Dead Zone.*

There was one bright spot. Papa had built a narrow aviary along a patio wall for his treasured canaries. A neat row of double-stacked bricks defined the perimeter, encompassing a system for hosing down bird droppings. There was a bubbling fountain for bird baths, and an arrangement of manzanita branches for perching. With a couple of bottles of Old Crow, he commissioned another Paisan (Italian buddy) to wallpaper a panoramic scene of Yosemite Valley over the entire stucco wall. You could hear the canaries singing Papa's praises as they dined on lady fingers and soft bib lettuce from his garden.

My thoughts were interrupted by an earnest lick to my knee. Tiny Tim had sprinted from the front porch with an unusually eager greeting. When I knelt down to give him a hug, I spotted the source of his enthusiasm—the lineup of kitchen ware beside the front door. A familiar sense of dread snaked its way up through my insides. I let out a mournful groan.

"Minestroneeee!"

Nothing was more formidable to me than Papa's minestrone. To the untrained eye, it was more stew than soup. Any unwitting soul referring to it as vegetable soup would elicit a pitiable absolution and be dismissed as "Americani."

It was the slime factor, as only a prosciutto bone could deliver, that separated minestrone from its rivals. Before the term "mouthfeel" was coined to describe a sensation made by a particular food in your mouth, the overcooked chunks of zucchini, cabbage, and Swiss chard reduced to fibrous strands and coated with layers of tummy-turning fat had set my retching reflex into overdrive. Retching into your plate was considered a slap in the face to our father. Who was then compelled to get up from the table and give your *culo* (rear end) a slap for disrespecting the minestrone. Minestrone had no respect for "mouthfeel."

Was I so wrapped up in Halloween that I hadn't noticed the warning signs of an impending minestrone? Papa's prep took days. Was I so enamored with my Dutch girl costume that I hadn't spotted the fava beans soaking on the kitchen counter or the scads of garlic and onion skins piled knee-high in the trash? Was I too busy tapping out Shirley Temple routines in my wooden shoes to pay attention to Papa's puttering in the garden? The mosaic of chopped vegetables had eluded me: zucchini, tomatoes, potatoes, carrots, parsley, wax beans, and Swiss chard laid out in neat rows on Papa's tired old cutting board. But, how, for crying out loud, did I miss that God-forsaken prosciutto bone stoutly wrapped with tendon, gristle, and two inches of choke-provoking fat? Was I too blinded by the braided Dutch girl wig I'd been prancing around in all week to see that grotesque pig appendage dangling from the patio's crossbeams?

How could Papa desecrate Halloween, the most sacred of kids' holidays, with his ungodly concoction? At our dinner table, refusing to eat your minestrone was a punishable offense. Even daddy's girl was not exempt. Halloween or no Halloween, I would not be allowed to leave the dinner table without finishing a big bowl of minestrone. The battle lines had been drawn—my gag reflex vs. a spanking.

I was alone in my battle. Everyone loved Papa's cooking, not just our family but the whole neighborhood. Pots and bowls lay in wait, ready to receive his blessing—the Pardini's cast iron, the Lavezzo's Revere Ware, Norma Costa's precious Tupperware, and Nella Lucchesi's green mixing bowl with the chipped rim and shower cap lid. The more pots the better. It meant fewer leftovers. Papa would depend on me to make the deliveries before dinnertime.

Tiny Tim had waited patiently while I stood staring down at the pots and bowls—contemplating my fate. When he scratched at the front door, I followed him into the house. I heard Papa in the patio whistling along with his canaries. I waved to him from the kitchen window. He winked and nodded. His wide muscular hands with short stubby fingers gripped the wooden paddle scavenged from the kitchen at Scoma's restaurant.

"Hello, Sussie girl!" Papa was in his zone, all right. He sounded chirpy.

"We're not having minestrone tonight, are we, Papa?" I was careful not to sound whiny.

"You kids shit like rabbits. You need a good bowl of minestrone to stick to your ribs."

Papa, an authority on bowel movements, deemed his minestrone a cure-all for everything from diarrhea to constipation. I wondered which one of us kids forgot to flush the toilet, again.

"But Papa, it's Halloween."

He was blowing on a spoonful of soup. I winced. Papa swallowed warily. He smacked his lips, tossed a couple of parmesan cheese rinds into the pot, and gave me a stern warning.

"You kids are not going out there to eat all that crap unless you have something good in your bellies."

"But Papa."

His jaw set tight. Through clenched teeth he warned.

"You're going to eat it . . . and like it. *End of estoria!*"

Papa's "*End of estoria!*" was code for "spanking." I had to think fast. I retreated to the bedroom I shared with my sister for advice on dodging any potential dinnertime drama, but she had holed herself up in the bathroom to avoid helping with the deliveries. I could plead with our Aunt Mary, next door, for a last-minute dinner invitation. It wouldn't be the first time my sympathetic Aunt squeezed one more at the Staffornini dinner table, despite Uncle Pete's objections not to "interfere." Unfortunately, any pleading would have to wait until after I made the deliveries.

"C'mon Sussie. The minestrone's waiting." Papa shouted.

I heard him send Tiny Tim to fetch me. I followed the tail-wagging beggar to the patio, where my father stood at the stove, stirring what looked to me like bubbling sludge. He had parked my red wagon at his feet with the pots and bowls resting on a wet towel. Carefully, he ladled the steaming soup with the reverence of a priest offering up communion at Sunday mass. My job was to pull the wagon up and down the block making deliveries ahead of the bewitching 6:00 dinner hour.

It was close to 5:00, I worked fast, the damp towel absorbed the shock and spills as I navigated curbs and asphalt. I was determined to finish before my Uncle Pete got home. As I traversed the neighborhood, I worked out my plan. I just needed my aunt to ask my Mom if I could have dinner with my cousins on account of it being Halloween and we'd all be going out together, anyway.

On my way home, the wagon was full. Eleanor Pardini had given me a plate of rice torta and Bob Costa a bright yellow bouquet from his rose garden. Nella Lucchesi promised a tray of enchiladas when the weather turned colder. By the time I finished explaining to the mailman what I was doing with a jar of cherries in grappa, I was too late. Standing in front of my aunt and uncle's house, I could see through the big plate glass window into their dining room. There they all were: my aunt, uncle, and cousins sitting down to dinner ... and my little brother, Johnny, who had begged my invitation for himself.

Papa must have heard me sneak through the front door.

"Elena, Sussie, soup's on!"

I panicked. Then, ran for the bedroom and smack into my minestrone-tolerant sister dressed in her gypsy costume.

"Help me!" I begged.

Elena had four years on me, a quick wit and a stubborn streak. Ushering me back into our room, she grabbed my Dutch girl costume.

"Quick, put this on!"

I watched my sister adjust the wings on the starched white bonnet and position the long, yellow yarn braids to fall across my pinafore.

"Elena, Sussie, get in here!"

Papa's command ricocheted down the hallway.

"There," Elena said, dabbing two rouge circles on my flushed cheeks. "Even our minestrone-crazed father wouldn't have the heart to spank a cute, little Dutch girl!"

The tug of my wooden shoes against the carpet cautioned me to stop at the doorway and take stock. My sister motioned with her eyes at Mom's terra-cotta crock on the kitchen table. Ever the patriarch, Papa sat at his place, soup ladle in hand, and a linen towel tucked under his chin (a necessary precaution for sucking the marrow from prosciutto bones).

"Sussie!"

The clomp, clomp, clomp of wooden shoes on linoleum floor startled the threesome. With more enthusiasm than talent, I tap-danced the only shuffle-shuffle-toe-kick step I knew. Taking a scene from a Shirley Temple movie, I sang "Magic Wooden Shoes" in a mock German accent to the delight of my mother and the snorting laughter of my sister.

"C'mon, it's time to eat!"

Papa's shout-out cut through my ballyhoo entrance like a machete. I felt my throat tighten as he ceremoniously ladled the soup, filling the bowls to the brim, then passing them to us from across the table. The holy sacrament of the blessed gag reflex. During the wait, Tiny Tim (a loyal scrap-eating ally), had been banished from under the table to the garage. Papa had had enough of his premature whining for leftover prosciutto parts. I was doomed. There was only so much I could cough into our cheap paper napkins and wad into my fist, out of Papa's sight line.

It was 6:30. I had half an hour to eat and dry the dishes before I could go trick-or-treating. I was a notoriously slow eater. Papa always made me sit at the table right up until his buddies arrived after dinner for coffee royales. Often, I'd have to sit with my half-eaten plate and listen to their "BS" sessions. Occasionally, Frank Pardini, Papa's best friend, would take pity on me.

"What's the matter, Sussie? Don't you like minestrone?" he'd say.

Bang! My wish for a Frank Pardini intervention dissolved when Papa banged the kitchen table with the ladle to get my attention.

"EAT IT!"

I glanced over at my sister. She motioned to me with her spoon, carefully piled high with elbow macaroni. What luck! Papa sometimes added pasta to the soup. Digging around for something edible would made it look like I was eating. By the time I had extracted all my macaroni, Elena had finished the last of the thick broth, leaving only a few fava beans and a bit of gristle at the bottom of her bowl. We both jumped up from our seats when we heard the doorbell ring.

"Sit down!"

Ten minutes to seven. Someone dared to intrude on the sacred dinner hour. In our neighborhood, trick-or-treating before 7:00 was frowned upon and parents let you know it. When Mom came back from answering the door with my sister's best friend, Fifi, in tow Elena let out a squeal.

"Papa, can I go?" she begged.

"You have time to do the dishes." Papa said reaching for the ladle. "Your friend can have a nice bowl of minestrone while she waits."

Papa was looking mighty benevolent ladling out that soup, so I played my trump card.

"Papa, can I go to the bathroom?"

Papa eyed me suspiciously, "Go, and come!" was his terse reply. He knew my stalling tactics.

215

I could hear the commotion of trick-or-treaters outside as I sat on the toilet, contemplating my predicament. Why was Papa being so mean? It was no secret that I was his favorite. Couldn't he see I had no stomach for his minestrone? Wasn't it enough everybody else loved it? When I heard my brother and cousins from next door getting ready to leave, I cranked open the bathroom window and called out.

"Johnny, come get me. Don't leave without me!"

I hurried out of the bathroom and sprang back to the kitchen table just as the doorbell rang. I was surprised to see all the dishes had been cleared, washed and put away—except for mine. Evidently, grateful for the "best minestrone she ever ate," Fifi had pitched in to help. The girls had been excused with Papa's blessing.

Mom parked herself by the front door ready to hand out candy. Now, it was just me, Papa, and a cold bowl of minestrone. He was clearly tired of waiting for me, and ready for his Lazy-Boy and an episode of "I Search for Adventure" on the TV.

"C'mon finish your soup!"

I took a spoonful into my mouth and rested the contents directly onto my tongue avoiding any contact with my teeth. A stream of drool started running down the corner of my mouth. Papa stood up.

"Swallow, damn it, Sussie!"

I swallowed hard. A saliva sucking fava bean and a nasty band of tendon triggered my gag reflex. Mom ran into the kitchen just as the doorbell rang.

"Oh, for god's sake, Primo," she cried. "It's Halloween!"

My brother burst in through the front door dressed as Davy Crockett, grabbing his coonskin hat off the coffee table.

"For Pete's sake, aren't you done yet? We're all waiting for you!"

On his way out, he dodged Frank Pardini dressed in a red bartender's jacket. Frank held up a couple of shot glasses in one hand, and a bottle of Old Crow in the other.

"C'mon Primo, let's go trick-or-treating!"

Papa motioned over at me. Frank took notice of the little Dutch girl sitting with her head down, then spotted the minestrone that had congealed around the spoon standing at attention in the middle of my bowl.

"What's the matter Sussie?" he said. "Don't you like your father's minestrone?"

With that, he scooped up a big spoonful and shoveled it into his mouth.

"Best one yet, Primo," he said. "Too bad you had to go looking all over Timbuktu for the Prosciutto bone."

Papa smiled. He looked across the table at me, grabbed his napkin and waved me over. I didn't flinch when he reached for one of my yarn braids and wiped a splatter of minestrone off the tip.

"C'mon, Sussie girl," he said. "We've both had enough."

My mother is not, and never was, a pine cone

Vanessa MacLaren-Wray

She was always tight-closed
held fast
refused to fall

In her letters
strewn like a mat of pine boughs
those knobby fingers open
  sharp with memory
   reeking of dust and oil from hard roads
   the traffic of an unbalanced world

Dodge arrow-sharp scales
scent seed memories
trace imaginary leaves
  gloaming ovals
  cotyledon shadows
  harbingers of change

She grasped time
root and stem and leaf
  the generations behind
  the generations to come
  held tight in silence
  blood between her fingers
  remembered and foreseen

Tea done, you sit in slippers, robe,
contemplate a tale untold.
To spread some words out flat,
let them become a map:
with insights, glimmer of a globe.

ABOUT THE AUTHORS

Tom Adams *(Ricky the Robot)*, a writer with eleven years of dedicated storytelling, finds himself in the fourth quarter of his life. Tom lives with his wife of thirty-seven years, a marriage and family counselor, along the coastline just south of San Francisco. A proud member of the CWC, Tom cherishes the sense of community and connection he shares with fellow writers. Additionally, he actively participates in two writing critique groups, valuing the feedback and insights they provide to refine his craft. Tom's writing journey has found recognition in *Wormwood Press Media* and *Change Seven* magazines.

Doug Baird *(Flight 904)* is an event producer, stage manager, and graphic designer in San Francisco, where his company, Doug Baird Productions, has managed events for nonprofit, corporate, and theatrical projects for over thirty years. Doug was a photography instructor at City College of San Francisco for ten years and has presented workshops at festivals and art colleges in Europe. In 2004, he co-founded and has continued to be the producer and artistic director of Performance Showcase, featuring the work of Bay Area artists performing contemporary music, dance, opera, and spoken word. His award-winning science-fiction/fantasy stories have placed at the CWC Literary Stage and appear in the anthologies *Carry the Light* and earlier issues of *Fault Zone*.

Sue Barizon *(Minestrone Wars* and *Is There a Teacher in the House?)*, a native San Franciscan, writes memoir, fiction, and poems based on her first-generation childhood experiences growing up in the suburbs. She brings a poignant sense of humor to her short stories, memoirs, essays, and poems. Her work has been published in the *Fault Zone* series and *Carry the Light* anthologies. She has appeared in CWC's first Reader's Theater: Women's Journeys. She's won numerous awards from the San Mateo County Fair including Writer of the Year and Best of Show. Her story, "Summer Bananas," appeared in *Fault Zone: Reverse*. Sue is an active member of the CWC writing community.

Eva Barrows (*Where There's Smoke*) is a San Francisco Bay Area freelance writer and editor. She writes for regional magazines *Edible Silicon Valley* and *PUNCH*. She served as Editor-in-Chief of the health and wellness magazine, *Live & Thrive CA*. Her short stories have appeared in the *Carry the Light* and *Fault Zone* anthologies. Her love of fun and upbeat poetry, short stories, and artwork led her to create *Imitation Fruit Literary Journal* (*www.imitationfruit.com*).

Scott Best (*Stage Names*) is a husband, father, and metaphorical lottery-winner living and working in Palo Alto, California. His essays about love and relationships are fueled by an abiding fear that in some alternate timeline, he missed out on exactly this life. His work has recently been featured in "Tiny Love Stories," part of the *New York Times* column Modern Love, the *Good Men Project* online journal, as well as his personal Medium page (@scottbest), (*scottbest.medium.com*). His other published writing is principally technical in nature, and his name can be found on over two hundred issued patents worldwide. It was long past time to innovate on a different type of writing, and he hopes you enjoy the result.

Jo Carpignano (*Ode to Autumn* and *A Big Day for Billy*) writes poetry, fiction, and memoir. She published a book of poems titled *Paper Wings* and is now working on a memoir of her Italian immigrant family.

Lawrence Cohn (*I Named Her Lola*) regards writing as a vital part of his life. His interest in how poetry and short stories contribute important ideas to uplift our existence has always been his purpose. He started writing poetry and short stories in elementary school and felt compelled to write poems on the back pages of exams. He has been published in *Littack Magazine* as part of the Vitalist Poetry Genre as well as various college journals. "Every day, I'm reminded of Poetry being an integral part of my life. If I go for a walk, watch a movie, have a discussion with a friend, an idea is always near the edge of what I'm doing."

Tim Flood *(The Stone)* Tim's memoir *Islands Apart*, published in 1999, sold more than two thousand copies. He began writing again after retiring. An autobiographical short story "Spaceman," appearing in *Fault Zone: Reverse*, was nominated for a Pushcart Prize. He is the membership chairman, website manager, and newsletter editor of the SF-Peninsula branch of the California Writers Club and was recently presented with the Jack London Award for his service to that writing community. He is seeking a publisher for his first novel, *The Flower of Canaan*, and is at work on his second.

Heather E. Folsom *(Haze)* lives and works in the San Francisco Bay Area. Heather has been a featured reader at Coastside Poetry, a selected reader at LitCamp's Lit Nights and Bay Area Book Festival events, and published in *Modern Haiku*. Heather blogs on gardening, writing, work, and more at *somethinghappensnext.com*.

David Harris *(Betrayal)* grew up in the Catskill mountains of New York and has lived in the Bay Area for more than 30 years. His short stories have been published in *Litbreak Magazine*, *The Concho River Review*, *Idle Ink*, *Calliope*, and he was longlisted for the *Dillydoun Review*'s 2022 Short Story Prize. He is a former journalist for Reuters News Agency and has worked as a corporate communications consultant and speechwriter.

Laurel Anne Hill *(Weird to the Third Power)*—author and former underground storage tank operator—classifies her recently published third novel, *Plague of Flies: Revolt of the Spirits, 1846*, as historical fantasy/magical realism. She has based a number of her over thirty published short stories in historical settings. Her second novel, *The Engine Woman's Light*, has won a total of thirteen honors and awards; so far, *Plague of Flies* has received seventeen awards plus positive professional reviews. Laurel joined CWC over twenty years ago, and has served as branch secretary, treasurer, and Fault Zone editor-in-chief. More about her can be found at *laurelannehill.com*.

Audrey Kalman (*Monsieur Ventilateur*) writes fiction with a dark edge about what goes awry when human connection is missing from our lives. She is the author of *What Remains Unsaid*, two other novels, and a fiction collection, *Tiny Shoes Dancing* (shortlisted for the 2019 Rubery Book Award). Her fiction and poetry have appeared in more than a dozen print and online journals. She co-created the Birth Your Truest Story writers' community (*www.birthyourtrueststory.com*) and offers editing and coaching services for writers. Previously, she served as president and vice president of the SF Peninsula branch of the CWC and as editor of *Fault Zone*. She is (perpetually) at work on another novel. Find out more at *audreykalman.com*.

Nirmy Kang (*A Life in Five Baths*) is a British-Punjabi writer who lives in the Bay Area. Her work (fiction, memoir, short stories) explores her plural heritage and the universality of our lived experiences irrespective of origin. She has been featured on NPR/KQED *Perspectives*, published in *Write Yourself Out of a Corner* (W. W. Norton & Co.), and longlisted for the Bridport and Fish Prizes.

Amy Kelm (*The Car Wash*) is a story nerd and struggling writer from San Mateo County. A former marketing executive, she now fights the losing battle to keep her hardwood floors free from dog hair and her children in the nest. She writes short stories and is currently mapping out her first novel. Her work has appeared previously in *Fault Zone: Over the Edge*, and *Fault Zone: Diverge*.

D.L. LaRoche (*The Visit*) Raised in the suburbs of St Louis, a young devotee of Mark Twain, Dave has rafted and swum the Missouri rivers and camped the Ozark woods. As a traveler, he has lived among the islands in Georgian Bay; in Syracuse, New York; Burlington, Vermont; Los Angeles; Dana Point, California; and now in the Bay Area. He is the father of five, married, and now spends time writing of the dilemma, angst, and joy associated with living in this complicated world.

Evelyn LaTorre *(Parted, Not Separated)* Ed.D., has been a member and on the board of the Fremont Area Writers chapter of CWC since its founding in 2009, as well as being a member of the SF Peninsula CWC branch. Her work has appeared in numerous venues, including the *California Literary Review*. Her book, *Between Inca Walls*, about falling in love while serving in the Peace Corps, was awarded the 2021 Peace Corps Experience prize. It has also won a first place Hearten Award from Chanticleer International Book Awards and a five-star rating by Readers Favorite. Her second memoir, *Love in Any Language*, has also garnered numerous five-star reviews. Her website is: *www.evelynlatorre.com*.

Lucretia Leong *(A Rendezvous with Time)* came to California from Hawaii in 2015 and resides in Burlingame. In between eating and sleeping, she spends her time writing, walking, watercolor painting, reading, swimming, and hula dancing. Her fiction piece "Manna from Heaven" was published in the Korean centennial anthology, *Yobo*, a Bamboo Ridge publication. Her memoir article "Where Have All My Nouns Gone" appeared in the *California Literary Review* in 2022.

Ida J. Lewenstein *(If I Let It . . .)* is a retired English as a Second Language (ESL) instructor of some twenty years who wears several hats. She has written poems, chants, and rhymes to reinforce in a fun way the structures she was teaching, and some of these have worked their way into imaginative story poems, mostly for children, that have been published in books—ten in all, with more to come. She has also published poems about conservation and environmental causes. Many of her poems have appeared in California Writers Club publications.

Vanessa MacLaren-Wray *(Cold Trap; My mother is not, and never was, a pine cone)* writes poetry, science fiction, and fantasy exploring communication and attachment in this messy universe of ours. She's the author of the Patchwork Universe series, including *All That Was Asked*, *Shadows of Insurrection*, and *Flames of Attrition*. She also writes for the Truck Stop at the Center of the Galaxy shared-universe consortium. She hosts regular online open mics for the California Writers Club and often guest hosts for the podcast *Small Publishing in a Big Universe*. When not arguing with her cats, she works on new stories, her email journal *Messages from the Oort Cloud*, and her website, *cometarytales.com*.

Ellen McBarnette (*To My Canadian Friend*) is a life-long storyteller whose earliest tales were transcribed by her mother on scrap paper. Ellen's career has taken her from the halls of Congress to boozy poetry slams. She has performed nonfiction memoir storytelling on the stage, occasionally making enough for cab fare home! She writes nonfiction, speculative fiction, and poetry. Today, she is active in the San Francisco literary community as organizer of the Afrosurreal Writers Workshop of California and board member of the SF chapter of the Women's National Book Association. Her short story "Negrita" appears in the anthology of speculative fiction, *Midnight and Indigo.*

Richard E. McCallum (*A Thousand Years*) obtained a B.S. in film and television from Montana State University in 1976 and a Master of Arts degree from USC-LA in cinema in 1983. Richard served in the U.S. Navy as a combat camera operator and traveled the world documenting military exercises and public-relations events. He has worked in the film and multimedia industries in Los Angeles and San Francisco.

Patricia McCombs (*My Maw 1957*) lives in the Bay Area and delights her grandchildren with stories of life in a small town in Alabama in the 1950s. She cannot imagine how the grandmother of 1957 would be able to navigate life in California in 2022.

Lisa Meltzer Penn (*Washing the Dishes*) has had short fiction and essays published in multiple *Fault Zone* anthologies, *Traveler's Tales: Spain, The Sand Hill Review, Fabula Argentea,* TMI Project's *Alone Together* pandemic series, *Migozine,* San Mateo County Library's *Story Café,* and others, and won Best of Show at the 2021 San Mateo County Fair. An early excerpt from *The Siren Dialogues* published in *Best of The Sand Hill Review* was nominated for a Pushcart Prize. Along with being president, founding anthology editor, and recipient of the coveted Jack London Award for the San Francisco Peninsula branch of the California Writers Club, she has worked as an editor at Macmillan and other major publishers. Keep up to date with Lisa at *lisameltzerpenn.com* and *lisameltzerpenn.com/blog.*

Margaret Nalbach (*Off to the Ostrich Races*) Retired for a number of years, making up stories about ostriches has been lots of fun. Being retired has meant writing stories, continuing world travels, avid reading, learning to be an artist, volunteering, and enjoying life away from the business world. For many years, home has been in the San Francisco Bay Area.

Bruce Neuburger (*The Fight; Pablo and Maria*) is a retired teacher. He has published one book, *Lettuce Wars*, and a number of articles for on-line publications. These are his first published stories. "The Fight" is based on an event his father was part of a month before emigrating from Germany. "Pablo and Maria" comes from experiences working in the fields of California in the 1970s during the period of political upsurge. Bruce worked in the lettuce fields nearly ten years before returning to school to become an ESL teacher, which he did for thirty years before his retirement.

Luanne Oleas (*The Man Who Loved Bridges*) worked as a weekly newspaper columnist with reprints of her articles appearing in *Readers Digest, Parenting Magazine*, and the *San Jose Mercury News*. She worked as a technical writer in Silicon Valley while writing two published novels, *Flying Blind: A Cropduster's Story* and *A Primrose in November*. She recently finished her latest novel, *When Alice Played the Lottery*, and is currently writing another, *Shedding Cats*, about a technical writer who has too many cats. In real life, Luanne has only one cat, Blackberry.

Korie Pelka (*What Color is My Empty Nest?*) has a background in directing theater which served her well during her twenty-five-year career as a communication professional in Silicon Valley. In 2015, she left the corporate world to discover her own voice in a new stage of life she calls her Third Act. She now spends her time as a certified coach, consultant, and writer. Her stories have been published in previous issues of *Fault Zone*, the *California Literary Review*, and *Spirited Voices*. She has won multiple Literary Stage awards at the San Mateo County Fair including 2021 California Writer of the Year. She chronicles her journey through her Third Act Gypsy blog, www.3rdactgypsy.com, and is busy working on a self-help memoir.

Miera Rao *(Shades of Blue)* writes fiction, nonfiction, and poetry. She was honored to accept the 2022 Effie Lee Morris Literary Award for Poetry, by the SF chapter of the Women's National Book Association, where her poem won first place. Her creative nonfiction won both first place and best of show at the Literary Stage in San Mateo County. Her short stories have been published previously in the *Fault Zone* series.

Cheryl Ray *(Alone in the Garden)* is a California native and lives with her husband, Bob, and their border terrier, Charlie, on the San Francisco Peninsula about one mile from the San Andreas fault. She writes creative nonfiction and short fiction. Her published articles include appearances in *Sail, Latitudes & Attitudes, Writers' Journal,* and *Spirited Voices.* Essays have been published in *The Girl's Book of Friendship, Elements of English*–a tenth-grade textbook—and *Fault Zone.* Together with her husband, she has sailed some thirty thousand nautical miles in the Pacific and Atlantic oceans. When Cheryl is not writing or reading, she enjoys exercise classes.

Carol Reade *(The Homecoming)* is a widely-cited academic author writing on the intersection of culture, societal conflict, and employee behavior in multinational companies. A graduate of the University of Wisconsin, Sophia University in Tokyo, and the London School of Economics, she is currently a professor of international management at San José State University's Lucas College of Business. In addition to her academic writing, Carol has published stories based on her experiences living and working overseas. She is developing additional stories based on her experiences as well as stories taken from her family history for publication, perhaps as memoir or historical fiction.

Harlan Suits *(The Ice Cave)* is a writer of nonfiction essays and travel pieces, especially on nature and adventure travel. He studied English and American literature at Stanford University and worked in corporate communications until his recent retirement. He is a lifelong mountaineer and backpacker and also plays French horn in several local amateur ensembles.

Anne Marie Wenzel (*To my mother on her tenth birthday*) was born in San Francisco and graduated from San Francisco State University, where she is Lecturer Emerita of Economics. She has studied poetry and creative writing through Left Margin Lit and Stanford Continuing Studies. Her poetry is published in *Humble Pie* and the *California Literary Review*. She is a third-generation Italian-American living on the San Francisco Peninsula, where she writes poetry and is at work on an historical novel set in early twentieth-century Northern California.

Alisha Willis (*Nodding into a Groove*) is a civil-service employee who enjoys writing poetry and fiction. Her publication history includes poems in *Fault Zone* and in two editions of *Spirited Voices*. Active in the SF Peninsula branch of the CWC, she has served as both treasurer and parliamentarian.

Mickie Winkler (*The Palo Alto Poop Patrol*) is an irreverent writer of short humor, author of *Politics, Police, and Other Earthling Antics*, and former Mayor of Menlo Park. Winkler failed to do what most incumbents do—get reelected. She launched her writing career with Amazon and was frequently published in the product-review sections. Needing to supplement her negative income as a writer, she decided to attend law school, and will graduate in 2027—if her application is accepted. Winkler "grew up" in NYC. Alas, the beautiful California weather which attracted her, is now marred by the new "fire season"—as documented in her story "California, There I Go." Will she move? Go to law school? Ever be published again? Check her out at MickieWinkler.com.

Nanci Woody (*You Can Go Now*) has been a writer her entire adult life. She started out writing and publishing textbooks (accounting and business math) and all the ancillaries while teaching at a local community college. She has since published a novel and many short stories and poems. She is currently putting the finishing touches on the pilot for a streaming series, conveying her novel, *Tears and Trombones*, to the screen.

The San Francisco Peninsula Branch of the California Writers Club encourages, champions, and cheers its members. A community of writers at every level in their journeys, members connect with other writers, find critique groups, share their work, and support one another.

The motto of the California Writers Club—founded in 1909—is "Writers Helping Writers." Our branch serves that motto through public workshops, meetings, and lively interaction through both in-person and online events from open mikes to social gatherings.

To connect with the club, visit
cwc-sfpeninsula.org

The Fault Zone series, launched in 2010, exemplifies the principle of Writers Helping Writers. Each edition is curated by an editorial team, who work with individual authors to fully develop their work, exercise revision skills, and learn about the publishing process, to bring the selected works to their best realization in the finished anthology.

The 2021 edition, *Fault Zone: Reverse*, earned the Independent Press Award for anthologies and was a finalist in the anthology category for the 16th annual National Indie Excellence Awards. Several works were nominated for a Pushcart Prize.

Learn how to contribute:
cwc-sfpeninsula.org/faultzoneseries

Printed in the USA
CPSIA information can be obtained
at www.ICGtesting.com
LVHW040238031223
765241LV00069B/2062